# THE RAVEN'S CHILDREN

## EMILY BARLOW

*Dedicated to Evelyn, who runs with the wolves in her dreams, and Ashford, who has always been the bear.*

# PROLOGUE

"*Gather round, all,*" *said the burly, blond man at the head of the Great Hall. "We have a special treat tonight! Magnus, the greatest skald of my father's time, has agreed to come out of retirement for one night to tell us a tale!" There was a great amount of gasping and general sounds of pleasant surprise among the throng in the Hall as its occupants converged on the dais. The man smiled and winked conspiratorially. "He says he's been working on this one as long as he can remember, so it's bound to be good."*

*Leaving space for the children to sit on the floor at the front, chairs and benches were assembled haphazardly around the raised platform, which now held a single, comfortable-looking chair. Once everyone found a seat and the murmur died down, a middle-aged woman, red of hair and long of limb, lovingly escorted an ancient man up onto the dais and into the waiting chair. She kissed him on the top of the head and took a seat on the edge of the platform. Smiling, the man held up a hand in supplication, then took a swig from the water skin he carried with him. He cleared his throat. "It is a very special tale I tell tonight," he began in a surprisingly rich and pleasant voice that carried easily to every corner of the space. "It is a story which was passed to me by my father and was ever my favorite as a lad. However, he had not the heart to tell it here while he lived." He paused to let the words sink in, relishing the eerie stillness they brought. "And so I bear it to you tonight, close to the end of my days in this world, that you might know the true stories of the great kings and queens of old." Gnarled hands and rheumy eyes raised to the heavens, he cried, "Odin, father of the gods! Lend me the aid of your raven, Munin, and his peerless memory this night! I weave before you the tale of King Hrafn and his queen, Lady Astrid, and the trials put before their children.*

*"It all began on the fateful night Queen Astrid the Beloved gave birth to triplets—and was called to the bosom of the gods..."*

The aging midwife let the limp hand in hers fall gently back onto the bed. Tenderly, she reached over and closed the woman's empty eyes, then pushed her damp, blonde hair back from her face.

The room was silent.

Suddenly, the stillness was broken by the wailing of the three tiny babies held in the arms of three of the scullery maids, summoned from their work in the kitchens to assist with the birthing.

The midwife shook her head. The woman had given birth months before her time. For the first few weeks everything had seemed fine, but after the first two months had passed she had begun to have pains. Despite spending the next four months bedridden, she had gone into arduous labor the day before and given birth early to three small, but miraculously healthy, children.

It was a wonder she hadn't died too soon to give birth. She'd been in and out of consciousness for the last few hours, waking up during contractions, muttering incoherently in between. During one period of semi-lucidity, she had clutched the midwife's arm and desperately instructed her that she was to remember three names in the order she gave them: Asbjorn, Audolf, and Ambjorg.

The midwife repeated them to herself as she looked at each child in turn. The firstborn, by about two minutes, was a round-faced boy; the second, a slightly thinner version of his brother; and the last–and smallest–was a dainty little girl. But how had the woman known there would be three? And the names...how could she know...?

"Her last words were their names," intoned the midwife. "Let them be known as Asbjorn the Bear, Audolf the Wolf, and Ambjorg the Eagle."

"Long may they live," came the somber reply.

*"The king was devastated by the death of his beloved wife. So great was his grief that he neither ate nor slept for three days…"*

The king watched as the ceremonial boat bore the body of his queen away over the quiet waters of the fjord. Except for the small lapping noises of the water on the rocks, all was quiet. The boat, carved stem to stern with runes and gilded with chains of flowers brought by mourners, glided noiselessly out toward the outlet of the fjord and the rocks that would sink even the sturdiest of unguided craft. Despite the crowd that surrounded him, King Hrafn felt more alone than ever.

Once the boat had slipped out of sight beneath the waves the king turned and began the ascent up the hill to his hall. He was followed by his thanes and retainers, their consorts, and, lastly, by the townspeople. No one seemed predisposed to talk; the queen had been loved by many and respected by all, and her death was a dark cloud blocking the sunlight of the entire kingdom.

The return trip to the hall was the most difficult path King Hrafn had ever trod. With every step the reality that his queen was gone drove into his heart; her burial at sea had finalized what he could still hardly believe. Months of worrying about her physical state had left him exhausted and gaunt with strain. Part of him wanted greatly to run to the highest cliff over the fjord and throw himself into the cold, unforgiving water so that he might join her in her final resting place. Were he still childless, perhaps that would have been his fate, but now there was more at stake. She had given her life to bear their children; to leave them orphaned would dishonor her memory.

Regardless, he knew he had to find his peace soon. His thanes had long wondered if he was too weak to hold the throne. Soon one of them would make a move, and he had to be prepared.

*"Years passed, and the children got older, as children do." The elderly man paused for refreshment from his water skin*

*and smiled at the red-haired woman seated below him. She returned his smile warmly, caught up in the tale. "It was then they began to understand that the peace-loving country they would one day serve was not always peaceful, and that sometimes peace must be bought with blood."*

# CHAPTER 1

"No fair!  You're cheating!"

"Am not!"

"Are too!"

"Am not!"

"Hey now, Dolf, how can she be cheating?" asked Asbjorn.

"None of the other kids can ever find me when we play hide-and-go-seek," Audolf answered, frowning.

"That's just 'cause I'm smarter than them."

"Now, Ambi, we know you're very smart, but are you sure you're not...you know, using certain things without thinking about it?" Asbjorn asked, attempting to look reproachful.

"And what 'things' would you be talking about?" asked Ambjorg, all innocence and sweetness.

"You know."

"Well...maybe," she admitted sheepishly. Dolf snorted. "I try not to, really I do!  It's just...I can't help it." She gave her brothers the saddest, most penitent expression she could manage.

Asbjorn glanced upward. There, spiraling above the trees just to the south, was the telltale eagle, wheeling away on the thermals.

"Let's play another game," he suggested as the eagle was lost to sight.

"What game?" asked Dolf, suddenly coming out of his sulk.

"It's called 'Studying our History Lesson,' and it starts with whoever can get inside the hall the fastest!" Asbjorn shouted as he raced off toward the great hall. Dolf and Ambi looked at each other indignantly and tore off after him.

Just past the steps up to the hall, the children slowed to an eager walk. Last time they were caught running in the hall they were forced to endure an extra hour of lessons with Geirvarr, their weapons teacher, since they appeared to have such boundless energy.

The great hall was a long, rectangular building made of rough-hewn logs. The lintel and doorposts were brightly painted and carved in the shapes of animals; ravens, bears, eagles, owls, wolves, and even reindeer pranced, glided, and loped around the door frame. Heavy, iron-bound doors proclaimed a simple phrase in runes etched into the hard wood:

*Gunnbjorn Ivarsson's Hall*

Currently, the large doors were thrown wide open to admit as much sunlight as possible, since the only illumination inside the hall came from narrow vents just beneath the eaves of the roof. In bad weather the vents would be covered with skins or oilcloth to keep the dirt floor inside the building dry. The smoke hole in the roof worked the same way, but since the weather was nice, it was left uncovered to let in more fresh air. The trestle tables set up for mealtimes were put away, and there were few people in the hall, since there was much work to do outdoors. A few women bustled hastily through the building carrying foodstuffs in preparation for the midday meal, still an hour away, but the hall was otherwise unoccupied.

"Where's Snorri?" asked Ambjorg, crestfallen, as the children strode through the door to the seemingly-empty hall. "He was supposed to have returned yesterday."

In response, a large shadow loomed out from behind the open door just behind Ambjorg and grabbed her slight figure, picking her up with one arm. She squealed and struggled for a moment before she realized that her brothers were grinning up at her assailant. Turning around in his firm grip, she found herself staring straight into the mirthful gray-green eyes of the skald. She beamed at him and threw both arms around his neck before he chuckled and gently set her down.

Although Snorri spent much of his time writing poems and practicing songs, no man would call him weak. He traveled the countryside part of the year, sharing poems and stories of the gods, heroes, wars, great deeds, and even some history. Of course, traveling had its dangers; besides the obvious predatory animals, there was also the occasional predatory human, and many a bandit had seen their end by Snorri's hand.

"I see old Geirvarr has been teaching you well, young lady," he said jovially. "I'm just glad you decided not to practice your eye gouges on me." He winked conspiratorially at Audolf and Asbjorn, whose grins widened.

"I beat Dolf yesterday at weapons practice," Ambjorg announced, standing up straight and puffing out her chest. Audolf scowled and stuck out his tongue petulantly in response.

"Well, well, I'm impressed!" Snorri sat down on a small stool and rested his back against the wall, letting the sunshine flowing through the open door warm his skin. Each time he came back to town it seemed a better place to stay indefinitely. Perhaps he should find a wife, settle down, start a farmstead and write ballads in his spare time. After all, the men of his generation had done so years ago and had successful farms and many children to show for it. What else should a man want in life?

"Snorri?" Ambjorg asked, poking at his knee inquisitively.

"What? Oh, I'm sorry, Ambi. I was woolgathering. My last trip was long, and I'm not getting any younger." He produced three reed mats from behind his stool and gestured for the children to sit. They plopped down onto the mats and lay, chins in hands, listening intently.

"So, with which tales shall I regale you today?" asked Snorri, settling in for an hour's worth of storytelling.

"Ooh, ooh, tell us about the beginning of the world!" insisted Asbjorn. "You promised last time!"

"How about the story of our grandfather and his many battles?" suggested Audolf.

"I want to hear about our mother," Ambjorg requested.

"One at a time, one at a time!" Snorri exclaimed. "Now, I think we should start with Asbjorn's request—the story of the beginning of the world as we know it." The children shifted, settled down, and waited expectantly for the tale to begin.

And so, for the next hour, Snorri spun the tale of the beginning of the world, of the ice giants, the fire giants, the nine realms of the great Tree, of mighty Odin and his rise to power among the gods. He told of the great serpent girding the world and the halls of Valhalla, where valorous men and women train for war and await the day of Ragnarok. All this the children took in with awe, though they had heard many of the tales before. Occasionally one would interrupt to ask a question, but for the most part, they listened in silent wonderment.

By the time Snorri finished, the preparations for the midday meal were almost complete. "Well, it looks like we've run out of time, as usual," Snorri remarked as the smells from the food that had appeared on the trestle tables wafted over to their corner of the hall.

"But you haven't told us about our grandfather!" protested Audolf.

"Or Mother," said Ambjorg, her jaw set in an accusatory manner.

"My deepest apologies to you both," replied Snorri. "We'll start with those first thing tomorrow. Don't you have kitchen duties today? I fear I've already made you late."

"Yes, Snorri," the three chorused, hanging their heads in disappointment.

"Well, then, off you go! I don't want you getting in trouble with the cook because I kept you late again." With that, the children said their goodbyes and trotted off to whatever scullery duties they were assigned for the day. Snorri watched them go, wondering for the thousandth time what would become of them. After all, with their father's health already beginning to fail, it wouldn't be long before the duties to which they were born were thrust upon them, prepared or not.

As if in answer to this thought, the king appeared in the great doorway. A tall man, though of slighter build than the skald, the king managed to dominate even the wide space left by the open doors. His shoulder-length blond hair blew gently in the soft breeze entering the hall despite the plain circlet he wore as a sign of his office. Upon seeing Snorri, he smiled warmly and started toward his longtime friend.

As the king came closer, Snorri recognized more signs of his illness than he had before he'd left. To the casual observer, he looked like any other man his age, but to Snorri, who had been his closest friend almost from birth, the king looked visibly older. His usually trim waistline looked thinner, his belt cinched a little tighter, and there was more of a hollowness to his cheeks than the skald would have liked. But the king strode purposefully to the corner Snorri occupied without any indication of infirmity. The skald stood and bowed slightly in greeting.

"Snorri, you of all people should know that I don't stand on ceremony," the king said, clasping the skald's hand warmly. His grip was still quite firm. "It's good to have you back. Of course, it would be nice to have you here permanently." He grinned sardonically.

"Duty calls, my king," Snorri replied with a flourish. "Besides, how else would we get news from the rest of the country? With the way the weather has been this past season, it's a wonder even I could get through to the northernmost settlements. The spring thaw came much later than it should have this year."

"It did, didn't it? How are things in the north?" The two men seated themselves at the head table and began to discuss the state of the kingdom as the midday meal was brought out. It consisted mostly of cheeses, breads, and fish, with a smattering of fruits and vegetables. Since the capital was built close to the fjords fishing was a large industry in the town, and the humid, temperate climate allowed for the growth of a broad range of crops.

Soon the hall was full of hungry workers and bustling kitchen staff who wasted no time in generating a boisterous buzz of conversation. Once they had completed their duties, Asbjorn, Audolf, and Ambjorg joined their father and the skald at the head table and tucked in with a will. Most of their father's conversation with the skald was drowned out by the general din in the hall, but Ambjorg, who sat closest, caught a few snippets of conversation.

"So the winter was hard on the northern settlements, then?" the king was saying. "Hmm…we'll see if we can't at least send some supplies up there to help with what was lost."

"Supplies may not appease certain of the settlers up there," Snorri warned. "Someone has spent the winter spreading the seeds of malcontent across the region. I think you know who I mean."

The king's expression darkened. "We will deal with that in due time. For now, our attention must stay on this superstition business. Is there any news about what's been happening there?"

"Not much," Snorri replied as he tore off another chunk of bread from the dark loaf before him. "Only that the northerners have adopted strange ways. There have even been whisperings of witchcraft."

"There are always whisperings of witchcraft when too many hard winters go by," responded the king as he chose an apple from a plate of fruit. "People fear what they don't know or understand. Regardless, we should keep an eye on these developments."

"Of course, sire," Snorri agreed as he helped himself to more baked fish. From there the conversation turned to the goings-on in the capital over the winter, and Ambjorg tuned it out. She'd heard enough to keep herself and her brothers satisfied for days.

"…And there was even talk of witches," finished Ambjorg.

"Of course that's what you'd remember," Audolf grumbled. "It's always about magic with you. Honestly. Nobody really believes in that stuff."

Asbjorn ignored him. "Regardless, there's obviously something going on in the north that concerns Father. What should we do to help him?"

"I don't see as there's anything we *can* do," said Ambi. "He's not doing anything about it himself—he said as much. I'm sure he knows what he's doing. For now, all we can do is stick to our chores—" Dolf mumbled incoherently until Ambi plowed ahead—"and keep him from having to worry about us, too."

"A good plan," Asbjorn agreed.

# CHAPTER 2

*Seven years later*

"Dolf, what *have* you done with that report? Father needs it for this afternoon's meeting." A high-strung Ambjorg paced what used to be their father's study, stopping here and there to paw her way through disheveled piles of parchment. "You know he's not as good with details as he used to be."

"I don't know, I told you!" Dolf put down the book he'd been trying to read and rolled hazel eyes at his sister over his perfect, straight nose. "I had it yesterday, and I put it there, on the shelf. I don't know what happened to it after that."

"Well, it's not—ah, here it is." Having located her quarry, Ambjorg straightened the parchment and looked over at her brother, who was lounging at the desk with his feet on the table-top. "You know," she began in a tired tone of voice, "you really should attend at least a few of these meetings. Even Asbjorn finds the time for one or two here and there." She drew herself up to her full height, nearly equal to his when both were standing, in an attempt to scold him more effectively.

"But you do such a wonderful job on your own, sister," Audolf replied as he swung his feet down from the table to meet her steel-gray gaze, his arms spread wide. "What assistance could I possibly offer?"

"Your presence is all that is required," came her icy reply. "A show of support for our father. The gods know he needs it right now. And besides, we must prove to the thanes that we are concerned with the running of the kingdom. If we do not, we will have a war on our hands as soon as…" She trailed off, unable to give voice to the cause for her concerns.

"Honestly, Ambi, do you really think that's going to happen?"

"I don't think, Dolf. I know. And had you been to any of these sessions in the past two years, you would, too." She swept from the room in an azure swirl of linen-clad frustration.

"Hmph." Audolf resumed his seat behind the desk, folding his lanky figure bonelessly into his favorite chair. "Don't need meetings to keep the thanes in order," he mumbled to himself, "just a bloody great show of force." He picked up his book and continued where he'd left off before their argument.

A few moments later a large shape in a deep red tunic and trousers passed by the study door, then stopped and stuck its head around the corner. "Dolf! Are you coming or what?" Asbjorn shifted his considerable mass into the doorway, arms akimbo. His short, chestnut-brown hair was mostly under control due to a valiant attempt at washing it the night before, but a few pieces peeked stubbornly over the back of his head. Still, Audolf had to admit his brother cut an imposing figure. *Much more imposing than mine, resemblance be damned.*

Sighing deeply, Audolf marked his page and put down the book. "First Ambi, now you, brother. Is this really necessary? I'm halfway through a piece on the uses of spearmen in large-scale combat."

"It is if you ever plan on having the opportunity to use what you're reading, there." Asbjorn brushed a stray piece of hair out of his face absently.

"So she's sold you on her conspiracy theories as well, eh? Fine; I give up." Audolf rose from behind the desk, straightened the deep green tunic that complemented his own carefully coifed brunette locks, and met his brother's hazel-eyed stare resignedly. "Lead on." He gestured expansively for Asbjorn to exit before him.

Turning on his heel, Asbjorn set off for the meeting hall at a brisk pace. Audolf kept up easily; though their builds were strikingly dissimilar, both young men were the same height, and their strides matched well. Having been confined to their quarters or the outlying buildings for most of the winter due to the weather, both enjoyed the brief time spent in the afternoon sun as they strode across the lawn. Though spring was well on its way, the air still held some of winter's chill, heralding a cool evening and frosty night.

As they approached the open front doors to the meeting hall they could tell the session had begun in earnest. Gunnvaror, one of the thanes from the southlands, was already presenting a case on the country's need to curtail its logging practices in the southern woodlands.

"Fellow thanes, if we continue to tax the forests by harvesting such large tracts of land, we won't be able to re-plant quickly enough to replace what we've taken. Already the game has begun to move far out of our regular hunting areas. Soon we won't have enough meat to feed our families. We cannot fish as you on the coast can do—come winter, my people will starve." Gunnvaror swept his gaze across the room, gauging the reactions to his plea. "I come here today to ask you to make every effort to conserve wood. Use logs from your stores; they season well, but leave them too long and they won't be usable. Patch your longboats instead of building new ones. If your lands contain forests, use them to supplement what you've set aside. Whatever you can do to limit your dependency on logs from the southern woodlands, I urge you to put into practice. And if there is anything I or my people can do to assist with your efforts, you have but to ask." The burly thane nodded to the assembly and resumed his seat.

Audolf and Asbjorn had managed to enter the meeting relatively unnoticed during Gunnvaror's speech and were now seated to the left of their father, who was listening attentively to the proceedings. Despite his weakening state of health, he sat stoic and erect at the head of the U-shaped table where his thanes met quarterly to discuss the state of the country. To the king's right sat Ambjorg, who mirrored her father's posture and bearing while shifting her steel-gray gaze across the assembly and back, reading the thanes' expressions and gauging their reactions to the topics at hand. Occasionally she would sift quietly through the papers on the table before her, glance at a page long enough to find whatever information she required, and return to her quiet surveillance.

Thane Rikaror, an older man and thane of the western coastal areas, rose to speak. "I see your plight, Gunnvaror, but how are my people to feed themselves if their boats will not float? We cannot fish by swimming to where the fish bite. Are the southern woodlands so overtaxed that my people must starve, too?" He sat down with an angry look toward Gunnvaror.

A general murmur of discontent arose from the gathering. "Thanes, please," began the king, "I'm sure there is a solution to this problem that will benefit all." His voice, despite his frail state, was still surprisingly strong, and it cut through the noise in the room. The mumbling faded as all heads turned toward their liege.

A quiet baritone voice broke the stillness. "If you will, my lord, my lands contain rich quarries of stone. My people have been successful in building homes out of stone and mortar for years. If our skills or materials may be of use elsewhere in the kingdom to help with this shortage—accounting for fair trade, of course—they are at the disposal of the thanes." Everyone turned to regard Thane Brandulfr, the youngest of their number and thane of the eastern mountainous areas.

Ambjorg leaned toward her father and whispered a few words in his ear. He nodded sagely, then regarded his gathered retainers, whose attention had returned to the king. "Thane Gunn-varor, if your people were to begin building their homes of stone and mortar, would this ease the draw on the woodlands in your domain?" The thane nodded. "Then it's settled. You and Thane Brandulfr may work out what you consider fair trade for materials and labor or training.

"As for the coastal lands," the king continued, "I believe a trade would be the best option. Thane Rikaror, your people are highly successful fishermen." The thane nodded proudly.     Ambjorg slid a sheet of parchment in front of her father unobtrusively. The king studied it for a brief moment, then addressed the thane again. "If my numbers are correct, you had a fair surplus of dried fish available at the end of last year's season, even beyond what was required to last your people through the winter." The thane nodded again, though somewhat warily. "Then it seems to me you should not mind trading on that surplus for wood to patch such fishing boats as you currently have." Rikaror calcu-lated mentally for a moment, then, unable to find a way around the fairness of the trade, shook his head. "Good," said the king, reclining in his seat. "So, in summary, Thane Gunnvaror will use stone in trade from Thane Brandulfr to build new homes from this day forth, and Thane Rikaror will discontinue the building of new boats in favor of trading surplus dried fish for patch wood from the southern forests. Does this seem fair to all?" Heads nodded around the room, a few rather unhappily. "Then I declare the matter settled.  What is our next topic for discussion?"

And so the afternoon continued, with thanes presenting their concerns and complaints and the king offering the fairest possible resolution for all parties involved. By the time the day's business was concluded the sun hung low in the sky and the evening's feast was already set in the great hall. Many of the thanes retired briefly to their guest quarters to freshen up before the meal. Ambjorg took her father's arm and led him from the meeting hall, followed closely by Audolf and Asbjorn.

"Today was good day, Father," she began. "We resolved quite a few complaints for the first day of meetings. That should set the stage for a productive quarterly gathering."

The king grimaced. "I would agree with you, Ambi, but recall who was absent from the group." He gave her a moment, then continued. "That does not bode well."

"Perhaps he was merely delayed," Asbjorn offered. "Travel has been hard this year, especially from the north."

"Asbjorn, you have always seen the best in people," mused the king. "Make sure that is a quality you do not lose. But do not let it blind you to what is happening around you." He stopped for a moment, coughed harshly, and continued walking.

They walked the rest of the way to the king's quarters in silence. Ambjorg gave her father into the care of his healer, then followed her brothers to the great hall, where the feast was laid and awaiting their presence. As usual, the hall was full to brimming, but the crowd at the trestle tables was different; the workers and retainers were eating at home with their families, and their places at table were supplanted by the visiting thanes and their retinues. Since this was the first meeting of the year, many of them brought their families with them, leaving one child, sibling, or spouse to manage the lands in their stead. It was an opportunity for their children to see the rest of the country and to meet the families of the other thanes. As such, it was a very festive occasion, and the hall was buzzing with conversation.

The chatter in the hall died as Ambjorg and her brothers mounted the few stairs onto the dais at the end of the hall containing the head table. Ambjorg leaned toward her brothers and whispered, "Who wants to do it this time?"

Audolf immediately opened his mouth to reply, but was cut off by his brother. "I'll do it," said Asbjorn as he straightened and turned to address the hall. Audolf frowned, but faced the assemblage quietly.

"Fellow thanes, we welcome you and your families to the first meeting of the year. As always, we offer you the hospitality of our hall and bid you enjoy yourselves. So, without further ado, let us feast!" Applause and a cheer rose from the crowd as Asbjorn seated his sister, then himself, and began to sate the surprising amount of hunger the work of the day had generated.

"Nicely done," murmured Ambjorg from his right.

"Thank you, sister," Asbjorn replied. "I thought I might save us from one of Dolf's soliloquies."

"It was *not* a soliloquy," Audolf interjected testily from his left. "I merely wrote a poem for the occasion. Besides, that was *years* ago, and it wasn't even my best work." He took a turkey leg from the platter before him and began to delicately remove the meat from the bone.

Asbjorn snorted and took a draught of mead. Ambjorg shook her head and studied the assemblage as she daintily sipped at her soup. "I like that not at all," she remarked as her gaze swept across the table on the far right-hand side of the hall.

"What? All I see is Thane Rikaror and his family…and who is that with his son?" asked Asbjorn.

"That's Thane Ingvarr's sister. She's much younger than the thane, and it's no secret that her brother has little love for any of the western families. That's trouble brewing, and no doubt."

Asbjorn nodded around a bite of honeyed bread. "Have a look at Thane Gunnvaror's table—is that Thane Eirikr's son sitting next to his youngest?"

Ambjorg nodded, her thick, honey-colored braid sliding over one shoulder as she turned to face her brother. "They seem to have taken quite a liking to each other. From what I understand, both their fathers approve of the relationship—their mothers, too—and a marriage between the two thanedoms might solidify the south even more. Eirikr's lands have been encroaching on Gunnvaror's as his thanedom has expanded, and there have been a number of small land disputes among both of their retainers, but they've all been handled without violence on both sides, and the borders have been redrawn amicably." Ambi set aside her empty soup bowl in favor of a plate of steamed greens.

The three ate in silence for a while, studying the assemblage and its dynamics. Occasionally a small child would break free from his or her parent and run, squealing happily, down the aisle between the benches.

Midway through the meal the idyllic atmosphere was broken as two figures appeared in the open doorway at the end of the hall. Both wore fur-trimmed cloaks of black despite the relative warmth of the evening, and both appeared to have been traveling all day.

"I am disappointed!" cried the larger of the two figures as he threw his arms open in an expansive gesture. "Here we've ridden all day, and still managed to nearly miss the evening's festivities." He threw back the hood of his cloak, revealing a weathered, late-middle-aged face with pale skin and icy blue eyes. His dark beard was lined in two places with silver, and his hair had matching shocks of gray at the temples. He was smiling, but the gesture never reached his eyes.

His counterpart also pulled back his hood, but with rather less flourish. He was a younger man, perhaps twenty, with the same dark hair and blue eyes as his father. But where the older man's expression was false, yet warm, his son's expression was cold and calculating. He surveyed the entire assembly before turning his glance onto the dais at the head of the room—and smiled as his gaze met Ambjorg's. She shivered at the predatory look on the man's face.

The sound of Asbjorn's chair slowly pushing away from his place at the table broke the abrupt silence. Audolf and Ambjorg quietly stood to his left and right, wary of the tension in the room.

"We're glad you were able to make it, Thane Alfgrimr,"

came a voice from the side door of the great hall. The assembled crowd stood as the king entered and made his way slowly onto the dais. "I was afraid, with all the news of problems with the northern roads, that you would not be joining us." He seated himself carefully with the surreptitious assistance of his sons, and reached for his plate.

At this signal, the rest of the hall resumed their seats. The northern thane and his son removed their cloaks and took places near the head of one of the center tables. Its previous occupants made more room than was required for the two of them to be seated.

The meal continued without further event. King Hrafn stayed long enough to complete his meal, then retired to his chambers for the night. Once the king had left, many of the older thanes and those with young children also retired to their quarters, leaving the younger members of the gathering to socialize. The trestle tables used for dinner were pushed aside to make room, and a few musicians made their way through the crowd to one of the now-unused tables. Soon lively music filled the hall and the first few dancers made their way out onto the makeshift floor.

"Well, looks like my part of the evening has finally started," said Audolf as he stood and surveyed the room, rubbing his hands together eagerly. "I'll be dancing if you need me." He traipsed down the stairs, picked out his first partner—a pretty young woman wearing a dress with a rather daring neckline—and headed out on to the floor.

Asbjorn stretched in his chair. "I think Dolf has the right idea, though not quite the right execution," he said as he stood and offered his hand to his sister. "We really should mingle a bit."

Ambjorg took the proffered hand and stood, adjusting her dress. "I suppose," she admitted. "But I refuse to dance unless it is absolutely necessary." She followed her brother down the stairs and into the waiting crowd.

Those left in the hall had split themselves into two large groups, one on each side of the hall, and each group contained smaller circles of conversation. On the left side of the room were the young men and older boys, while the right side of the room was dominated by the young women. Occasionally one of the men would drift across the room and ask a lady to dance, and they would make their way to the center of the hall; otherwise, the groups stayed largely separate.

Asbjorn, upon leaving the dais, strolled toward a group of young men in the midst of a heated conversation on hunting.

"I'm telling you, I made the shot from a hundred yards! My father's lands have the best bowyers in the country."

"I still don't believe it," replied a thin, brown-haired youth. "A hundred yards? In the trees? And you managed to take down a full-grown stag with one arrow?" He snorted. "I'll believe it when I see it."

"You couldn't even pull a bow that large!" the first speaker retorted.

"I wouldn't have to. Hunting isn't all about how fine a bow you own, after all. It's about how you approach the stag..." Asbjorn drifted away from the first group and closer to another. This one was comprised of older members, including one or two of the younger thanes.

"I hear things have been bad in the north this year," one was saying. "The gods know winter was hard enough on us, and we never have it half as bad as the northern thanedoms."

"We haven't had much word on it, ourselves," replied one of the southern thanes' sons. "By the time word from the north reaches us, you're better off believing only a quarter of it. The last skald to come through told tales of witches with strange animals. Can you believe it?"

Thane Brandulfr, who had been listening in on the conversation, spoke up. "I'd wager more of it is true than we care to believe. My people have been seeing strange things in the forests of late, and a few have gone into the woods and never returned. The few passes across the mountains are no longer safe. Since the winter was so harsh we were snowed in for months longer than usual, and when the thaws came, they washed out the mountain roads to the point where they cannot be traveled. It will take most of the summer to get them back into shape."

There was silence for a moment while everyone internalized the thane's statements. Then one of the lesser thanes' sons spoke up. "Well, Brandulfr, you know that my father's people are always willing to help. Just send us word if you need some extra provisions, maybe a bit of manpower, and we'll see what we can spare."

"Your offer is much appreciated, Ingvarr," replied the thane. "We'll keep it in mind."

From there the conversation turned to the smaller goings-on of the families involved in the discussion. Asbjorn lost interest and drifted around the remaining groups on his side of the room, quietly gleaning what information he could from the ongoing discussions, though he learned little of interest.

Meanwhile, across the room, Ambjorg was trapped in a discussion with one of the younger groups on, of all things, boys. Currently, she was attempting to dissuade one of the younger girls from getting involved with a young man quite a few years older than she.

"But he's so noble!" the girl replied to her latest entreaty. "I'm sure he would be a wonderful thane!"

"He's headstrong and rash," replied Ambjorg derisively. "He would, indeed, *not* make a good thane." Her reasoning was interrupted by a young woman, who had inserted herself into the group without anyone's notice.

"Excuse me, Lady Ambjorg, but I was wondering if you had a moment?" Ambjorg looked up and met the deep brown eyes of Eyildr, her closest childhood friend. She winked almost imperceptibly, and Ambjorg's carefully schooled expression barely hid her relief.

"Yes, of course," she replied, excusing herself from her previous group of ladies. Once they were well away from the group, she turned to Eyildr. "I cannot thank you enough—what an empty-headed lot they are! Were we like that when we were younger?"

"Of course not," snorted Eyildr. "We were raised better. I daresay this generation is a bit spoiled." She seated herself on one of the unoccupied benches at the end of the room and patted the seat next to her. "Do have a seat, Ambi—we have a lot of catching up to do!"

Ambjorg joined her on the bench. "It's been so long! We've missed you at the last few meetings. Where have you been?"

"Quite busy, actually," Eyildr replied. "Father has had me going on rounds with him and Davyn now. In fact, the reason I haven't been here the past few meetings is that he's left me in charge of his lands."

"Really?" Ambjorg's eyebrows rose in surprise. "As close are you are to the northlands?"

Eyildr nodded. "He's been teaching me arms, too. He's also put out word that anyone—man or woman—who wishes to learn to fight may study for an hour a day with his armsmaster. The classes have been full to brimming the past few months."

"I'd like to admit to surprise on that count, but I'm afraid I can't. Your father is a very practical man, and I'm hearing things out of the north that frighten me."

"So are we. In fact, Father has made a few trips up there himself, ostensibly to do some trading and talk to some of the other lesser thanes. His reception on each successive trip has been more chilly, if you'll pardon the turn of phrase." She leaned closer to Ambjorg. "I'd keep a close eye on Thane Alfgrimr and his son, if I were you. I wouldn't put it past them to do something despicable while they were here." She straightened, then looked past Ambjorg. Her expression brightened. "My lord Asbjorn!" she exclaimed, standing. "So good to see you again."

"Your presence has been missed these past few meetings," rumbled Asbjorn. "Ambi, I do apologize, but if you don't mind, I would like to deprive you of a conversation partner for a while. Eyildr, would you care to dance?" He extended a polite hand.

Eyildr smiled warmly. "I would love to, my lord," she replied, and they wandered off toward the dance floor, leaving Ambjorg alone with her thoughts. She settled onto the bench and surveyed the assembled youths for a time, watching their social interactions with a detached interest.

"My lady, do you not dance?" The warm baritone voice startled her out of her reverie. Thane Brandulfr was standing at a polite distance to her right, eyeing her curiously.

Ambjorg regained her composure quickly. "Not when I can avoid it," she replied with a small smile.

"Ah. Well, do let me know if your feelings on the matter

change." He smiled, inclined his head, and rejoined the young men on the other side of the room.

Ambjorg found herself for the first time reconsidering her usual policy. She was in the midst of this internal debate when a lanky, dark-haired figure flopped down onto the bench next to her.

"Beautiful night, isn't it?" the young man asked, his voice a reedy tenor. His ice-blue eyes were gazing out the open doors to the hall and reclining against the table behind the bench, his elbows resting on the table behind him. His feet were crossed at the ankles, showing off his well-worn black riding boots, which matched the rest of his attire.

"Indeed," replied Ambjorg coldly. "If you will excuse me, I have business elsewhere." She rose and turned to leave.

Alflakr caught her arm as she turned. His grip was firm, almost painful, as he held her wrist. "Please, don't let me drive you away from your seat. I merely wished to speak with you." His eyes held her gaze for a moment, the same rapacious look in them she'd shuddered at earlier when he'd entered the hall.

"Is there a problem here?" asked a quiet voice behind Ambjorg. She turned to see Thane Brandulfr standing behind her, a hard expression on his face. His gaze turned to the young man's hand on Ambjorg's wrist.

Letting go, the man shrugged and stood. "None that I can see—the lady and I were just talking."

The thane's expression narrowed slightly, but he did not press the issue. "My apologies, then—I believe the lady had promised me a dance." He turned his gaze from the young man and extended his hand to Ambjorg. "My lady?"

She hesitated a moment, then placed her hand in his. It was warm and surprisingly callused. With a last look at the young man, the thane led her onto the dance floor.

"You needn't have done that," Ambjorg stated flatly as they began to dance. He wasn't much taller than she, and their strides matched well. "I could have easily taken care of it myself."

"I know," he replied quietly, gazing warily over her shoulder. "If you'll beg my pardon, I felt an opportunity to show my support for your family was important enough to endure your chagrin." They moved with the music in silence for a few moments. "It appears your would-be admirer has found a new target." Brandulfr nodded vaguely in the direction of the group of vapid young women Ambjorg had left earlier in the evening. Ambjorg rolled her eyes before she could stop herself. The thane chuckled deep in his throat. "I see you have little use for either hunter or hunted."

"I do not generally associate with many of the younger ladies, no," Ambjorg replied as neutrally as possible.

Brandulfr chuckled again. "You don't seem one for idle gossip." They slowed to a halt as the song ended. Brandulfr took Ambjorg's hand, bowed slightly, and said, "My thanks for the dance. You should do so more often; you're quite graceful. Now, if you will excuse me, I must speak with Ingvarr." He inclined his head as Ambjorg retrieved her hand and strode off toward a group of young men close by.

Ambjorg, still slightly bemused by the entire turn of events, strolled back to the young ladies' side of the hall and took a seat on one of the benches close to a group of ladies. Within moments, Eyildr and Asbjorn joined her, hand in hand, on the bench.

"What was that all about?" asked Eyildr, her fine brow furrowed with curiosity. "I don't think I've ever seen you dance at a meeting. And with Thane Brandulfr?"

Ambjorg shook herself from her state of mild confusion. "He was saving me, actually, from the attentions of one Alflakr Alfgrimrsson." She gave them a moment for the statement to sink in and shuddered quietly. "It was quite gentlemanly of him."

Asbjorn growled softly. "I knew I didn't like the look of that northern boy," he grumbled. "Did he hurt you?"

"No," replied Ambjorg absently. "But I don't like the way he looks at me. It's like a wolf who's stalking a rabbit."

Eyildr laughed. "What, you mean the same look your brother Dolf has at this very moment? He's spent the last three dances with the same girl." All three turned to see Audolf dancing very closely with a pretty brown-haired girl of about sixteen. Both appeared to be completely oblivious to the rest of the world. Ambjorg rolled her eyes, and Asbjorn chuckled. "It's a different girl every meeting," he said. "He always ends up with a broken heart, but at least he hasn't ended up with a child yet. Of course, there's a first time for everything." Shaking his head, he separated himself from Eyildr and rose. "Sorry, ladies, but it looks as if a few of the men are retiring for the night, and I must finish my rounds before they're gone. Don't wait up for me. Eyildr, a pleasure, as always." His eyes sparkled as he kissed her hand, then left Eyildr and Ambjorg alone on the bench.

The group of young ladies had moved away and were currently fawning over Alflakr, who appeared to relish the attention. Ambjorg turned her back to the group in disgust. "Wish me luck in avoiding him over the next few days; I have a feeling I haven't seen the last of Alflakr."

Eyildr, whose eyes had been following Asbjorn, turned her attention to Ambjorg, then scanned the rest of the room. "I don't think you'll have to worry over much," she said. "Now that Asbjorn knows what's happened, I doubt he'll let Alflakr anywhere near you. And it appears you have a second guardian, as well." She nodded vaguely toward the group of young men speaking with Thane Brandulfr. "Thane Brandulfr has also been keeping an eye on you since your dance.

"Speaking of Thane Brandulfr, what's he like? I've never spoken with him, but the word amongst the girls is that he's polite, but cold. They all think he's attractive, though." She studied Ambjorg's expression for a moment. "What do you think?"

Ambjorg paused for a moment. "To be honest, I'm not exactly sure," she replied cautiously. "He's very polite, but I wouldn't consider him cold. Just quiet. I believe we spoke all of about three sentences."

Eyildr giggled. "But do you think he's attractive? I certainly do, though he's not my type. Dark hair, gray eyes, tall, muscular build…I'll bet he's one of the thanes who goes out and works with his people."

"I'm sure of it," replied Ambjorg. "His hands are as rough as any mill worker's." She sat quietly for a moment, pondering. "I suppose he's attractive. But it's not as if I have the time or energy for such things; with Father's illness, Dolf, Asbi and I are picking up most of the slack. In fact, I should be getting to bed—we have meetings first thing in the morning." She took Eyildr's hand, squeezed it, and said, "I'm so glad you came. It's so good to see a friendly face I know I can trust. There are so few        of those here anymore." With that, she turned and left the hall.

Eyildr watched her go, concern in her eyes. She had known Ambjorg and her brothers since they were children together; her father had sent her to live with family close by every summer until she was thirteen. When she'd last seen the siblings, they'd been the same age as her and looked it; now they were all seventeen, but Eyildr looked the youngest by far. Ambjorg wore more than her years in her expression and bearing, though her face and body were still young and lithe. Asbjorn had a look of responsibility about him she hadn't remembered from the last time she'd visited. Audolf looked much the same, but on the same token, seemed a bit more preoccupied with things other than drinking and women than she'd expected, this night being the exception.

As she stood and glanced around the hall, Eyildr noticed Thane Brandulfr's eyes skim over the now-empty bench beside her, then bid his companions good night and retire from the hall. Leaving the younger ladies to their fawning, she followed suit.

# CHAPTER 3

The next morning Ambjorg and Asbjorn were up early and in their father's chambers an hour before the day's meetings were scheduled to start. The three of them had a small breakfast in the king's sitting room, over which they discussed what they'd learned.

"I hear from Eyildr that tensions are mounting in the north," began Ambjorg. "Her father is giving weapons training to all who wish to learn. She's also been the one looking after his lands while he's been gone on expeditions into the northlands. According to her, even the lesser thanes north of their lands are becoming less and less hospitable."

"I wouldn't be surprised if Alfgrimr was spreading rumors to make the more southern thanes unpopular," replied the king as he chose a piece of fruit from the heaping tray in the center of the table around which they sat. "The problem is, we don't know what rumors he's spreading. We need more information on his movements."

It was about this time that Audolf made his disheveled and bleary-eyed appearance, perhaps a touch moreso than usual. He made his way as unobtrusively as possible into the small chamber and eyed the pastries on the table before him dubiously. Seating himself, he took some toast from the stack next to the fruit. "Morning," he grumbled, and chewed on his toast.

"Good of you to join us," Ambjorg replied curtly.

"Cut him a little slack, Ambi," Asbjorn said. "He was up late last night getting us information, weren't you, Dolf?"

Audolf nodded. "Arnhildr is the second daughter of one of the lesser northern thanes. We spent most of the evening together." He took another bite of his toast and spoke around the mouthful of bread. "She's convinced that her father is half crazy. He went to a meeting of all the thanes in the north, and when he came back, he spoke of strange things—creatures of magic, witches, warlocks, and the like. Said he'd met one in the far north, some peculiar woman from across the mountains. Anyhow, it seems that most of the northern thanes have been growing restless; the winter was harsh, and they feel like the rest of the thanedoms shorted them on aid. Basically, it sounds like the whole area is a hotbed of unrest." He reached for the pot of honey before him, obviously starting to awaken more fully.

King Hrafn nodded. "So I'd surmised. The question is, how do we deal with this? I would prefer a method that does not involve bloodshed."

The four of them sat quietly for a few moments, thoughtfully munching on their meal. "I think we need to find out more," Ambjorg suggested after a while. "Perhaps if we can get some information that might discredit the fomenter of these sentiments…"

"Like we have to guess who that is," Dolf mumbled.

Asbjorn nodded. "I think it's pretty obvious, as well, but the obvious answer isn't always the right one. I'll keep a sharp ear out, and I'll put the word out...elsewhere…to look for things out of the ordinary. Dolf, you might do, as well." His brother nodded "Ambi, keep your eyes peeled; it seems you have Alflakr's attention, so you might be able to catch him at something unsavory." She nodded her assent.

"I'll keep a weather eye out, too," she said as she finished her repast.

The king wiped his mouth with a plain linen napkin. There were few fineries in his personal chambers; he was a man who believed in living simply. "I'll leave most of the information gathering to you three. Even the council sessions tire me so these days." He sank back in his chair, seeming to shrink before their eyes.

"Father, as we've said before, we can stand in your stead at the meetings. You can save your energy for other things," pleaded Ambjorg. She laid a hand on her father's arm, feeling the clammy chill of his skin despite the warmth of the morning and his chambers.

Hrafn patted her hand. "I appreciate the sentiment, Ambjorg, but I really must be in attendance. As touchy as things are right now, our country cannot afford for me to show too much weakness. You saw what almost happened at dinner last night."

"Yes, Father, but I'm sure we could've handled that. Somehow." Ambjorg sighed. "At any rate, I think I will head to the meeting chambers a bit early. I have some more reading to do." She rose from the table, taking with her a sheaf of parchment, and swept out of the room.

Asbjorn stood, then stretched. "I think I shall take a walk," he said. "We have a good half hour before the meetings start, and I have business in the woods." Without further ado, he lumbered out of the chamber.

"Well, if everyone else is leaving, I suppose I shall stay and keep you company, Father," Audolf said, moving to take a seat closer to the king.

"Don't worry about me, son," said Hrafn, waving him off. "I'm due with my healer before the session starts. She'll see me to the meeting chambers, where I'm sure Ambi will meet me." Audolf looked dubious, but he nodded. "Then I suppose I, too, shall take a walk. I'll see you in a half hour or so, Father." He rose and left the chamber.

Once the room was empty, King Hrafn let himself deflate. His inexplicable illness was getting the better of him, and he knew it. He was trying to hang onto life long enough to clear up this mess in the north, and after that, it would be up to his children. *I'll be seeing you soon enough, my Astrid,* he thought. *Until the time is right, give me strength.*

Asbjorn strolled across the meadows outside the great hall, headed toward a large copse of trees just to the southwest. The day was warming up quickly, and before long he was sweating in his brown linen shirt and loose trousers. He reached the copse and stood for a moment in the shade under the closest tree, enjoying the cool breeze fanning him from beneath the low-hanging tree branches.

Soon enough he heard footsteps behind him. Turning, he found Audolf jogging across the field and into the copse behind him. "I see you had the same thought as I," Asbjorn said as his brother slowed to a halt, barely breathing hard. "I'll take the west end of the grove."

"I'll head east, then," replied Audolf, and they turned and went their separate ways.

Asbjorn pushed through the thickening brush, shrugging off a few thistles and thorns as he passed. When he felt he was far enough into the copse, he stopped and stood for a moment next to a large birch tree. Closing his eyes, he rubbed his back on the bark of the tree as if to scratch an itch and concentrated.

Soon there was a rustling in the brush ahead of him. He opened his eyes and a large, brown bear poked its head out of the nearest thicket. It sniffed its way over to where Asbjorn was standing and grunted, looking up at him expectantly.

Asbjorn squatted before the bear and rested his forehead between its ears. What passed between them was silent, an unspoken and brief communion. When Asbjorn straightened, they looked at each other for a moment before the bear wandered off through the thicket from whence it had come, perhaps with a bit more purpose. Likewise, Asbjorn turned and found his way back out of the grove.

On the other side of the stand of trees, Audolf found a comfortable clearing bedded with loam and sat down, legs crossed beneath him. He closed his eyes, and very softly, he howled.

A few moments later, a lean, four-legged figure emerged into the clearing, its yellow eyes fixed on Audolf. The wolf approached him warily. Audolf looked deep into its eyes for a few moments, fixating intently on the wolf, then broke the stare. The wolf took one last look at Audolf, then turned and left the clearing.

Dusting himself off, Audolf headed back the way he'd come, meeting Asbjorn at the edge of the trees. Neither spoke as they headed back to the compound and the meeting chambers.

Ambjorg entered the empty meeting chamber. She took her usual seat to the right of the king's and set down her sheaf of parchments. Sighing in resignation, she began to leaf through them, looking for certain bits of information buried within the reports.

Minutes passed, and eventually Audolf and Asbjorn entered the chamber. "Ah, good, we're still early," said Asbjorn as he took his seat to the left of the king's. Audolf flopped down into his seat, which was just to the left of Asbjorn's. Together, the four seats for the king and his offspring took up one end of the rectangle of tables set up for the council sessions. The rest was filled semi-arbitrarily by the thanes and retainers in attendance. The chamber itself was not overly large, but it contained four windows, two on each of the long sides of the rectangular room, which were often opened to allow the breeze to pass through. This early in the morning they were closed and the chamber was comfortably cool.

"Anything interesting in your stack of reports, Ambi?" asked Audolf as he picked idly at a string on the corner of his good red tunic.

"Stop playing with your tunic. And not yet, but I'm sure there's something here; I just haven't found it yet." She shuffled the parchment she'd been reading behind the rest of the stack and started on the next one.

"Can I help?" asked Asbjorn.

Ambjorg handed him the back half of the sheaf she held. "I've been through these already. If you'd like, you may read them and see what you can find. I'm mostly looking for small details that don't fit—numbers that don't add up, discrepancies, whatever's there. See if you can find anything." She went back to the parchment in her hand.

Asbjorn looked at the first parchment. It was titled *Population Count—Southern Thanedoms, First Quarter*. He skimmed the report, then looked at the second—*Population Count—Northern Thanedoms, First Quarter*. What on earth was she looking for in the general census records? Asbjorn sighed and began to review the reports.

After a few minutes, the thanes began to trickle in. A few brought their oldest sons or daughters to give them experience in the management of the thanedoms as they related to the whole of the country. Since the table was not large enough to fit the thanes and their children, chairs were set along the walls of the chamber behind the ones set at the table. By the time Ambjorg realized the day's participants were arriving a few of these were already filled. She looked up in time to see her friend Eyildr enter just behind her father, Thane Vidar, who smiled at Ambjorg. She returned the gesture warmly, then went back to her reading.

Soon most of the seats at the table were filled and about half the seats behind the table were occupied. The seats nearest the door at the far end of the room were left empty for any latecomers. Ambjorg, judging the time close to when her father should be arriving, set down her papers and slipped out the door to await him.

She didn't have to wait long; no sooner had she entered the hallway than he rounded the corner on the arm of his healer. The middle-aged woman handed him off to Ambjorg, who took his arm and held the door for him as he entered the chamber.

The gentle hum of conversation ceased as the king entered and took his seat. None of the thanes stood when he entered; in this room, it was understood that all were equals. He was merely the facilitator. Nonetheless, he nodded in greeting and was seated.

As soon as everyone was settled the council meeting began in earnest. Much had been resolved the previous day, but much was left undone, and as soon as one topic was solved, another was brought forward. Thane Gunnvaror was just beginning a report on trade with the southerners when the meeting was interrupted by the boisterous entrance of Thane Alfgrimr and his son.

"Here, hand me that, you lackwit," he was saying as the two entered the room. He held a rolled-up parchment in his left hand, and his son had a dissatisfied look about him  Alfgrimr smiled winningly, the expression still not reaching his eyes, and took in the thanes in attendance. "Please excuse our late arrival, my lords," he said. "We had a few…familial difficulties this morning." He took a seat near the door, motioning for his son to take the seat behind him. "Pray continue, Thane Gunnvaror."

The southern thane scowled for a moment, then continued with his report. Ambjorg looked up from her reports long enough to note where the thane was sitting and caught Alflakr staring at her, his hungry eyes boring into hers. She turned away and found her gaze caught momentarily in Thane Brandulfur's steel-hued stare. He nodded almost imperceptibly and turned his attention back to Thane Gunnvaror. Ambjorg realized she hadn't seen him enter and was mildly embarrassed by the fact. She returned to her reports to keep from dwelling on the thought.

The rest of the morning went uneventfully. Despite the hard winter, conditions were good in much of the kingdom; the western shores had yielded a good catch so far, and while the southern forests had been logged a bit extensively, the measures taken the day before would keep them from shrinking irreparably. The mountain-dwelling people in the east had found ore deposits and were beginning to mine for iron as they quarried stone for their masonry, and the thanes just north of the capital expected a good harvest in the fall. Overall, few could complain.

They broke for lunch around noon and headed en masse toward the great hall, where a luncheon of cold meats, cheeses, and breads was already laid out and waiting. The younger members in attendance pounced on the victuals, some of them making sandwiches out of the available supplies and carrying them out into the meadow to enjoy the balmy weather. Many of the older thanes sat at the arranged tables, still talking over the topics at hand.

Asbjorn made his way around the tables, looking for a place to eat his sandwich. He found a spot on a bench between two of the lesser mid-kingdom thanes. "Mind if I join you?" he asked.

"Not at all," said the one to his left. "Please." He gestured to the seat beside him. "We were just discussing our choices in crops this year. Agvior here tells me his people are planting more barley than they did last year, but I can't for the life of me understand why." Asbjorn listened to both sides of the discussion for a while and decided that while neither thane was completely correct in his assessment of the situation, they got along amicably enough.

Meanwhile, Audolf took some of the meat and cheese, made a few lunch rolls, and headed out onto the lawn. He was immediately joined by most of the young ladies in attendance, some of whom were not attending the meetings but had come to the great hall in anticipation of the lunch break. He listened to their gossip and chatter, interjecting a few things here and there to steer the conversation a bit, and generally enjoyed himself for a while.

Ambjorg, on the other hand, nibbled on some of the cheese from the table, then surreptitiously folded a few pieces of meat into a napkin along with an extra piece of cheese and slipped out of the great hall. She made her way across the side courtyard and into the tallest of the surrounding buildings—a watchtower three stories high. Since it was built on the highest of the area's rolling hills, it didn't need to be any taller. Climbing the stairs, she entered the topmost room, which was open to the midday breeze, and unfolded her napkin on the sill. She laid a piece of the meat from her luncheon on the sill, then stepped to the side and leaned on the low wall surrounding the room to survey the cloudscapes before her.

Before long, she heard a keening cry from overhead, and a gray-and-white speckled figure plummeted from the sky, landing on the sill. Cocking its head at her, it picked up the proffered piece of meat and gulped it down in one go. Ambjorg stretched her arm out toward the bird and it carefully stepped onto her wrist, needle-sharp talons barely grazing her skin. She stroked the feathers between its wings and on its chest and it closed its eyes and ducked its head with pleasure. When it finally opened its eyes, she stared into them for a moment, seemingly lost in their raptorous depths, then continued stroking its feathers. After a while, she set another piece of meat on the sill and held her arm up for the eagle to step forward. It gulped down the second piece of meat as quickly as the first, then stared at her for a moment before swooping down from the tower. As warm as the day was, it soon found a thermal to ride and became a tiny speck in the distance.

Ambjorg lingered on the tower's topmost deck for a while. It was one of her favorite retreats when she wished to think without interruptions or needed time alone.

After a few minutes she heard the door below her open and close, then footsteps on the stairway. Unsure of who might have seen her enter the tower, she turned to face the door, carefully schooling her expression into neutrality.

Moments later Thane Brandulfr turned the corner, starting

when he discovered the tower was not empty. "My lady," he said almost reflexively as he regained his composure. "I'm sorry—I didn't expect to find anyone up here. I heard the view was quite spectacular and thought I might have a look before being subjected to another afternoon of confinement. I shall return at another time." He bowed slightly, then turned to leave.

"Please don't let me deprive you of the fresh air; it's particularly refreshing up here," Ambjorg replied. Brandulfr turned again and regarded her for a moment, then nodded and made his way up the rest of the stairs. He took up a place a discreet distance to her left and leaned his forearms on the wall, gazing out into the distance. He'd rolled up his shirtsleeves to the elbows due to the heat of the day, and she noticed that his forearms were well-muscled—the sign of a tradesman, not a merchant or noble. Ambjorg surmised that the rumors of him working with his retainers were probably true.

She resumed both her place on the wall and her reverie, despite the fact that she was acutely aware of the thane's presence to her left. He seemed content with silence. As they watched, the clouds overhead floated idly by, seemingly oblivious to the goings-on below them.

The thane's voice broke their individual contemplation. "It appears I had heard correctly—the view is quite remarkable from here," he mused quietly.

"I'm sure it's nothing like what you're used to," replied Ambjorg absently. "I've never visited the mountains, but I'd imagine the vistas you see every day must be much grander."

"It's different," said Brandulfr distantly. "Everything is so… flat…down here. So much more gentle. The mountains are all harsh angles and crags, deep crevasses and valleys, and painted white with snow for much of the year. It's nice to see a landscape with color and warmth." He glanced toward the great hall, where people had begun filing out toward the meeting chambers. "It appears the meetings are resuming; may I accompany you back to the meeting hall?" He turned to Ambjorg and offered her his arm.

She hesitated, very briefly, then nodded. "Thank you, Thane Brandulfr," she said as she slipped her hand through the crook of his arm.

"The pleasure is mine, my lady," he replied.

They strolled across the lawns and back to the meeting hall in silence, reaching it just in time for the last of the stragglers to resume their seats. Ambjorg nodded to Thane Brandulfr and took her place to the right of her father, who seemed not to notice she'd reentered the room. Two reports sat side by side on the table before him, and he seemed to be comparing them to one another. As she took her seat, the king, without looking up from his reports, asked quietly, "Your brothers could not find you during luncheon, nor could they readily account for all in attendance here. You are well, I trust?" King Hrafn regarded his daughter, a look of fatherly concern on his face.

"Quite well, Father," Ambjorg replied.

"Good." The king glanced at his reports one last time, then addressed the gathering. "Have we all returned?" A few glances around the room and nods from the other attendees affirmed the fact that all were present. "Then let us continue. Before our break for lunch we heard from Thane Eirikr; who was next on the docket?"

One of the lesser thanes from the west stood. "I believe I was next, my lord," he began in a quavering voice. "My people are concerned over the recent border disputes with Thane Rikaror's retainers…"

The afternoon wore on. As the sun passed its zenith and began its descent the room warmed and the windows were opened to allow the slight breeze to pass through. Despite the breath of wind, most of the thanes were sweating and tempers began to flare. Audolf asked to see one of Ambjorg's stack of reports and used the parchment as a fan to cool himself. Only the king seemed unaffected by the heat. Finally, as the sun kissed the tree line, King Hrafn called a halt to the proceedings.

"I believe we've covered most of what was slated for today," he said, pushing himself carefully to his feet, "and I'm sure we could all use a cool drink. Dinner should be set in the great hall within the hour. Please make yourselves comfortable until then." With a nod to the thanes, he took Asbjorn's arm and moved cautiously out the door, followed by Audolf, then Ambjorg, her stack of parchment balanced in the crook of her arm. The rest of the thanes rose, stretched, and began to converse in low voices as they filed slowly out of the room. Last to leave was Thane Alfgrimr, who paused in the doorway and gazed momentarily at the large chair at the opposite end of the room before following his son into the hallway beyond.

Asbjorn escorted the king back to his chambers, accompanied closely by his siblings. "I think things are going quite well, Father," he remarked as they traversed the open-air hallways between the meeting chambers and the king's rooms.

"I would tend to agree, Asbjorn," the king replied. "However, I believe the worst is yet to come. The first few days of meetings are often the easiest, and we have yet to hear from the thanes of some of the larger areas. Keep your eyes and ears open for word on what might be coming in the next few days." They stopped as they reached the door to the king's chambers. "I don't believe I shall join you at the evening meal; today's proceedings have wearied me." He regarded each of his children for a moment, then patted Asbjorn's bulky arm. "I know I needn't worry with you three to manage things." With that, he turned and opened the door to his suite. His children turned to leave, Audolf slouching off toward his quarters, Asbjorn striding across the lawn, and Ambjorg headed to the study to file her reports from the day's discussions.

"Ambjorg." She turned, surprised, to see her father standing with his hand on the door to his suite. "Will you join me for a moment? The report filing can wait." He entered the room beyond, leaving her to rush to catch the door. Once inside, the king seated himself at the small, round table in the center of the room and poured himself a glass of water from the pitcher before him. "Would you care for a drink?" he asked.

"No, thank you, Father," Ambjorg replied. She sat across from him, back straight, and laid her papers on her lap, folding her hands on top of them.

King Hrafn sipped his water for a moment, then spoke without meeting her eye. "I would speak to you as a father to his daughter for a time, Ambi," he began. "Surely you must know that one day, you shall marry and have a family." He paused, gauging her reaction from the corner of his eye. When he did not continue, Ambjorg spoke.

"Of course, Father," she said carefully.

He nodded, studying the water in his glass. "In fact, you are not much younger now than your mother was when she and I were wed." Though he still studied the water, his eyes no longer saw the glass's contents. "I know you feel you must take care of me in my illness, and I know you feel your responsibilities moreso than your brothers, but if I may, I would like to give you a small piece of advice: do not let your responsibilities become your life. Your brothers share the responsibilities of managing the kingdom and still find ways to enjoy the free time they have."

"I do enjoy my free time, Father," Ambjorg protested mildly. "Sometimes I spend hours alone in the watchtower, seeing as the eagle sees, watching him hunt…" She trailed off.

"I know," her father replied, holding a placating hand before him. "But young women your age generally spend time with friends, or courting young men." He smiled wanly. "I hear you have caught the eye of more than one of the young men in attendance this spring."

Ambjorg shivered. "Unless you mean Alflakr Alfgrimrsson, who is a highly unsavory character, I'm sure I don't know what you mean." She poured herself a half-full glass of water from the pitcher on the table.

King Hrafn leaned toward her conspiratorially. "I can honestly say that I have never, in the three years he has been a thane, seen Thane Brandulfr escort a young woman anywhere, in public or private. And the word is he asked you to dance last night—and you accepted." He leaned back in his chair and smiled slyly.

Blushing, Ambjorg said, "Well, simply because you have not witnessed it does not mean it has never occurred. In any case, I only danced with him to escape the attentions of Alflakr." She hid behind her water glass.

The king chuckled. "You could do much worse than Thane Brandulfr. He's only four years your elder, you know." He set his glass down and refilled it from the pitcher. "He's also a well-respected thane, especially by his people, and that speaks highly of him. The easterners do not suffer an incompetent to lead them.

"At any rate, all I am suggesting is that you consider my

advice. I will not always be here to give it, and it would ease my mind to know that you and your brothers are taken care of when I am gone." With that, King Hrafn drained his second glass of water and stood, if unsteadily. "Now, if you will excuse me, I think I will take a nap. Too much maundering has made me sleepy." Ambjorg stood and moved around the table to steady him, but stopped when he waved her away. "It isn't far to my bedchamber. I'll be fine. You go and get ready for supper." The king shuffled off toward his bed.

Ambjorg stood by the table for a moment, unsure of what to say. In the end, she retrieved her parchment sheets from where she'd set them on the table when she stood and quietly left the chamber.

"I thought I might find you here," Asbjorn said gently, the smile on his face evident in his voice.

Eyildr turned, startled from her reverie on the bank of the tiny rill that crossed the copse of trees near the great hall. As her widened eyes took in the great silhouette that was Asbjorn, backed as he was by the sun, she smiled. "You know how much I love this place," she said, trailing her fingers in the chilly waters.

"Father says this was one of Mother's favorite retreats," Asbjorn replied as he seated himself next to her on a moss-covered rock.

"Was it?" Eyildr responded. "You never told me that." She dried her hand on the hem of her skirt and slowly turned to face him. "Is it true that she walked with Freyja?" she asked.

Asbjorn paused for a moment, picking up a small rock and tossing it into the chuckling waters of the stream. "I don't know," he replied at last. "All I know is that she…knew things…like where the winter would be hardest and when the storms of late fall would hit the coast." He picked up another rock. "I wish I could've known her."

The two fell silent for a time. Eyildr shifted closer to Asbjorn and laid her hand over his atop the mossy rock. After a while, she spoke. "It seems the meetings are going well," she prompted.

"Aye, but Father seems to think the worst is yet to come."

Eyildr nodded. "Something's brewing with Thane Alfgrimr, though I'm not quite sure what it is. He's been entirely too accommodating thus far, and he's managed to keep that son of his in check, insofar as that is possible." Despite herself, she shivered. "I've heard stories of that one and his, well, escapades."

Asbjorn's eyes narrowed and he put an arm around Eyildr, drawing her close. "Then stay close to me and he shall not bother you," he declared. "Nor shall any other man, if I have my say about it." He grew silent for a moment, lost in thought.

"What troubles you?" Eyildr asked, shifting so that she could see Asbjorn's face.

He frowned slightly. "Only that all too soon, you and your father will return to your holdings, and I won't be able to watch over you. If things in the north go awry, your father's lands will be among the first to feel the troubles." He sighed.

"I know," she replied, "but you will have to trust in my family's ability to see things through. He may be irresponsible, but my brother is steadfast in his loyalty to his family, and Father is wise in his age." She stood, extending her hand to Asbjorn. "Come, let us walk for a while, then go and prepare ourselves for dinner."

He took her hand, but instead of pulling himself upward, he tugged her onto his lap. Giggling, Eyildr let herself be wrapped in a gigantic bear hug and squeezed against his chest. She listened to his heart beating a strong tattoo against her cheek. "You know I would be lost if anything happened to you," he said quietly as she shifted to rest her head on his shoulder.

"I know," she replied. "But we each have our duties, yours to your father and our country, and mine to my father and his holdings." Eyildr sat up and took his face in both of her hands. "But I promise I shall visit as often as possible from now on." She let her hands fall to her lap. "I'd have come back sooner, but I wasn't sure…" She let her words trail off as she dropped her gaze.

"You weren't sure of what? Of me?" Asbjorn lifted her chin with a finger so that he could meet her gaze. "Eyildr, I have never had eyes for any but you. I have known since you fostered here so many years ago that there could never be anyone else. Any doubt I might've had was washed away as soon as I saw your face three days ago. So if you doubt, do not doubt me." He let his hand fall from beneath her chin.

"But…there are so many others…and many more beautiful…" she began.

Asbjorn stopped her with a finger to her lips. "None so beautiful as you," he said, smiling. "And if you don't believe me, ask the three or four other young men I've had to discourage over the last few days."

"Surely not," Eyildr replied.

"Oh, most definitely! One almost came to blows, though I daresay I'd have had the advantage in that fight." He chuckled, then realized that Eyildr had gone very still. "What's wrong? Have I said something to upset you?"

She sniffled almost imperceptibly. "No," she replied. "It's just…I…don't know what to say." When she finally met his gaze, her eyes were bright with barely-repressed tears.

Asbjorn's expression clouded. "I've upset you," he said and began the process of disentangling himself to stand up.

Eyildr caught his hands, taking them both in her own, her long, fine-boned fingers barely reaching across Asbjorn's great, callused paws. "Please, don't leave. You haven't upset me," she said through the tears that had begun to trail down her cheeks. She smiled up at him. "It's just that—well, I didn't dare to hope that you would wait for me to return. I had no right, no claim to you, and I was certain that if I hoped, you would find someone else and I would be forgotten." It was her turn to lay a finger across Asbjorn's lips to silence his protests. "Now I see that is not the case. I shall never doubt again." Very gently, she removed her finger and replaced it with her lips.

After a few moments, and once Eyildr had dried her tears, they stood, hand in hand, and strolled out of the copse.

Audolf checked his reflection again in the slightly battered steel mirror hung in his bedroom. For the third time that evening, he stripped off the tunic he'd put on and threw it onto his bed. This time he followed it, flopping down across his pillows face-down.

*What am I going to do?* he mused as he buried his face in a pillow and growled. *Arnhildr is getting insistent, and if her reputation is to be believed, I'm surprised someone hasn't gotten her with child already.* He rolled over onto his back, lacing his fingers behind his head. *That's not a chance I want to take. But how do I tell her that without completely putting her off? She's been a font of information thus far, and if I spurn her, she's likely to turn the rest of the ladies against me.* He sighed. Why did information gathering have to be this difficult?

Resignedly, he stood and donned the third tunic again. Perhaps if he simply avoided her? No, that would ruin his own reputation. Rumors would fly that he was afraid to bed a woman, or worse, that he was unable to. But maybe if he began a few rumors of his own along the same lines he'd already heard, then switched his attentions to another target…

That idea had potential. He ruminated on the subject, choosing a plausible story that wasn't too damaging to Arnhildr's already-tarnished reputation and deciding which of the other ladies would be the most useful to ply.

As he put the finishing touches on his wardrobe, Audolf decided that information gathering could be fun, after all.

The evening meal was once again a very relaxed affair. Since the king himself was not in attendance, Asbjorn began the feast, then chatted idly with his siblings about the day's events. Ambjorg noticed that there was a certain lightness to her brother's spirit and wondered what could have caused it—until she realized that his eyes kept straying back to Eyildr, her childhood friend and confidant. She smiled.

Dolf was also slightly distracted, but covered his nerves with a smile and a joke wherever he could interject one. As soon as the meal was finished, he excused himself from the head table and made a beeline for the first group of young men he saw. Ambjorg and her other sibling wondered absently at his behavior as they ate.

When Asbjorn had finished his meal and noticed that Ambjorg was picking at the remnants of hers, he turned to his sister. "Ambi…I have something to ask you," he stated uncomfortably as he shifted in his seat.

"Anything, brother," Ambjorg replied, slightly puzzled.

"It's…I…well, it's like this," Asbjorn began. "I know that you and Eyildr have been close friends for a very long time, and, well, I've always thought she was a very fine young woman, and…oh, Hel." He ran a hand through his unruly mop of hair self-consciously. "I guess what I'm saying is, would it bother you—would you mind—if Eyildr and I…" He trailed off, looking sheepishly at his sister.

Ambjorg laughed. "Of course not, Asbjorn!" She threw her arms around her brother's neck. "In fact, I'd be extremely happy for you both. You have no idea how long she has pined after you!" Letting go, she studied the relief on her brother's face. "But I do thank you for taking my feelings into consideration." She pushed her chair back and stood. "Now, if you don't mind, I'd like to go have a word with her."

Asbjorn caught her hand momentarily. "Just be careful—I haven't actually asked her yet," he warned.

"Not to worry, brother," Ambjorg replied with a wink. "I'm sure she's prepared for that eventuality." With that, she glided down the steps of the dais and toward her waiting companion.

The dancing that evening was even more animated than the previous night's; less than an hour after the meal few were left conversing near the walls. Ambjorg and Eyildr spoke for quite some time, heads close together to better listen over the growing din of music and voices. Eventually, Asbjorn came to claim his dancing partner, and Ambjorg found a quiet, out-of-the-way place to observe the revelry.

Audolf had firmly ensconced himself in a corner with two or three other young men and a carafe of wine. None of them seemed interested in participating in the more social activities at the party. Occasionally, one would glance over at the group of ladies frequented by Arnhildr, then shake his head and pour himself more wine. Ambjorg wondered at her brother's sudden change in behavior, but for once, trusted in his judgment.

Notably absent from the evening meal and following festivities were Thane Alfgrimr and his son, Alflakr. Ambjorg was not in the least upset by this, except for the fact that it meant she could find no excuse to invite the attentions of Thane Brandulfr, who seemed perfectly content to sip wine with a few of his comrades and exchange hunting stories. Only once during the evening did his eyes find Ambjorg, to whom he nodded deferentially, then returned to his conversation. This bothered Ambjorg, though she couldn't define a reason for her malcontent, and she retired to her bed earlier than usual, leaving her brothers to enjoy the jovial atmosphere.

The next few days followed much the same; the daily meetings were productive, though progressively more heated, as the king had prophesied. The evening meals were followed by lively revelry, during which Audolf changed dance partners every night and Asbjorn stayed close by Eyildr. Thane Brandulfr maintained his distance from Ambjorg to her growing chagrin, but managed to stay within sight of her whenever Alflakr Alfgrimrsson was about (though this last escaped her notice).

It was mid-afternoon of the final day of meetings when Thane Alfgrimr finally spoke his thoughts. The morning's discussions had been brief, consisting mostly of a review of the conclusions made on the previous days, and they had broken for lunch early with the hope of concluding the day's business ahead of schedule. All the items on the agenda had been covered when Thane Alfgrimr stood to be recognized.

"I see you have something to discuss, Thane Alfgrimr," said the king from the other end of the tables. "You are recognized. Please present your topic."

"Thank you, my lord," the thane replied. "First, let me say that I feel these proceedings have been most enlightening and productive. My thanks to all who have attended and helped to make it so." He inclined his head to the assembly and received a few nods in return. "I do not wish to keep us any longer than is required, but I do note that one auspicious point has not been covered." He turned to address the king directly. "My lord King Hrafn, with all due respect, I would inquire about the succession to the throne." The sudden silence in the room was palpable. Almost as one, the thanes turned to regard the king, who sat unmoving at the head of the room. "You have three very able children of the same age, my lord. How will you choose your successor?"

The king was silent for a moment. "I have thought long and hard about the issue of succession, Thane Alfgrimr," he replied, "and I believe I have a solution to the problem, though I would appreciate the chance to discuss it with my children before presenting it here."

Thane Alfgrimr nodded. "Of course, my lord. But seeing as how our assembly would need a chance to ratify your decision, as is customary, I was wondering if such a thing might be accomplished before the end of our council this spring."

The king inhaled deeply, holding his breath for a moment, then exhaling slowly. "If the thanes will agree to stay on for one more day, we shall speak of this on the morrow. All in favor?" Heads around the room nodded slowly. "Then let us adjourn, for today's business is finished and I wish some time with my family." The king stood with the assistance of Asbjorn and left the room, followed by his children.

Their slow journey to the king's chambers was silent, each lost in his or her own thoughts on the discussion to come. When they reached their destination, Audolf opened the door for his father and siblings, then closed it firmly, locking it behind him. Ambjorg poured each of them a glass of water from the pitcher on the table around which they took their seats.

The king took a swallow of his water. "Asbjorn, would you check to be sure the windows are firmly closed—and that we are alone? I trust not that this matter was brought up for our discussion." Asbjorn nodded and rose to check the windows. "Audolf, help your brother." Audolf nodded and started toward the opposite end of the room as Asbjorn. "Ambjorg, can you get an overhead view of the building? Is anyone close by?" Ambjorg closed her eyes for a moment, then shook her head.

"No one is close by, Father," she replied as she opened her eyes. King Hrafn closed his eyes for a moment, seemingly lost in thought, then nodded. Audolf thought he heard the cry of a raven as he closed the last window in the room.

Asbjorn and Audolf resumed their seats, looking to their father expectantly. The king gathered his thoughts and began to speak. "I'm sure you've all been wondering for some time now how we would resolve the matter of succession, seeing as how there are three of you and only one of me." The three siblings shrugged nonchalantly.

"We always thought you would have a plan, Father," Audolf answered for all of them.

The king smiled. "I do, in fact." He produced a parchment from a hidden compartment on the table around which they sat. "This parchment outlines the plan I set down for the succession to the throne, as witnessed three days ago by Thanes Gunnvaror, Rikaror, and Brandulfr. Exact copies of this document with original signatures can be found in the study and hidden in one of the stones in the watchtower, in case this copy is lost or otherwise altered.

"I shall let you all read the document itself, but first, let me give you a summary of its contents. Since all three of you are healthy and fit to rule, I see no reason to choose only one of you to succeed me. You work together beautifully and, indeed, are at your best when you can converse with one another. As such, I have chosen you all as my successors." He sat back in his chair, leaving the parchment on the table. Ambjorg reached down and carefully picked it up, reading quickly as the king continued. "It shall work like this: for the first year following my death, you shall all sit the throne as equal rulers. I've already had two extra seats made; the craftsman has been sworn to secrecy, but he knows what to do when the time comes. After the first year has passed, you will take turns, each ruling for a year. During that time, the other two may do as they see fit, acting as advisors when available, possibly traveling the country or raising families during their off time. During times of war or strife, all three shall return to the throne until matters return to normal. In the event of illness or temporary disablement, the next year's on-duty ruler will act as on-duty until the scheduled ruler is fit."

The three siblings sat quietly, ruminating on the subject, as Ambjorg read the document. "Father, this does not take into account the next generation of succession," she said as she finished reading.

"That is an intentional omission," Hrafn replied. "Since none of you are married, it is an omission I feel I can make. I trust in your abilities to decide what's best for the country once the decision must be made."

The four of them sat quietly in thought. Finally, Asbjorn spoke up. "Have you specified the order of rotation, Father?"

"It's in the document," Ambjorg replied, handing it to    Asbjorn. "I'm to be first, then you, then Dolf." Asbjorn read through the document, if a bit more slowly than his sister.

"What about ratification?" asked Audolf. "This is a bit radical and unprecedented. Are you sure the thanes will accept it?"

"The undersigned support it fully," Hrafn replied, "and the lesser thanes of their areas will follow their lead. To be honest, I'm not sure what will happen with the northern thanes. Alfgrimr is likely to buck it, though I have a feeling he'll be sorely outvoted, but that may mean that a few of the lesser thanes in his area could vote against it, as well." He turned to Asbjorn. "Either way, Eyildr's father and his holders are likely to be in a very difficult position." Asbjorn's brow knitted as he considered this point.

"What about the three of you?" asked the king. "What do you think of this plan? Do you accept it? I admit I crafted it without your input, which was a bit callous of me, but I felt I could be more fair to you all if I did so."

The siblings exchanged glances, a wordless communication passing between them. "We do, Father," Ambjorg replied for all of them. "In fact, we couldn't have come up with something better ourselves, and we understand your reasons for your actions." Asbjorn and Audolf nodded their assent.

King Hrafn relaxed visibly. "Then it is decided," he declared. "Now all that's left to do is to have it ratified, which will happen on the morrow. I shall sleep better this night with all this behind us." The king regarded his children fondly for a moment. "It has been a long time since we sat together as a family," he said wistfully. "It makes me glad that we can do so now, despite the busy nature of our lives and our duties." He finished his glass of water and gestured for Ambjorg to pass him the pitcher. She stood instead and refilled his glass.

"Your mother would be so proud of you all," he said, smiling. "You each have something of her, you know. Asbjorn, you have her gentle nature; Audolf, her sense of adventure; and Ambjorg—you have her smile and her deep understanding of our people. There is nothing she couldn't accomplish if she put her mind to it, and when the three of you work together, the same holds true." King Hrafn gazed upon his children for a while, then straightened in his chair. "But enough of my sentimental woolgathering. Tell me of your doings these past few days, for surely you have all done something other than sit in those boring meetings all day!"

Audolf grinned wolfishly. "Well, I think Asbjorn has spent most of his time with E-yil-dr," he said, drawing her name out in a sing-song fashion.

Asbjorn shoved him sideways in his seat. "Of course I have—and don't tell me you're not jealous of me for being able to spend my days with a real lady, unlike those with whom you've been associating." Audolf scowled at his brother.

"Well, I finally got rid of Arnhildr. She was getting a bit pushy, and honestly, she's not worth the trouble. I found out what I could from her, then just helped substantiate a few of the rumors going around about her—and there are plenty, believe me. She hasn't wanted anything to do with me for days." He leaned back in his seat and put his feet up on the coffee table, being careful not to overturn the water pitcher or glasses. "Though she does have a rather pretty friend."

"Don't tell me you're going to start mooning over her," Ambjorg retorted, rolling her eyes. "She has to be the most vapid and useless woman to enter the great hall in ages. Besides, I hear someone else has his eye on her already." She took a dainty sip of her water to hide her smile.

"Really? Who? I'll fix his hay wagon…" Audolf began.

The four sat, talking idly, until time for the evening meal. As the siblings rose to leave, the king rose with them. "I believe I'm feeling better than I have in days," he said. "Would one of you do me the honor of escorting me to the great hall? I would like to dine with my people tonight."

Ambjorg placed the succession document, which lay forgotten on the coffee table, back into its hiding place, then offered her father her arm. "I shall be happy to," she replied with a smile. The king returned it fondly, then took her arm and let his children act as his honor guard on his way to the great hall.

As they entered the hall, a hush fell over the assembled thanes and their families. The king patted Ambjorg's hand, then released her arm and mounted the steps to the dais under his own power. After exchanging a look, the siblings followed and stood before their seats at the head table. Drawing himself up to his full height, the king stood proudly before his seat and said the words to begin the meal in a clear, strong baritone voice. The assembly responded with a hearty cheer, and the first courses of the meal were served.

The meal wore on and the king did not appear to wilt as was normally the case; in fact, he seemed to draw strength from the people around him. Nor did he retire to his chambers immediately after dinner; instead, he spent a half hour or so speaking with various thanes and their families. At one point, he sat in conference with the thanes who had witnessed his succession statement for a few minutes, after which all three nodded, then dispersed to speak with the lesser thanes of their respective areas. Only when the king had received a brief look and a nod from each did he announce that he would retire to his chambers for the night.

The king's healer met him at the door to the great hall and assured Ambjorg, who had followed her father out, that she would see the king safely to his chambers. Even as she fretted over him a bit, the king smiled at her, the same smile she remembered from her childhood and a more carefree smile than she'd seen him wear in ages, and reassured her that he would be fine. With that, he bade her good night, and walked, erect and unaided, toward his chambers.

Ambjorg returned to the great hall to find her brothers waiting just inside the door. "Is he all right?" Audolf asked.

"I think so," Ambjorg replied carefully. "His healer is seeing him to his chambers."

"I haven't seen Father so animated in ages," said Dolf. "Do you think he's finally starting to get better?"

Asbjorn stood quietly, his brow knitted in thought. "I'm not so sure, Dolf," he said finally. "Sometimes, they say that people seem to suddenly recover just before…" He trailed off, unable to finish his sentence.

The three stood for a moment in silent contemplation. "Should we go to him? Stay with him tonight, just in case?" asked Audolf.

"I don't think so," replied Ambjorg. "He's likely to be very tired, however well he may have looked, and he made it clear that he needed no help getting back to his chambers. I think he wants some time alone."

Asbjorn nodded. "Then we'll respect his wishes. Come! Let us enjoy the last night of celebration!" He put his arms around his siblings and herded them towards the dance floor. "I might even steal a dance out of my sister tonight." Ambjorg gave a small smile. "There's my girl," he said, letting go of Audolf. "Shall we?" She nodded and followed him out onto the floor.

As soon as the king rounded the first bend in the hallway, he looked to his healer for support. Leaning heavily on the woman, he made his way slowly back to his chamber door.

"Thank you," he said as they arrived, "but I shan't be needing you this evening."

"My lord, you are exhausted," the healer began. "You know how bad days like this are on your joints—you need your medicines."

The king smiled wearily. "I know where they are," he said, "and I've seen you mix them enough times that I could do it in my sleep—which I may have to do if I don't make it into my bedchamber soon." He patted his long-time caregiver's hand. "Thank you for your concern, but I think I'll make it one more night without your help." Smiling wanly, he made his way into his chambers, then locked and bolted the door.

Seating himself carefully in his favorite chair, he waited.

He might have dozed off, but some time later, King Hrafn heard one of the windows in his bedchamber creak inward. Snapping himself fully awake, he sat up in his chair, almost as straight as he had earlier in the evening. He heard someone slip through the open window, then draw back his bedclothes. When it was discovered that he wasn't in his bed, booted footsteps rang out across the stone floor toward the sitting room where he was seated.

"It's about time you got here," the king began. "Let me see your face before you do what we both know you've come to do." A figure rounded his chair, then stood before him, dressed entirely in black. He was cloaked and hooded, a tall, lanky figure, but his eyes, ice-blue, shone out from beneath the hood. "Ah," the king said in reply, nodding. "I had thought to see your father, but I suppose it follows that he would send his son to do his work." The king poured two glasses of water, sliding one across the table. "Will you drink with me before completing your task?" Without waiting for a reply, he took a drink from his glass and set it back on the table.

"I shall enjoy watching you expire," said the cloaked figure as he moved toward the king. Removing a small packet of paper from his cloak, he opened it and upended the contents into the king's glass. "Then our kingdom will see the strength a true ruler can wield."

The king held his head high. "You do not understand true strength," he replied.

"Quiet, fool!" The figure moved quickly, snatching open the hidden compartment on the table before him and removing the document it contained. The king feigned surprise and reached toward the document.

"Please, no," he said desperately. "Kill me, but leave the document intact. There are those who know of it—they'll catch you for sure—"

"Silence, I said!" The man crumpled the paper, then reached for the nearest candle to set the paper ablaze. "Your so-called plans will die with you. Now, drink!"

"You think I would willingly drink your poison?" the king asked, snorting derisively.

"Then I will force it down your throat!" the man cried, grasping the king's collar and tilting his head back forcibly. King Hrafn fought back, but only feebly, for he was still weakened by the evening's energy expenditures. His younger, stronger attacker forced open his mouth and poured the contents down his gullet. He managed to spit some of it back into the man's face before reflexively swallowing a good mouthful of the tainted water. Crowing in triumph, the man sprang back, taking the glass with him. He opened a window and dumped the remainder of the poisoned liquid onto the grass outside. Then, after refilling the glass halfway and replacing it on the table, he left the way he'd come.

King Hrafn sat back in his chair and attempted to regain his dignity as he waited to die.

Some time and a dance with Audolf later, Ambjorg found Eyildr sitting quietly in a corner with Asbjorn. She hovered close by, waiting to be noticed, and soon Eyildr saw her and motioned her over. Asbjorn excused himself quietly and left, heading for Audolf's group of conversationalists.

"What's wrong with you tonight, dear?" Eyildr asked, concerned. "You've been preoccupied all evening. It's the last night of meeting! You should be enjoying yourself." She took one of Ambjorg's hands in her own.

Ambjorg squeezed her hand. "It's Father," she replied, collapsing onto the seat next to Eyildr. "I'm just worried, is all. He looked so hale this evening." She fussed with her honey-blond hair for a moment, a rare nervous habit. "I worry that he's overtaxed himself, or that it's a sign of…of…" She trailed off.

Eyildr smiled sympathetically. "I'm sure he'll be fine in the morning," she said, "if a little tired. He's probably just happy that the meetings are almost over. Look around—everyone seems as if a weight has been lifted from their shoulders." Ambjorg looked around her, and indeed, the entire assembly seemed lighter. She smiled at Eyildr.

"You're right," she said. "I just can't help but worry about him. I suppose I feel it's my job, since Mother isn't here to do it."

"You do a fine job taking care of him in her stead," Eyildr replied. "But I'm sure she wouldn't want you missing out on tonight's festivities because she isn't around to worry for you." Standing, she drew Ambjorg to her feet. "Come! If you won't dance with the menfolk then I shall have to dance with you instead!" Giggling, she pulled the both of them onto the dance floor. Ambjorg couldn't help but giggle with her as Eyildr, barely the shorter of the two, bowed and took her hand.

They danced the remainder of the song, taking turns at leading and laughing like schoolgirls. A couple of the older boys joined in, one pantomiming a young girl as the other led him around the dance floor. By the time the song ended, most of the youth was on its feet, and half were dancing with partners of the same gender. Laughter filled the great hall as the couples bowed to one another and left the floor.

Panting and chuckling, Eyildr and Ambjorg resumed their seats at the end of the hall. "I've noticed," said Eyildr between breaths, "that your thane is nowhere to be seen tonight."

"'My' thane? Oh, you mean Thane Brandulfr," replied Ambjorg, catching her breath as well. "I hadn't noticed, myself. Besides, he's paid me absolutely no mind the last three days or so." A thoughtful expression crossed her face. "Three days…I wonder…" She stood suddenly, startling Eyildr. "I'm sorry, but I have to go. I'd like to do some thinking."

"Headed to the watchtower, then?" Eyildr asked as she stood.

"Yes," Ambjorg replied. "Thank you for the dance," she said, a twinkle in her eye. "See you on the morrow?"

"Of course," Eyildr replied, giving Ambjorg a sisterly hug. "See you first thing in the morning." She watched Ambjorg leave with a curious expression on her face.

Ambjorg made a beeline for the watchtower, walking quickly. She thought for a moment that she saw a silhouette outlined against the night sky, but in the darkness, she couldn't be sure. Regardless, she unbound her hair, removing the metal rod around which it was wrapped. It wasn't terribly sharp, but it was pointed at one end, and used properly, as Weaponsmaster Geir-varr had trained her, it could be deadly.

She mounted the stairs quietly and carefully, the linen of her skirts making the gentlest of sounds as she spiraled upwards through the torchlight. When she came to the doorway at the top of the stairs, she studied the figure leaning on the crenelated wall for a moment before replacing the rod in her hair and approaching the wall a few feet away.

They both stood in silence for a while before Ambjorg spoke. "You've been avoiding me, Thane Brandulfr," she said quietly.

"I have," he agreed.

"You knew of my father's plans." He nodded silently, his silhouette barely perceptible in the starlight. "And you support them?" He nodded again. "Even though they could very well start a war with the north?" Again, a nod, if slower. "And Thane Gunnvaror? And Thane Rikaror? They acknowledge this, as well?" Another nod.

They stood in silence for a few minutes, each with their own thoughts. Finally, Thane Brandulfr broke the silence. "You're not cross with me?" he asked, turning her direction for the first time since she joined him on the tower.

"No," she replied simply. "I think I understand your reasons. If you had spent much of your time with me during the meetings, once it was discovered that you helped witness Father's succession plan your motives in supporting it could be questioned, and that might undermine its ratification." She paused, watching as an owl swooped from a nearby rooftop to catch its unsuspecting prey, a tiny field mouse. "Am I correct?"

The thane nodded.

"I see." Ambjorg paused for a moment, then turned to leave.

"My lady." She half turned to see him push away from the parapet and turn to face her. In the soft glow from the torch-lit hallway, she could almost make out his expression, but not quite. "Will you visit my holdings sometime? See the snow-covered vistas you spoke of before?" He stood still, tensed, as he awaited her response.

She smiled, knowing he could not see it in the darkness, but that he would hear it in her reply. "I would love to, Thane Brandulfr," she replied.

He relaxed visibly. "I shall look forward to it," he said, bowing. She inclined her head and started back down the stairs.

Just as she reached the doorway out onto the night-covered grounds, she heard dozens of ravens call and take to the sky from the rooftops of the royal quarters. "Father!" she cried as she broke into a dead run.

A few steps later, she heard Thane Brandulfr catch her up. "What's wrong?" he asked as they ran.

"Something's happened," she replied breathlessly. "I think…" She couldn't let herself finish the sentence, and they ran on in silence, their ragged breathing keeping time with their feet.

Audolf and Asbjorn met them at the entrance to the king's chambers, Eyildr not far behind. "You heard it, too?" Dolf asked unnecessarily as they all stopped outside the door. Asbjorn pounded on the door. "Father!" he called. After receiving no response, he tried the door. "Locked," he said. Ambjorg fumbled about a hidden pocket on her skirts and came up with a key. Pushing past her brother, she jammed the key in the lock and shoved on the door. "Barred!" she cried.

Asbjorn pulled her out of the way. "Stand back!" he yelled. With a bellow, he launched himself at the door. Audolf could hear the bar crack as it bent under the pressure, but it held fast. Asbjorn launched himself at the door a second time, this time with Thane Brandulfr's assistance, and the bar gave way. The five of them poured into the room, only to stop suddenly as they took in the scene before them. The king sat, fully clothed, in his favorite chair, hands on the armrests, head lolled to one side. His sightless eyes stared at the floor beside his chair.

Ambjorg, the first to move, fell to her knees beside the chair and grasped one of his thin hands. It was even colder than usual. "Father…" she whispered, tears sliding down her cheeks. Her single-word utterance seemed to unfreeze the rest of those in attendance, and Asbjorn let out a bellow of rage and despair. Audolf looked blankly on the scene as if he didn't quite understand what was happening around him. Eyildr placed a hand over her mouth, then reached out with her other to give comfort to Asbjorn, who was audibly sobbing, his hand over his eyes. Last of all, Thane Brandulfr placed a tentative hand on Ambjorg's shoulder. "My lady," he said. She turned her face to him, tears streaming down her cheeks Closing her eyes for a moment, she laid a hand atop his, then nodded. Wiping at her still-streaming eyes, she shook herself, then cast around the table. "The document," she said, fumbling blindly at the catch for the hidden compartment. When it opened, she bit back a sob. "It's gone."

"There are duplicates," Thane Brandulfr reminded her gently. "I'll go retrieve one." He turned on his heel.

Ambjorg caught him by the wrist. "Please," she said plaintively. "Don't go." She fought back another sob. "Father…"

Audolf, still seemingly in a daze, wandered up to Ambjorg. "I'll go look. Where did they hide the copies?"

"Are you sure you want to go, Dolf?" Eyildr asked, looking up from Asbjorn's side. Her face was also tear-streaked.

"Someone has to," he replied, "and I'm in shock, so I might as well use it to be helpful. 'Sides, I won't be leaving any of you alone. I'll check the study first." He turned and headed for the study.

"Someone…someone should get the healer," Ambjorg said. "She'll know what to do. Eyildr, will you stay with Asbjorn?" Her companion nodded. "Keep watch for a few minutes. I'll be back soon." She started toward the door. After a significant look from Eyildr, Thane Brandulfr followed her out.

Everything after that happened very quickly. Ambjorg met the healer as she rounded the next corner and told her what had happened. Nodding slowly, she followed her back to the king's chambers, where she closed King Hrafn's eyes and had Audolf, who had returned with another copy of the document tucked safely in his shirt, and Asbjorn, whose sobs were subsiding, help her lift the king onto his bed to be laid in state.

Once word had circulated of the king's death, the revelry in the great hall ceased abruptly. A few of the women began to weep, and the men grew quiet. One by one and two by two, they filed out of the great hall to take the news to those who had already gone to bed.

Back in the king's chambers, the siblings, plus Eyildr and Thane Brandulfr, sat in silence. The door to the corridor had been closed, but the door to the king's bedchamber stood open, more through a desire to keep watch over his body than for any perceived closeness. Eventually Asbjorn cried himself to sleep on

Eyildr's shoulder, and she followed him into slumber soon after. Audolf, still in shock over the night's events, was nodding in one of the chairs in the sitting room. Only Ambjorg sat wide awake in one of the chairs in the small dining area attached to the sitting room. She had stopped crying, but otherwise hadn't spoken since summoning the healer.

Thane Brandulfr rose from the sitting room, took a blanket from a chest near the coffee table, and covered Asbjorn and Eyildr with it. After doing the same for Audolf, he joined Ambjorg at the dining table. "Won't you try to get some sleep, like the others?" he asked.

"I couldn't," Ambjorg replied woodenly. "Besides, someone should stay awake to keep watch. If she were still alive, it would be Mother's duty. Since she is not, it falls to me." She stared down at her hands resting on the table. "Father always said I had her hands. I wish I'd known her." She fell silent once again.

After a time, Thane Brandulfr spoke again. "I don't remember her well," he said, "since I was only four when she died, but I remember visiting here once and seeing her briefly." Ambjorg looked at him quizzically. "The queen. Your mother."

Her expression turned to mild surprise. "You saw her?" she asked. "What did she look like? Do you remember?"

"As I said, not well, but enough to know that you very much resemble her," he replied softly. "She had the most beautiful honey-colored hair that she kept long, much like you keep yours, and soft, gray eyes that smiled all the time. I thought she was almost as beautiful as my mother." He smiled in remembrance. "Of course, I thought my mother was the most beautiful woman in the world, so that was quite a comparison."

"What's your mother like?" Ambjorg asked.

"She was a very singular woman," he replied. Ambjorg's expression fell as she caught the past tense in his statement.

"My apologies—I didn't know," she said.

"No apologies necessary," the thane replied. "As you said, you didn't know. She died when I was seven."

"So young," Ambjorg replied. "Is your father still living, then?"

The thane shook his head. "He was killed in the same avalanche that took my mother. Our whole house was buried, as was his smithy and my mother's workshop. I was playing in the woods with a friend, miles away. By the time I got home, half the town had arrived and was trying to dig out the house." He shook his head again. "It was no use; the only things that were salvageable were some of Father's tools. We never did find my parents."

Ambjorg reached across the table and placed a hand atop his. "I'm so sorry," she said.

The thane patted her hand and smiled thinly. "It's been many years," he said. "I've moved on. It's what they would've wanted." Ambjorg smiled back just as wanly and withdrew her hand. They sat together in silence for some time. Eventually, Ambjorg rose and wandered to the door to the garden, undoing the latch. She slipped outside to enjoy the coolness of the night air.

As she wandered the garden, Ambjorg found herself just outside her father's bedchamber window. She looked sorrowfully in on him, lying so motionless on his own bed, until she realized something wasn't quite right. Taking a second, closer look, she noticed that the latch to the window was broken and stood ever so slightly open. She hurried back to the garden door and called to Thane Brandulfr, who rose and looked at her quizzically. Motioning for him to follow her, she hurried back around the side of the building. "Look," she said, pointing, as the thane made his way around the corner. He gazed into the window. "No no no, at the window, the window!" Finally he noticed the broken latch and his eyes narrowed.

"Tell me, when you left the great hall this evening, was Thane Alfgrimr still there?" he asked. She thought for a moment, then nodded. "What about his son?" Ambjorg hesitated.

"I'm not sure," she replied slowly.

Thane Brandulfr growled softly, then turned and went back inside. Shaking Audolf fully awake, he asked him the same question. "Dunno, I think so," he said muzzily as he awoke. "Wait— yes, yes he was! He'd just come back from relieving himself not fifteen minutes earlier. Made a big deal about it, if you ask me." A look crossed his face. "You mean to say…" He shot up from the chair, and only Thane Brandulfr's greater size kept him from hitting the door, a murderous expression on his face. "I'll kill him! Let me go!" He struggled against the thane's firm restraint.

"Audolf, no!" Ambjorg pleaded. "We can't prove anything, and going after him would only make things worse. You're still grief-stricken; we all are. Let's wait until we have something concrete before we seek out justice." Audolf relaxed in Thane Brandulfr's grip and sagged back into his chair. "It's a good thing you didn't wake up Asbjorn, either; I don't think the four of us put together could keep him from killing someone if we told him, so let's try to keep this quiet until after Alfgrimr and his horrible son have departed. Perhaps they'll find a way to incriminate themselves somehow."

"But why would they do such a thing?" Audolf asked, barely smothering his anger.

"Because they're making a play for the ruling of the kingdom, that's why," Thane Brandulfr replied, closing the garden door and latching it behind him. "Your father saw it coming, which is why he had us witness the creation of the documents like the one you carry. Keep it on your person at all times. They've already proven that they'll kill to achieve their goals, so keep that in mind if you see them in the next few days and don't give them an excuse for a fight. They fight dirty, and it isn't worth it." The thane ran a hand through his dark hair, exhaling slowly. "Didn't you wonder why Alfgrimr waited until the last day of the meetings to ask about the succession? Don't you find it a bit odd that the day he asks about it, the king dies in his sleep, seemingly of the illness which has consumed him these past decades, and leaves the issue of the succession unresolved until after the funeral?"

"Why didn't he speak of this to us sooner?" lamented Ambjorg.

"Because he didn't want any of you to stumble onto anything and put yourselves in harm's way," the thane replied. "This way, he was their only target. Whatever might have happened, he knew that war was brewing in the north, and he wanted all three of you alive and healthy to protect the kingdom. It wasn't fair to you, I'll admit that, but I trust that you'll see his logic and that he felt he had to put the needs of the kingdom first." Thane Brandulfr sat himself across from Audolf, still closest to the door.

Audolf exhaled in a burst of frustration. "He knew he was likely to die, and yet he did nothing to stop it! I don't understand."

"I think I do," Ambjorg said quietly. "How long has—had—Father suffered? He clung to life as tenaciously as he could until we were old enough to rule in his stead. Think about the responsibilities he's given us in the last year; they were all a sort of test to be sure we were ready. He's always known that things would be unstable once he passed, especially with there being three of us and none of us counted as eldest, so he's taken all the steps he can to make things as manageable as possible. And you know how much he missed Mother." Her throat caught on this last word, and she sat in silence for a time. "At any rate, they're together now, and I'm sure he did everything he could for us."

Audolf ruminated on Ambjorg's words. "I suppose you're right," he said finally. "It's very selfish of me to think as I have been. Father gave so much of himself to make sure we could carry on after he was gone. It's not fair for me to blame him for any of this." He sat, mollified, and wrapped his blanket tighter around his body.

"Aren't you cold, my lady?" Thane Brandulfr asked as he realized Ambjorg was still in the short-sleeved linen dress she'd worn earlier.

"If I am, I don't feel it," she replied. "Besides, it's helping to keep me awake." Despite herself, she shivered slightly.

The thane rose and gathered another blanket from the chest next to the wall, draping it over her shoulders before resuming his chair. She nodded her thanks absently and wrapped it around her lean form. Soon her shivering subsided, and she made her way back out into the garden in silence to wait for the dawn.

The next day dawned gray and cloudy. It was as if the land itself wept for its fallen king; the birds gave muted song as he was carried by his sons and thanes from his chamber on a litter of oak and ash. They bore his body a mile or so to the sea, followed closely by Ambjorg and Eyildr, then the thanes, lead by Thanes

Brandulfr, Gunnvaror, and Rikaror. Thane Alfgrimr and his son were in attendance, but followed in the middle of the entourage where they could remain fairly anonymous. The procession of mourners extended back as far as the eye could see.

Once they reached the coast, a boat was brought forth, intricately carved at prow and stern with the heads of fearsome dragons. It was a single-masted craft with a lone white sail whipping in the wind. Otherwise, it looked like any of the dozens of fishing boats nearby. It was just large enough to fit the body of the king, which was lowered onto a platform built into the bottom of the boat. Ambjorg and Eyildr and many of the women placed flowers into the boat as they processed past to pay their last respects to King Hrafn. Finally, once the last of the mourners had left, Asbjorn and Audolf, with the help of a few of the thanes, set the sail and shoved the boat off the sand and into the fjord.

The three siblings watched from shore until they could no longer see the craft bearing their father's body toward the rocks ahead. Once the white sail sank from view they climbed the path leading from the beach and headed home.

Later that afternoon a council was held regarding the succession to the throne. By the time the siblings had followed the last of the mourners back to the great hall the craftsman of whom King Hrafn had spoken had already set two new thrones, identical to the original in every way, onto the dais. The new sovereigns made their way through the hall full of sympathetic eyes and down the corridor to the meeting room, which fell silent when they entered. Asbjorn took up his father's seat at the head of the table, Ambjorg to his right, Audolf to his left, and the assembled thanes took their seats.

"In light of the circumstances, let us make this brief," Asbjorn began. "We have in our possession a copy of our father's last will, witnessed by three of the thanes, stating his intentions for the succession of the throne." Audolf produced the document from within his tunic. She couldn't be sure, but Ambjorg thought she saw a flicker of disapproval flash across Thane Alfgrimr's face before he schooled his expression once again. Asbjorn continued. "It states that the succession will occur thus: that for the first year after his death—" his voice caught for a moment, but he plowed forward "—all three of us shall rule in equal stead. For each year thereafter…" He continued outlining the plan for the succession of the throne without pause for comment. "Thus it was stated and thus it shall be, as ratified by this council. All in favor?" Thanes Gunnvaror, Brandulfr, and Rikaror raised their hands, followed quickly by the lesser thanes of the south, east, and west. Thane Vidar, Eyildr's father, raised his hand, as well. One or two of the smaller northern thanes also raised their hands, but Thane Alfgrimr kept his hand quite noticeably on the table in front of him. Regardless, a three-quarters majority was easily reached and the plan for succession was approved. Soon after the meeting was adjourned, and the thanes began to make their plans for returning to their holdings.

Ambjorg, Asbjorn, and Audolf made their way out onto the lawn outside the great hall to take in what scant warmth they could from a break in the clouds. None of them spoke for a while. Eventually, they realized they'd wandered over to the copse of trees across from the hall. Asbjorn silently left the group and headed to the west as Audolf did the same to the east, leaving Ambjorg to make her way back up the gentle slope past the great hall to the watchtower.

She climbed the steps slowly, lost in thought and memory. When she reached the top, she closed her eyes for a moment, feeling the chill wind ruffle her loosely-coiffed hair…her feathers…

Soon she was soaring with the eagle crying above her head. She let loose her hair to feel the wind as he felt it, watching through his eyes as her own tresses whipped back and forth in a sudden gust. For a moment, she was liberated from all her burdens, all her cares. For one moment, she was free.

Just then, she noticed through the eagle's razor-sharp vision a figure paused on the stairs behind her. She tightened her grip on the rod she'd removed from her hair and waited, still facing the parapet wall, to see what the figure would do. It started forward just enough into the light for her to see who it was, then paused, turned, and started back down the stairs.

"Did you think to leave without saying goodbye?" she said, turning and opening her eyes. Thane Brandulfr froze on the staircase, one hand trailing the wall. Straightening, he turned to face her.

"You shouldn't be up here alone, my lady," he said.

"I'm not," she replied, the ghost of a smile dancing around her face. As the thane sought for a response, she continued. "Besides, it's not as if I'm completely helpless." She wound her long hair back around the metal rod and into a loose bun to keep it out of her face. The thane took note of the implement and raised an eyebrow momentarily. "I heard you coming, after all."

Thane Brandulfr, who was secure in his ability to stalk a hind at ten feet without it spooking—and on a windless day, at that—wondered at that for a moment, then moved on with his thoughts. "I came to see if there was any way I could assist you before returning to my people," he said. "Is there anything you require of me before I leave?"

Ambjorg thought for a moment, unable to find a reason for him to stay. She shook her head. "I could not ask of you any more than you've already done," she replied. "Thank you for your help yesterday, and this morning. My brothers and I are in your debt."

He shook his head. "I only did what was required of me by my own honor, my lady," he replied. "It was the least I could do. All I could ask in repayment is that you do the same for someone else, should the opportunity arise." With that, he bowed. "I must take my leave if I am to reach the first inn by nightfall. If I may?"

Ambjorg descended a few stairs to catch up with the thane. Reflexively, he offered her his arm. She took it, laying her gloved hand atop the sleeve of his leather overcoat. "You may. If it please you, I shall see you off."

"As you will, my lady," he replied, and they started down the stairs.

Asbjorn made his way distractedly through the copse of trees. Eventually, he stumbled upon the clearing he realized he'd been subconsciously looking for. Closing his eyes, he sat care-fully on a bed of last autumn's pine needles at the base of a large tree. He shifted back and forth, scratching his back on the rough bark of the pine tree…the birch tree…

Then he was snuffling through the brush after the scent of some spring berries and maybe, if he was lucky, a beehive. He was still famished after spending the entire winter holed up in his cave, sleeping off his fat, and he could use some nice, juicy ber-ries—or maybe a good, plump hare—to start rebuilding his girth for next year's hibernation.

The thought of juicy berries made the bear thirsty, so he trundled down to the small stream that crossed the grove. As he lapped at the water, he realized suddenly that he was being watched. Just downstream, a tall woman with brown eyes and matching hair sat still as a stone, eyes wide with fear.

Asbjorn, realizing it was the bear who was scaring Eyildr half to death, asked the bear to head upstream, out of sight, to get his drink. With a grunt, the bear complied, and Asbjorn opened his eyes, stood, and began to make his way toward the rill.

Eyildr watched, wide-eyed, as the bear snorted, then trundled off upstream in search of something else, though what it could want over the tender morsel she must be, she had no idea. She turned—and found herself face to face with a beautiful, vaguely familiar gray-eyed woman.

Eyildr jumped. "I-I'm sorry, I d-didn't hear you arrive," she stuttered.

The woman laughed, a sound that seemed to carry the laugh of thousands of women of all ages, yet at the same time belonged only to one. "It is I who should apologize, my dear," she said. "I forget that my feet make no sound unless I wish it so." Her voice, a soft alto, blended with the gurgling stream, a counterpoint to its melody. Suddenly, the slight breeze seemed to affect her, tousling her long, golden hair and sending leaves skirling around her plainly-clad figure. She extended her hand. "Walk with me, child. I would speak with you of the days to come."

Eyildr, her mind reeling, took the woman's hand and followed her into the forest.

Audolf trudged aimlessly through the forest, finding eventually that his feet had carried him to the same place they always did. He slumped down in the middle of the clearing, crossing his legs and folding himself onto the loam. Finding a small stick nearby, he began to dig a hole in the dirt in front of him, single-mindedly attempting to make it as deep as he possibly could.

Soon, a four-legged figure appeared at the edge of the clearing. It was joined by another, and another, until eight pairs of eyes ringed the clearing. Audolf raised his head and met the eyes of the first wolf. As one, the pack raised their heads to the sky and howled.

After a moment, Audolf joined them.

Asbjorn traipsed through the forest toward the rill, buoyed by the chance to see Eyildr before she left for her father's holdings. But when he arrived, she wasn't there. He cast about for a moment, looking for signs of her passing, and found none. He consulted with the bear, who was still upstream trying to catch a fish. All he received in return was a vague notion of "safe," combined with an image of two large, gray human eyes.

That made no sense. Eyildr's eyes were brown, not gray. Was she with Ambjorg? But Ambjorg hadn't entered the copse with them, and if he knew her half as well as he thought, she was at the watchtower, doing the same thing he'd come here to do.

Nose to the ground, he kept searching for signs of her whereabouts, finding nothing until he heard the baying of wolves to his right. Finally, he left the rill and headed toward the sound of the mournful howling, knowing he would find his brother there. Together, they might find Eyildr.

The wolves went silent before Asbjorn burst into the clearing Audolf had inhabited. He stopped to catch his breath. "Eyildr," he puffed. "Have you…seen her?" He leaned over with his hands on his knees to catch his breath.

"No, brother," Audolf replied. "Want me to check with the pack?"

"Please," Asbjorn panted. "I know…she was in the grove… saw her…bear…" He trailed off and waved his hand toward his brother.

Audolf closed his eyes, asking the pack if they had run across her scent or seen her on their trip to the clearing. They scented the wind, then replied in their strange way of thought. It had taken him quite some time to decipher how the pack functioned.

"They haven't seen or smelled her since they got here, but they say there's a smell on the wind that means the copse is… well, the closest human approximation is 'safe,'" he replied. "What it means to them is more like 'free from interference of other packs or lone wolves or predators.'"

Asbjorn sighed as he finally caught his breath. "Strange," he said. "I got the same kind of feeling from the bear—that, and an image of a pair of gray human eyes."

Audolf shrugged. "I would trust the animals on this one, brother," he said, standing as the pack disappeared back into the forest. "Come, let's head back to the great hall to bid our farewells."

Asbjorn reluctantly followed his brother back toward the hall.

A short while later Eyildr strolled out of the copse in something of a daze. In her hand she held a single green leaf from an alder tree. Despite its trip through the copse clutched in her hand, it bore no signs of bruising or mistreatment. She folded it carefully and tucked it into a pocket on her riding leathers.

When she looked up, she saw Asbjorn walking purposefully toward her. "There you are! Where did you go? I saw you enter the grove, but when I went to look by the stream, you were gone."

"I took a walk," she replied. "When I didn't see you by the stream, I decided I wanted to stretch my legs before spending the rest of the evening a-horseback." She looked away. Asbjorn studied her with a curious expression, but dropped the subject.

"Shall I see you and your father off?" he asked as they walked toward the stables.

"I'd love for you to," she replied as he took her hand.

Soon the thanes were gone and the great hall was once again empty, though the emptiness seemed more pervasive than it had before. Ambjorg walked through the hall and to her father's chambers, now empty. She met Audolf on the way and Asbjorn at the door.

They entered silently, closing the door behind them. Some thoughtful soul had replaced the bar on the door so that it would function properly. Without a word, they lowered themselves into three of the four chairs in the sitting room, and Ambjorg poured them each a glass of water. She hesitated at the fourth glass on the table, then picked it up and stowed it in a small drawer on the table made for such a purpose.

"So what do we do now?" Audolf asked.

"What Father wanted us to do," Asbjorn replied solemnly. "We protect this land and its people from harm and continue the peace and prosperity he so carefully fostered."

"Even if we have to go to war to do so?" Ambjorg asked, chagrined.

Asbjorn nodded. "Even so."

# CHAPTER 4

Audolf leaned toward his sister. "Do we really have to sit up here, dressed like this, all day?"

"Yes, Audolf, all day," she hissed back angrily. "I know it's hot, but these holders have traveled a very long way for us to hear their pleas. Listening to them is the least we can do." She turned her attention back to the holders who were speaking.

It was late summer, and the past few months had been a blur. When they weren't hearing complaints from holders from all over the country they were responding to written complaints from the thanes, or writing reports, or filing reports, or, very occasionally, helping the nearby holders with their duties. Anymore, spending a day with a holder on his farm was a welcome break from the monotony.

Finally the man finished speaking, and Asbjorn, who was on primary duty that day, contemplated for a moment before suggesting a course of action that should seem fair to both parties involved. When they agreed, he thanked them, and they left the hall.

Slumping in his chair, Asbjorn looked to his sister. "Are there any more today?" he asked plaintively.

Ambjorg checked her roster. "Looks like that was the last of them," she replied, exhaling and relaxing a bit herself. "I think I'll head up to the watchtower."

Audolf's stomach growled. "Think I'll head down to the kitchens, see if I can get a snack," he said, stretching as he stood. Asbjorn poked him in the stomach, causing him to fold in half mid-stretch.

"You're always eating, Dolf, and you never gain a pound!" he exclaimed. Standing, he did some stretching of his own—watching his brother for retaliation the entire time—and started down the dais. "It's a nap for me, I think. This heat makes me sleepy." He yawned, half for effect.

Dolf caught him halfway down the stairs, reaching down a stair or two to grind his knuckles into the top of his brother's head. "You're always sleepy," Dolf grumbled as Asbjorn reached backward to grab at him. He danced out of the way. "Not up for a little exercise? Maybe a bit of swordplay?" He grabbed a roll of parchment off the table Ambjorg was clearing and pantomimed an exchange of blows. She grabbed the parchment on his backswing and glared at him before going back to gathering and organizing the papers.

Asbjorn looked down at his midsection, then back at his brother, and sighed. "I suppose I could use the exercise," he admitted, "especially after spending the entire day sitting in front of this table." Audolf darted past him and down the rest of the stairs, haring off toward the armory. Asbjorn looked to his sister. "Care to join us, Ambi? I know you've been wanting to get more arms practice in."

"Thanks, Asbi, but I think I'll pass today; I did an extended session with the weaponsmaster yesterday and I'm still feeling it, especially after spending the entire day sitting in front of this table." She smiled at her brother. "Go on—I'll finish cleaning up and re-file these." Regardless, he helped her bundle the assorted parchments into a manageable stack before heading toward the armory.

Ambjorg lifted the stack of parchments and made her way carefully down stairs she couldn't see to navigate. Lifting her chin to see over the stack of reports, she successfully traversed the sparsely-populated hallways between the great hall and the study, where the reports would be filed. Organizing them didn't take long; she had a habit of stacking them properly as they were used through the day, so she didn't spend much time re-filing the reports they'd used or written. Soon enough she was striding through the gardens toward the watchtower, still her favorite solitary retreat.

She climbed the stairs, checking as was her recent habit with whatever eagle happened to be nearby—as one always was—that the tower was empty before finishing the journey up the stairs. She closed the gate at the top of the stairs and stared out at the landscape before her.

It was still full summer, and the land was green and vibrant. The rolling hills were a patchwork of green fields, mostly planted in the spring, with maturing crops blanketing the farmland. Here and there a stream cut through the regimented patterns of the cropland, adding silver-blue streaks of natural randomness to the vista.

Though she had seen the same view all her life, Ambjorg never ceased to be amazed by it. She spent a few moments admiring its beauty, then closed her eyes and saw it as the eagle soaring above her saw. Flashes of movement occasionally caught its eye—a female, this time, and hunting to feed her young. Ambjorg sensed from the mother eagle's mental image that they would be ready to fly soon.

She broke contact with the mother eagle and found another, an adolescent male whom she followed for some time before he flew beyond her range. Finally, she found the one she'd been looking for. This eagle had just finished flying a circuit of the northern parts of the realm within a few days' flight of the capital. Ambjorg consulted its strange and quirky memory to see if she could find any signs of the problems rumored to be brewing there. As usual, she found little; it seemed the unrest in the north had quieted compared with months prior, though she didn't trust the relative peace. She indicated that the tired eagle should rest for a moment on the watchtower wall. He complied, roosting a few feet from her as she opened the pouch she'd brought with her. It contained a small, carefully-wrapped pile of diced meat, which she unwrapped and laid on the parapet wall. The exhausted bird let out a cry and hopped over to the pile, greedily gulping the first few bites. She smiled, running a finger down its back between its folded wings, and left it to its meal.

When she returned to the study to make note of what she'd just learned, she found a small pile of letters awaiting someone's attention. Sighing resignedly to herself, she perused the stack. Letters from holders…the usual letter for Asbjorn from Eyildr… another letter for Dolf…a letter from Thane Brandulfr…

She paused, looking back over the parchment envelope bearing the thane's seal. Curiosity soon overcame her and she slid a small knife under the seal. It hadn't been broken, which was a relief; occasionally, the letters from elsewhere in the kingdom showed signs they'd been tampered with. They were all most careful about what they wrote.

*My lords and lady,* the letter began, *I hope this letter finds you well. I know your attentions could be better spent elsewhere, so I shall be brief—my holders are planning a late summer festival like no other this year. We would be honored if you could spare the time to attend, as the festival is meant to honor your collective ascension to the throne, but we will understand if your duties keep you from attending. The messenger sent with this missive will await your reply. By my hand and seal, Thane Brandulfr.*

Their last conversation before her father's death rang out in her mind. *Will you visit my holdings sometime? See the snow-covered vistas you spoke of before?* Ambjorg couldn't help but feel the letter was meant for her moreso than her brothers, but she resolved to present it to them as a collective invitation, regardless.

Skipping the rest of the mail, she took the letter in hand and went to find her brothers.

"You're…getting out…of shape," Audolf panted, leaning on his wooden practice sword.

"You're not…so spry right now…yourself," Asbjorn replied, leaning likewise on his own practice weapon. As usual, their sparring session had drawn a crowd of onlookers. Once it ended the crowd dispersed in twos and threes.

They looked up to see Ambjorg approaching purposefully, parchment in hand. Audolf rolled his eyes. "What's she found us to do now?" he asked reproachfully. "Can't we get fifteen minutes' peace?" Asbjorn shrugged in reply and started toward their sister.

"How would you two feel about a short vacation?" she asked. Dumbfounded, her brothers shrugged, waiting for an explanation. "I have a letter from one of the thanes requesting our presence at his holders' late summer festival, which is to be held in our honor this year."

Audolf took the letter from her. "Ooh, from Thane Brandulfr, no less," he replied, grinning. "I'm sure Sis would lo-o-ove to see him again." He made a kissy face at Ambjorg, who scowled back.

"The messenger he sent is waiting for a reply," she continued. "I don't see a reason to make him wait any longer than is necessary. What do you say? Should we go?"

Asbjorn contemplated for a moment. "One of us should probably stay here," he decided, "to be sure nothing goes awry. But I see no reason two of us can't go and have a little time off." Audolf nodded his assent. "I'll stay," Asbjorn continued. "I've about got the hang of the day-to-day workings of things, and the gods know you've needed a break, Ambi." She looked away, unwilling to admit even to her brother that she'd been working too hard. "Dolf, why don't you go with her? You'll both be better off traveling together, and I know you're itching to be out of the direct path of responsibility for a while." Audolf grinned wolfishly at him. "Besides, wasn't there a certain lesser thane's daughter you had your eye on a while back?" Now it was Dolf's turn to avoid his brother's gaze.

Asbjorn chuckled. "Go, then, and send your reply—you and Dolf shall attend." He racked his practice weapon and padding, gesturing for Audolf to do the same.

"And you, brother, shall stay here and write your daily letters to Eyildr," Ambjorg retorted with a sly smile.

Asbjorn's already ruddy face darkened by a few shades, starting with his ears. "I do not write her daily," he replied, indignant.

"Fine, then," Ambjorg cast over her shoulder as she headed back toward the study. "Every other day."

Grumbling, Asbjorn headed off to his rooms to clean up.

When she returned to the study, Ambjorg penned a hasty but polite reply to the thane's invitation, graciously accepting for herself and her brother. The messenger who brought the invitation was lounging in the stables, but he stood immediately as she entered the barn. "My lady," he said, performing a hasty and unpracticed bow. "I am to receive your response and deliver it directly to Thane Brandulfr. Do you require anything else of me?"

"When is the festival?" she asked as she handed him the parchment envelope sealed with the new royal crest: a bear silhouette with a wolf superimposed and facing opposite, an eagle flying just above their heads. It changed with each ruler according to his or her wishes.

"Nine days hence, in my hometown," the man replied, tucking the parchment into a waterproof leather satchel, which he slung over his shoulder.

"Nine days…" Ambjorg mused. "A good number. It bodes well for our journey. What of the roads? Are they in good condition for travel?"

"Excellent, my lady," the messenger replied.

"And are they safe?"

"Were when I passed through," he said. "But I've heard tell of brigands roundabout the halfway point, right between our holding and the next. You'll find none past the foothills, though. Our thane makes sure them that preys on his people only do so once."

Ambjorg thought for a moment, but no further questions came to mind. "Thank you, good fellow, and take care on your journey home; we wish to share the celebration with you, as well as the rest of your kinsfolk." The man nodded, sketched another hasty bow, and mounted his horse. Within a few moments he was over the horizon and out of sight.

Ambjorg studied the late afternoon sky. The sun dipped low in its track, setting the tips of the trees aflame to the west. Soon it would be dinnertime in the great hall and she still had reports to write and mail to finish sorting and prioritizing. Sighing, she turned and headed back toward the hall.

Sunrise three days later saw Ambjorg and Audolf in the stables, checking over their gear. Neither had packed much; four days of trail rations and a couple sets of clothes for their time in the eastern mountains, plus basic survival gear should they have to cross country at any point. Both wore riding leathers, though

Ambjorg seemed ill at ease. "I would've preferred a split skirt," she remarked when Audolf teased her about her self-consciousness.

"Nonsense, sister," he replied. "The leather holds up to any weather, and if we have to cross country, you'll be thankful for it. It also acts as an extra layer between you and someone else's blade." He paused, regarding his sister for a moment. "I think it rather suits you. Let's just hope Thane Brandulfr agrees." She shot him a murderous look from across the back of the mare she had chosen for their trip.

"Don't worry about him, sweetling," she murmured to the horse. "We'll show him how to ride, won't we?" The mare whickered and tossed her head, reaching around to sniff at the cloak folded over Ambjorg's arm. The day was already warming, and while she wouldn't need it for warmth, she had a feeling it would be welcome in the days to come if the clouds on the eastern horizon matured.

Checking the sword fastened firmly to her saddle and the unstrung bow jutting from her pack, she made one last circle around her mount, trailing a hand down her flank to keep her from spooking as she walked behind the mare. She checked all four hooves to be sure the mare's shoes were secure and to look for rocks lodged in the soft part of her hoof. When everything was finished to her satisfaction, she straightened and went to help her brother.

Audolf was in the midst of saddling his mount. He had chosen a rather headstrong stallion, a beautiful steed, but difficult to manage. Currently, he was struggling to tighten the belly band on his saddle. "Bastard keeps puffing out his ribs," he complained as he pulled on the cinch. Ambjorg slapped the unruly mount's heaving side with one hand and gestured to her brother with the other.

"Hurry, while he's still inhaling," she said. Audolf tightened the cinch. She checked it, then proceeded to help her brother finish saddling the beast. "You'll have to use a firm hand with this one," she remarked as the stallion shivered in his traces. "Are you sure you want to take him instead of that lovely gelding in the corner stall? I'll wait for you to get him saddled."

"And ride into town on anything less than this beauty?" Audolf snorted, and the stallion echoed him. "Never. I'll deal with him."

"All right then—it's your backside," Ambjorg replied, easily finding her seat on the mare. She clicked her tongue and they set off.

Asbjorn was waiting for them by the copse of trees. He stretched, yawned, and rubbed his eyes, then waved as they approached. "Had to see you off," he said as they drew alongside him. "Wouldn't do for me not to." He handed each of them a small package, wrapped in heavy butcher's paper. "Honey loaf," he whispered conspiratorially. "I filched it from the kitchens this morning. It won't last long, but it should see you down the road today." He patted each of their mounts in turn. The mare leaned into his hand, but the stallion danced sideways a step or two. "I see you're taking the feisty one, Dolf," Asbjorn remarked. "You sure you wouldn't rather have the gelding?"

"Not in a million years," Audolf replied.

His brother shrugged. "Have it your way. I'm sure Ambi warned you?" At Ambjorg's nod, he quirked his mouth and patted his brother on the leg. "Fine, then—it's your backside."

"Heyla, I don't think either of you are giving me much credit for my horsemanship. I'll be fine! He's just a beast, after all." The "beast" shied sideways again, tossing his head, and Audolf almost lost his grip on the reigns.

Ambjorg rolled her eyes. Asbjorn smothered a chuckle, then took his sister's hand for a moment, squeezing it before letting go. "Take care on the journey," he said, patting her mount on the rump. "Now get going! The day isn't getting any younger, you know!" With that, he waved and started toward the great hall.

Shaking her head, Ambjorg let Audolf take the lead as they started down the road to the mountains.

The first few days of the five-day journey passed uneventfully. There were inns spaced regularly down the road, so they spent the night each night in relative comfort. During the day they were paced by a silent honor guard which changed as they entered and left pack territories. Ambjorg kept one eye in the sky at all times, on the lookout for brigands and other unsavories.

On the fourth day of their journey Ambjorg stopped them mid-stride in the middle of the path. "We should cut across country for a while," she suggested, finding a game trail that branched off the main road.

"See something we should worry about?" Audolf asked.

"I'm not sure, but I'd rather not find out, if you don't mind," Ambjorg replied, and she nudged her mount toward the game trail.

Audolf cut his mount in front of hers. "I'll go first, then," he said. "You haven't even been camping in years. I've at least been hunting on a regular basis." Deciding that it was not the time for an argument, Ambjorg allowed him to lead.

They followed the game trail for some time, keeping the foothills ahead of them and slightly to the left. Once they'd traveled out of earshot or view of the main road they veered off the game trail when it continued southward and struck out due east to parallel the road. Ambjorg kept an eye on the movement she'd see on the road earlier in the day and was rewarded with a clear view of the brigands she thought she'd seen setting up an ambush a few miles down the road. They were breaking down the trip wire they had set up across the road earlier in the day. She shared her discovery with her brother, who narrowed his eyes, but continued on.

Around dusk, they made camp. Since there were no inns they didn't bother to head back toward the road, but found a suitable clearing a few miles away from the main thoroughfare. There was a stream close by which they used to water the horses and fill their water skins, and Ambjorg bathed and washed out her leathers, which were covered in dust from days on the road. The water was chilly, almost frigid, but she felt it was worth braving the cold to get clean.

Finally, they built a small fire and dug some of the trail rations out of their bags. After sharing a few stories and remembrances of their childhood they rolled out their bedrolls and laid down to rest, secure in the knowledge that the silent, yellow eyes in the woods would keep watch and keep them safe.

The fifth day of their journey dawned bright and warm. As soon as Ambjorg gave the all-clear, she and Audolf returned to the road to follow it the rest of the way to their destination. Even this close to the foothills the temperatures rose to an uncomfortable level by midday. The days and evenings were warm, but the nights were still comfortably cool.

As they climbed the foothills of the eastern mountains the vegetation beside the road became more and more sparse. Eventually the only plants clinging to the base of the mountains were pine and fir trees and the occasional scrub bush. Every now and then a blue spruce would poke its head through a clump of pines, adding a dot of color to the landscape; otherwise, everything to the side of the path was dark green or gray. The grasses this far up the hillsides were not the verdant carpet they were used to seeing, but instead were tall, spindly stalks of greenish yellow, waving in the wind. Despite its seeming desolation, the landscape had an austere elegance all its own.

They paused at midday to rest the horses, who had begun to show signs of their weariness sooner than normal. A small rill cut through the rocks just off the path nearby and they watered the horses at it carefully, then allowed them to graze on the tall grass for a short while. Audolf consulted the map they'd brought with them. "We should be about…here," he said, stabbing at a point on the map with his finger. "We crossed into Thane Brandulfr's holdings sometime yesterday. At the rate we're moving we should reach the town of Thorsbrand by nightfall, and that's with sparing the horses quite a bit. They don't seem to do as well in these mountains." He rolled the map back up and replaced it in his saddlebags.

Ambjorg grudgingly admitted to herself that her brother had become a better horseman in the five days they'd been on the road. Granted, three of those days he hadn't had to saddle his beast in the morning and had grumbled about his sore buttocks, but he'd done well enough on the fourth day without the help of a stable boy, and the stallion had seemed willing enough to follow his direction for most of the day. He kept a tight reign on his mount when necessary and seemed more at ease than when they'd left.

Judging that the horses had enjoyed the sweet grass long enough, they re-mounted and continued eastward—and upward. Soon the trail became steeper, and they dismounted to ease the burden on their mounts as they climbed a knoll covered in scree. Once they'd made the other side with a minimum of scratches and falls they re-mounted and moved on.

Early evening saw the two siblings slouching in the saddles of tired mounts as they rode into the town of Thorsbrand. Seeing the end of their journey near they sat up straighter and attempted to look as presentable as possible. Audolf brushed off his leathers to remove the worst of the road dust, and Ambjorg tossed her single, long braid back over her shoulder, shifting in her saddle to ease the stiffness in her joints. As they approached the outer walls a wide-eyed child went sprinting off into town, calling before him, "They're here! They're here!" Holders and craftsmen and their families came to the doors of the dwellings and shops lining the streets. Smiling at the massing crowd, the siblings waved in greeting as they rode. Cheers and children's laughter followed them through the streets.

The gravel-paved road led them into the town square, which was little more than a broad path winding around a fenced garden. Around the square sat the inn—a good-sized building that appeared to have more common room area than accommodations—and various shops and craft workshops, including a good-sized smithy. As they approached, they could see the glow of the forge, cherry-red in the slowly fading light. The smith was at the anvil, his apprentice working the bellows, but he looked up as they passed.

Gray eyes met gray, and Ambjorg realized that the smith was not a smith at all. Blinking in surprise, he set aside the iron rod he'd been working with, leaving it on the side of the forge. He placed a hand on the shoulder of the boy working the bellows and spoke to him briefly. The boy nodded, then started racking the tools left out on the workbench and anvil. The erstwhile smith picked up a rag and wiped his hands clean of the soot they'd acquired.

Ambjorg had stopped her mount in front of the smithy. Audolf, blissfully unaware, continued on a few lengths before realizing he'd left his sister behind. His mount complained at the sudden change of direction as he rode back to the open front of the smithy, a quizzical look on his face until he saw Thane Brandulfr remove his heavy leather apron and hang it next to the workbench.

"Thane Brandulfr!" he exclaimed. "It's good to see you." He dismounted somewhat stiffly despite his best efforts and tossed the reins of his mount over its head to use them as a lead rope.

The thane nodded, bowing slightly. "My lord," he replied, clasping hands with Audolf briefly. Turning to Ambjorg, he offered her his hand. "My lady," he said with a slightly deeper bow. Instead of taking his hand, she handed him the reins of her mare and dismounted unaided with the fluid grace of an accomplished rider. There were a few nods from the crowd that had gathered.

"Thane Brandulfr," she replied, inclining her head toward him with a triumphant twinkle in her eye. Taking her actions in stride, the thane tossed the reins over her mare's head and began to lead it through the town square. Audolf fell in beside Thane Brandulfr, and Ambjorg beside her brother. "I see you and your holders are faring well," she offered.

He nodded as he led them past more houses and shops and down the other side of the main thoroughfare. "Despite the hard winter, we've had a good spring planting and the crops look healthy, such as they are. The deer and small game populations are smaller than in recent years, but that's to be expected, and there is still plenty to feed the mouths we have through the next winter." He turned toward the siblings. "I must apologize for not greeting you sooner," he said. "I tend to lose track of time in the smithy. The town smith had an accident last week and has been unable to work since, and there are always horses that need shoeing."

"Were you a smith before you were thane, then?" Audolf asked.

Thane Brandulfr shrugged. "My father was a smith," he replied. "I know something of the trade." They walked silently for a while, the siblings smiling and waving at the townspeople and children lining their path. "I hope you don't mind," the thane began as they rounded a corner, "but I've taken the liberty of airing out two of the guest rooms in my home. They're a bit better-appointed and a great deal more private than the inn in the town, and it's not often they see occupants. Will this be acceptable for your accommodations?"

"Sounds fine to me," Audolf replied, then belatedly looked to his sister. "That is, if it's all right with Ambjorg."

She appeared to consider for a moment, then nodded. "It shall be our pleasure to guest with you," she replied, eyes on the road before them. Audolf exhaled, and even Thane Brandulfr seemed slightly more at ease. They continued to nod greetings and wave to the townspeople as they made their way down the street.

As they turned a final corner the thane's dwelling loomed into view. It was a rectangular two-story structure made entirely of gray stone with windows dotting the front of the building and stacks for two chimneys visible above the slate roof. As they approached the building they were greeted by a carved oaken door, polished, but worn, with a large brass knocker and matching handle. Thane Brandulfr handed the reins of Ambjorg's horse to one of the men following them, gesturing for Audolf to do the same with his, and pushed open the door.

The room beyond looked as if it belonged in a hunting lodge. An elk's head stared at them with empty glass eyes from above the doorway to the next room. The stone floor was covered in a bearskin rug, and the back of each chair in the sitting room was draped with the pelt of some smaller creature—one with a beaver, one a hare. Audolf's eyes lingered on the bearskin rug before they made their way into the next room, a formal dining room. This room had an air of disuse; the candelabrum on the table sported a thin layer of dust, as did the table and its green runner with gold trim. They moved quickly on through the attached study, which had seen much recent use based on its state of general disarray, and up the stairs to the second level.

The guest rooms were the first two doors at the top of the stairs. Thane Brandulfr showed them to their rooms, then showed them the upstairs jakes, complete with bathtub. "Dinner will be ready in about an hour," he said, "which should give you a bit of time to recover from your journey. My assistant, Agvarr, will be upstairs with your saddlebags shortly." With a nod to both of his guests, he left them to settle into their quarters.

Audolf threw himself onto his bed in full sprawl. "Ah, this feels wonderful," he sighed as he kicked off his boots.

"You really should clean up before you touch anything," Ambjorg said from the doorway as she gently pulled the braid out of her hair. "You're filthy."

"So are you," Audolf observed, and he threw a pillow at his sister.

She dodged it, then picked it up off the floor. "Yes, but I plan on taking a bath as soon as is humanly possible," she said as she tossed the pillow back onto Audolf's bed. About that time, Agvarr appeared at the top of the staircase, carrying a set of saddlebags. He was an older man, perhaps fifty, but managed the saddlebags quite well despite his apparent age.

"My lady," he said, "I brought yours up first, thinkin' you might want first crack at your things for a bath." He set her saddlebags just inside the door to her room. "I'll be right back up with some hot water." Straightening, he hurried back down the stairs.

Ambjorg arched an eyebrow at her brother. "Looks like I'll get my wish," she said. Soon, Agvarr reappeared carrying two buckets of steaming water. He dumped them into the tub, then turned a knob above the spigot and let the tub fill the rest of the way with cool water from the cistern outside. "I can fetch a few more buckets if you'd like it hotter," he offered.

"Oh no, I'm sure it will be just fine," Ambjorg replied, smiling. "It's been a warm trip, so I think I'd rather take a lukewarm bath. I appreciate the effort."

"Whoops—almost forgot." Agvarr dug around in his pocket for a moment, then produced a cake of soap. "My wife sent you this. She makes some of the best lavender soap this side o' the southlands. Said you might like to feel like a lady again after such a journey." He presented the soap to Ambjorg.

She took it, taking in the heady scent of lavender. "Thank her for me, Agvarr—it smells wonderful!"

He nodded. "I shall, my lady. Now, if you'll excuse me, I must retrieve my lord's baggage, then attend to dinner." Bowing, he headed back down the stairs.

Ambjorg dug in her things for a suitable change of clothes and the small brush she'd packed. "I'll be in the bath," she called across the hall as she passed Audolf's room. He grunted in response, still sprawled on his bed.

Laying out her change of clothes on the counter in the bathroom, Ambjorg stripped off her dusty, sweat-soaked riding leathers before realizing that the curtains on the bathroom window were open. Holding her leathers in front of her, she leaned down and peeked over the sill—and her breath caught in her throat. The holding backed onto a steep slope, almost a cliff, that plunged into a deep valley. Beyond the ravine the northern section of the mountain range thrust skyward. The tips of the highest peaks were wreathed with clouds, but the summits of the lesser slopes were visible and still capped with snow despite the warmth of the season. Looking out on the range of mountains before her, Ambjorg couldn't imagine crossing them, and suddenly understood the importance of the single pass through the mountains.

Remembering the quickly-cooling bath behind her, she closed the drapes and eased herself into the tub, leaving her leathers in a pile on the floor. The water was just warm enough to ease her muscles after a long day's ride. She ducked her head under the water and began to wash her hair, using the lavender soap from Agvarr's wife to help remove all traces of dirt first from her hair, then from the rest of her body. She scrubbed at her skin until it was pink before she truly felt clean.

Setting the soap aside, she hoisted herself out of the tub and pulled the plug in the bottom to allow the water to drain. She dripped on the carpet for a moment before finding a towel in one of the cupboards, then dried herself off and wrapped the towel around her hair, squeezing it to remove the excess water. When she was certain it wouldn't drip she unwound the towel and hung it over the side of the tub, then donned the blue linen dress she'd brought. It was long-sleeved, but light, and should be comfortable even if the evening became chilly.

She was halfway through brushing her hair when Audolf knocked on the door. "Sis? Did you fall asleep in there?"

"No," she called through the door. "I'm brushing my hair—a

moment, if you please." Gathering her dirty leathers and the rest of her things, she opened the door. "I'll finish in my room. The bathroom is all yours." She swept off down the hallway to her room and closed the door.

Audolf grumbled after her. "She gets first bath—and the one with warm water, at that—and still acts like I'm being a nuisance for asking if she's through." Sighing, he closed the door, put down his change of clothes, and turned the knob to fill the tub.

Dinner was a casual affair served in a smaller dining area off the sitting room they'd crossed when they'd first entered the house. The fare was plain, but well-prepared: roasted mutton with baked potatoes and a leafy summer green on the side tossed with lentils. The meat was pleasantly spiced, and there was butter for the potatoes and the dark bread served hot from the oven. A dry white wine rounded out the meal.

Over dinner Audolf and the thane exchanged news from different parts of the kingdom. Thane Brandulfr had heard little from the northern reaches, but had heard from the southern and western; they had begun to put into play the plan the king had endorsed a few months earlier. The southland forests were set to recover within a few years, and the fishing on the coast was as successful as ever. Audolf was able to fill them in on some of the news from the north, but since there wasn't much concrete to tell, he merely mentioned that tensions were growing between the northern reaches and the rest of the country and left it at that.

Ambjorg ate in silence, for the most part. She interjected a time or two to expound on one of Audolf's points or to add a tidbit of information she'd run across, but otherwise she allowed Audolf's garrulous nature to dominate the conversation. When she'd finished eating Agvarr reappeared and took away her plate. She thanked him, receiving a smile in return, and excused herself from the table.

As she passed through the sitting room on her way to the front door she couldn't help but shiver as she saw the bearskin rug. She hurried past, out the door and into the pleasant night air. It was full dark, but there were lights on in the town, and the townspeople scurried from house to house, sometimes carrying bundles tightly to their chests. They looked purposeful but not rushed.

Ambjorg strolled around the back of the holding, careful to keep her distance from the slope ahead, and found a small porch attached to the back of the first floor. She seated herself on the single step and closed her eyes, searching the wind and finding the familiar feel of an eagle coming home to roost for the night. It was another female with a nest of three young—a large clutch for her breed—and they were hungry. She carried with her two small mice and a squirrel.

Drawing her attention back to the porch, Ambjorg smiled. Even in such seemingly inhospitable surroundings, life carried on. She mused on that for a while as she gazed at the stars above. It was a new moon, so the sky was dusted with them, an uninterrupted stream of glittering points marching across the heavens.

The door behind her creaked open slowly. "Might I join you?" Thane Brandulfr asked as he leaned around the doorway.

"As you will," Ambjorg replied. She moved over to make room on the stair for him to pass. Instead, he sat down on the stair beside her and followed her gaze into the starscape above.

They sat quietly for some time, contemplating the celestial vistas before them. Thane Brandulfr broke the silence. "Your brother has retired for the evening," he said in a soft voice. "He is exhausted from your journey. Are you not also tired, my lady?"

She shook her head, smiling. "My brother is not accustomed to spending time a-horseback," she replied. "I am not yet tired enough to sleep."

"As my lady wishes."

They fell silent once again, though each struggled inwardly to find words to fill the void of conversation. "The festival begins on the morrow," the thane offered. Ambjorg nodded.

"We've been looking forward to the festivities," she replied. "It's been some time since we had cause to celebrate." Still studying the night sky, she pulled her hair over her shoulder and absently began to braid it.

"Word among the thanes is that the three of you are doing a fine job of managing the kingdom," said Thane Brandulfr. "You

have their approval thus far, and I don't see that changing any-
time soon."

"We had heard as much, but it's good to hear it from a trusted source," Ambjorg replied.

"I'm glad you think of me as such," he replied.

Ambjorg undid the braid she'd done in her hair and began
to braid it again in the dark. She was acutely aware of both the
thane's physical proximity to her and the words neither of them
spoke, but both understood. She snuck a glance at Thane Brandulfr out of the corner of her eye. He sat stoically not a foot
from her, his knees drawn up and resting on the ground below
the step, arms folded and resting atop his knees. She could tell
he'd washed since working in the smithy, but his hands were still
stained a faint black, visible even by the dim starlight.

"I daresay there are few thanes who could replace one of
their village craftspeople, even for a short time," she ventured,
nodding toward his hands. He glanced at them, then shrugged.

"I do as I am able," he replied. "It is within my skill, and
without a metalworker, my people cannot prosper. Wagons and
carts break frequently on the rocky terrain up here, horses slip
shoes, coopers need barrel bindings…" He trailed off, then continued. "Smithing was good enough work for my father. Thane or
not, it will ever be good enough work for me."

Ambjorg smiled at him. "I'm sure he'd be proud of
you." She turned back to the stars. "I can only hope I do mine as
much honor as you do yours."

The thane hesitated for a moment, then laid a hand gently on
her shoulder. Without looking back at him, she reached up and
covered it with her own for a moment, then stood. "Tired or not, I
should be getting to bed," she remarked. "Please thank Agvarr for
the enjoyable meal and for all his help this evening."

Thane Brandulfr stood and opened the door for her. "I shall,
my lady," he replied as he followed her inside.

The next morning Ambjorg rose soon after dawn. She left
Audolf snoring loudly in his room and crept downstairs to see if
the house was awake. Just to the left of the staircase was the en-

trance to the kitchen, from which issued a clattering of pots, pans, and other dishes, punctuated by the occasional curse. The voice was not what she expected; for one, it was female.

"Can't find a damned thing in this kitchen," it muttered. Ambjorg turned a corner to see a portly, older woman rummaging through the cabinets. "Man has no organizational skills." She stood on her toes, reaching for a cast-iron griddle on the top shelf of a cupboard that was just beyond her reach.

Seeing an opportunity to be helpful, Ambjorg swept into the room, reached over the woman's head, and retrieved the griddle. "Thank you, dearie," the woman said absently, then turned abruptly. "Oh! Good morning, milady! Didn't expect to see you up early, what with the long trip and all." She bustled over to the stove and set down the griddle. Wiping her hands on her apron, she bobbed a quick curtsy. "I be Ingr, Agvarr's wife. He's busy with the festival today, so the cookin' and waitin' on and such falls to me. Be you wantin' anything in particular for breakfast?" Ambjorg shook her head. "All right, then, eggs and pancakes it be." Ingr busied herself about the stove and pantry and left Ambjorg to find an out-of-the-way corner. After a few near misses, she found a stool next to the island in the kitchen and set it in a corner, taking a seat.

"Do you think his lordship will be joining us for breakfast?" Ingr asked as she began to mix the pancake batter in a large wooden bowl.

"Is Thane Brandulfr not yet awake, then?" Ambjorg replied, curious.

Ingr laughed. "Oh, most certainly! Our Bran was up with the dawn—said he had some work to finish out at the smithy. I spoke of milady's brother." Stoking the fire in the wood-burning stove, she poured the first few pancakes onto the heated griddle.

"I should think he'll be along in an hour or so," Ambjorg said. "He's not an early riser as a rule, and the trip was hard on him." *Our Bran?* she thought.

"Poor dearie," Ingr replied as she beat eggs in another wooden bowl. "It is a dreadful long way. O' course, it's not so bad if you take the valley road." At Ambjorg's puzzled expression, she rolled her eyes. "Did Bran not tell you? I shall have his hide! Nobody uses the old road up the mountain anymore. It's in horrible shape—there's another, newer road, wide enough for the traders' carts to pass. Does switchbacks up the mountainside and comes out just below the town. We'll be sure you leave with it marked on such maps as you may have." She flipped the first of the pancakes expertly.

"Is there anything I can do to help?" Ambjorg inquired, shifting anxiously on her stool.

"No, no, I wouldn't hear of it!" Ingr declared. "'Sides, Bran'd have my hide for lettin' you get your hands dirty. You're our guest, and it's not often we get to do for others around here, so if you don't mind, we'll be waitin' on you as often as possible." She flipped the pancakes back over, judged them ready for consumption, and slid them off onto an earthenware plate. "Eggs'll be ready in a moment," she said as she slid the plate and a fork toward Ambjorg. "You're welcome to break your fast wherever you like—I'd recommend the back porch, m'self, as the view is splendid. Here, have some syrup." She produced a small flask of sweet, amber liquid from a cabinet under the island.

Ambjorg took a small bite of one of the pancakes. They were light, fluffy, and perfectly cooked. She poured a judicious amount of the syrup onto them, then waited for it to soak in. "Thank you, Ingr—they're delicious," she said as she started in on her breakfast. Before she'd finished the first quarter of the pancakes, Ingr slid a generous helping of scrambled eggs onto her plate.

"Be needin' that later," she surmised. "Festival days are always busy. Lots to do during the day and plenty of music for dancin' 'round the bonfire." She grinned at Ambjorg. "That is, if you're young enough to be dancin'. I haven't gotten Agvarr off his lazy behind in years! Now go—head out to yon porch and enjoy your breakfast while I clean up a bit here." Ambjorg thanked her again and started toward the back door. "And take your time—when you're finished, we'll do something with your hair," Ingr called after her. Smiling, Ambjorg quietly opened the back door and eased out onto the porch.

Ingr was right; the view was breathtaking. The same panorama she'd admired from the bathroom window the evening before was lit from the opposite side, and she could almost see the sunlight seeping down toward the bottom of the ravine before her. Her breakfast forgotten, she spent a long moment simply enjoying the view. The morning's birdsong had begun in earnest and provided a boisterous melody as a counterpoint to the peaceful scene before her.

Remembering her breakfast, she consumed it as quickly as manners would allow and soon found an empty plate staring back at her. Taking one last look at the ever-brightening mountaintops, she went back inside. Ingr was still in the kitchen, washing the cooking implements used for her breakfast. "Are you sure I can't help?" Ambjorg asked again as she handed her dish to the older woman.

"Wouldn't hear of it, milady," Ingr replied, taking her dirty dishes from her and washing them in the oversized sink. She dried them with a towel hung over her shoulder, then replaced them in the cupboard before turning to face Ambjorg. "Is that what you plan on wearing to the festival?" Ambjorg nodded in reply. "Then I believe I have just the thing to go with it for your hair," Ingr decided. "Come, milady—I shall fetch a few ribbons. A nice blue and gray should match well." She started off toward one of the rooms on the back side of the house, which might once have been servants' quarters, but now had become something of a catch-all room for various odds and ends. Digging through one of the stacks produced two matching blue ribbons and a third deep gray one. "Knew I kept these for a reason," Ingr declared. "Now, if you'll just have a seat, milady—" she indicated a short stool half obscured by a pile of knickknacks "—I'll see what I can do." Ambjorg shifted the detritus from the stool and seated herself, narrowly avoiding painful a run-in with a rogue pincushion she'd missed. "It's been some time since my daughter was around to let me braid her hair for her. Such beautiful hair she has, a nice, deep brown." Ingr brushed Ambjorg's hair out until it shone. "Why, I remember once…"

Ingr's soliloquy continued through the considerable amount of time it took to intricately braid the entirety of Ambjorg's hair and covered her family, to whom her daughters were married, their children, their holdings, and many other family details. Ambjorg listened enough to recall that one of the daughters had moved to the southlands with her new husband and was expecting her first child, but soon could no longer keep track of the particulars. When she'd finished she held up a small steel mirror for Ambjorg to observe her handiwork. "What does my lady think?" She had started a braid on each side of Ambjorg's head close to the brow, then brought it around the hairline over her ear and down to the nape of her neck. At the base of her neck the two braids met with a third taken from the top of her hairline, and all three braids were then braided together and hung down her back. The two blue ribbons were wound into the braids on the sides of her head, while the gray ribbon was wound into the center section. Overall the effect was quite striking, yet still highly practical.

"It looks wonderful!" Ambjorg exclaimed as she turned her head back and forth to get a proper look. "Thank you, Ingr!"

"My pleasure, milady—I do the best I can," she replied, beaming. "Now, the day is still young, but the town should be busy. If you follow the road to the town square, you'll run right into the festival grounds. There's plenty to see and do there, and you might even run into our Bran as he finishes his work at the smithy."

"I shall have to have a look," Ambjorg answered.

"Go then, milady, and I shall wait for your brother to rise." Ingr busied herself reorganizing a small pile of trinkets in one corner of the room, mumbling to herself. Taking this as a tacit dismissal, Ambjorg strode through the house and out the front door.

The town was, indeed, buzzing with activity, and the closer she got to the town square the more people thronged the streets. All of them seemed to be carrying something—wood planking for the merchant stands around the square, baskets of items for sale, bushels of summer greens. Heads turned as she passed, and a few had the presence of mind to bow or curtsy awkwardly. She nodded and smiled reassuringly and they continued about their duties.

Ambjorg decided to stroll through the square and down a few of the smaller lanes between groups of houses. As she passed the smithy she found herself craning her head to look for the thane, but his back was to her as he fired a piece of metal in the forge. Not wishing to draw attention to herself, she continued around the square and down one of the smaller lanes off the main thoroughfare. Here, children chased a ball down the lane, crowing with raucous laughter when one came within a hair's breadth of catching it, then accidentally kicked it further. A few chickens spooked from around a discarded heel of bread as the children raced by.

Suddenly a woman turned the corner at the end of the lane, frantically looking about in a panic. Spotting Ambjorg, she ran down the lane, picking up her skirts to keep from tripping over children or chickens. "Help! Please, you must help me! It's my husband!" the woman cried, breathless. She reached Ambjorg and took hold of her arm with a white-knuckled grip. "My husband—he's been taken!"

Ambjorg took the woman by the hand and led her toward the smithy. "Come—we'll find Thane Brandulfr. Taken by whom?" she asked as they trotted through the square.

"A—a *thing*!" the woman replied. "It was horrible! All tall and covered in fur…" She trailed off at the horror of her recollection. Not knowing what to say, Ambjorg fell silent as they approached the smithy. The thane was still heating the piece of metal she'd seen him preparing to work when she'd passed before, and she approached him cautiously, laying a hand on his shoulder. "Thane Brandulfr, there is a woman here who claims her husband has been taken by some sort of creature," she began.

"He was!" the woman cried. "Plucked from the porch as if he were a rag doll! Please, you must believe me!" Tears rolled down her ruddy cheeks in salted rivulets as she clutched at Ambjorg's arm.

Thane Brandulfr set his tools on the hearth and shared a glance with the boy working the bellows. The boy immediately ceased his pumping and began to bank the fire in the forge, putting up tools as he went. The thane approached the woman calmly, removing his elbow-length leather gloves and apron as he approached. "You say he was taken? When?" he asked in a quiet voice.

"J-just now!" she replied. "I came straight here fast as I

could."

"Did you see where it went?"

"North, I think."

He contemplated for a moment, then nodded and burst into action. "We'll need a search party," he said to the closest townsman. "Gather every able-bodied man you can find. Make certain they are armed—longbows, if they have them. We'll leave from the holding as soon as we have enough; it can't have gotten far." With that, he set out for his home at an easy lope.

Ambjorg, momentarily bewildered by the entire turn of events, caught him easily. "My brother and I shall go with you," she said as she drew abreast of him.

He glanced at her sidelong. "Certainly not, my lady," he replied. "You aren't familiar with the terrain. One slip could cost you your life. What's more, we hunt a very dangerous creature; I could not put you at such risk."

"I don't recall giving you a choice," she replied coldly.

The thane slowed to a walk as they reached the holding. He looked at Ambjorg for a long, interminable moment, then nodded. "As you will, my lady, but you will go with one of my men. We travel in groups of two or more, never less. You must listen carefully to anything he may tell you to do; it could save your life. Did you bring a weapon?" She nodded. "Good. Keep it close at hand."

"I shall go and fetch Audolf," she said, hurrying into the house and up the stairs. Thane Brandulfr headed for the other end of the house.

She met Audolf on his way down. "Come," she said, taking him by the sleeve.

"But I just woke up!" he protested around a yawn.

"We're joining a search party," she continued despite his protest. "One of the men in the village was taken by some horrible creature, and we're going to help find him." She pushed Audolf toward his room. "Change into your riding leathers, and see if you can't find a pack nearby while you're at it—the sooner we can catch a scent, the sooner we're likely to find him." Crossing the hall, she dug around for her leathers—but couldn't find them.

"Dolf! My leathers! Where'd they go?"

"I think Agvarr took them yesterday," he called from his room. "I'll run downstairs and look for them."

Ambjorg paced the length of her room for a few minutes while Audolf bounded down the stairs. Soon he raced back up, two sets of riding leathers in hand. "They're a bit damp; apparently Agvarr was kind enough to wash them yesterday and they haven't fully dried yet." He handed her the smaller of the leathers, then dashed across the hall and closed the door.

Following suit, Ambjorg stripped quickly and was soon dressed in her leathers, boots and all. She followed down the stairs a step behind Audolf, both strapping swords to their hips as they went. The weight of the weapon felt comforting, but odd; neither was used to carrying it on a regular basis.

By the time they'd changed and made their way outside a sizable group of men was assembled on the front lawn. Most of them had shortbows or staves, but some were armed with swords, axes, or longbows. A few raised an eyebrow at the siblings' appearance, but not a word was said as Thane Brandulfr emerged from the front door, longbow in hand and broadsword strapped to his back. "We keep to the same line as usual," he instructed in a voice loud enough to carry to the back of the group. "Same rules as last time: each pair keeps the pair to their left within sight. If you see or hear something, start the call to stop; if you hear the call to stop, pass it along." He pointed at a young man at the front of the crowd. "Ingvaror, you will pair up with his lordship and her ladyship." Ingvaror nodded and moved to their side. "The creature has a head start on us, but it's carrying weight, which should slow it down. We must hurry if we aim to catch it." With that, he turned and started down the road at a ground-eating pace.

Ingvaror turned to the siblings. "If you'll follow me, milord, milady," he said, following the thane, "we'll be crossing some difficult terrain today. It's a good thing you've got a good set of leathers—might have to do some climbing to get where we're going. Either way, it'll keep the thistles off." They were about in the middle of the search party, which so far seemed amoebic in shape. "We'll be right in the middle of the line. Good place to be, if you ask me; got help to either side if you need it. The ends are where things can get a bit hairy." After a short ways they turned off the road, and the siblings watched as the group fanned out into a wide line moving through the trees. "Should probably keep the noise down if we can," Ingvaror suggested as he guided them down a gentle slope into their place within the line. They placed their feet carefully as the line of villagers swept into the forest.

Ambjorg let Ingvaror take the lead and dropped back a pace or two to speak with Audolf. Leaning her head close to her brother's she whispered, "Were you able to find anything?"

He nodded. "There's a pack close by," he replied in kind, "but they're different from the ones back home. Wilder, somehow. They like this thing no better than we, though—it doesn't just go after humans." He hesitated.

"There's something else, isn't there?"

Audolf nodded. "It…well, it's a carnivore," he replied. "You can guess why it's snatching people and animals." Ambjorg nodded slowly. "Anyway, I've asked that they scent for it, and they've agreed to help and leave the search party alone. We just have to listen for the calls."

"I'll keep an eye in the sky, too," said Ambjorg. They moved apart and each split their attention between navigating the rough, downhill terrain and checking with their respective reconnaissance contributors. The going was easy for the most part, but it occurred to Audolf that the return journey might not be so.

After a few minutes of walking Audolf's head snapped up and a lone howl split the air directly ahead of them. "They've caught his scent," he murmured to Ambjorg out of the corner of his mouth. "We're on a direct path to the source." She nodded and they continued, eyes peeled and heads swiveling. A few of the men spooked at the eerie sound, but said nothing. The thick woodland was preternaturally quiet after the wolf's call died.

The search party continued for another ten minutes or so before Audolf approached his sister again. "We should be close," he whispered. "Very close. The image I got from the pack was right around here somewhere." He cast about for any sign of something out of the ordinary.

Ambjorg slowed for a moment, finding the eagle she'd flown with the previous evening. It was out hunting nearby for small creatures to feed its young. She felt guilty about asking it to help them, but she promised herself she wouldn't keep its attention long enough for its brood to go hungry that night. She couldn't stop moving for long, but she paused long enough to get a good mental image of the area they traversed. To their right was an outcropping the party had split to navigate around with the intent of meeting back up on the other side; to their left the woods extended on a long downward slope. There was something about the outcropping, though, that stuck in her mind—something on the face on the far side, where it dropped off so suddenly…

The eagle focused on the outcropping with its needle-sharp vision. There, at the opening of a shallow cave—a fresh splatter of blood.

She swallowed. "Dolf?" she whispered, motioning for him to come closer. "The outcropping—there's a cave on the other side. It's in there." Audolf nodded.

"Let's wait until we're on the other side to say anything," he suggested. Ambjorg nodded and resumed her distance. As soon as they passed the rock face Audolf tapped their guide on the shoulder and pointed toward the shelf they'd just passed. Ingvaror nodded and followed his finger, then did a double take as he noticed the red stain on the ledge near the cave. Raising his hands, he formed them into an odd shape and blew, producing a hollow, fluting sound intended to mimic the cry of a ground-dwelling bird. They heard the call pass down both sides of the line of searchers and watched as the ends of the line looped around and quietly drew in toward the middle. Soon a group of tense men stood silent in the shadow of the outcropping, staring at the cave entrance.

"It's too far up the cliff face for us to climb up to it," one of the men pointed out in a whisper. "Might could lower a rope off the top, though."

"Think it's still in there?" asked another.

"We'll operate under the assumption that it is," replied the thane. He looked to one of the younger men in the group, a boy of about fourteen, and gestured toward one of the nearby trees. "Think you could shin up that tree and tell us for sure?" The boy nodded eagerly and squirreled up the tree. In moments he was lost to the full summer foliage. A quiet, anxious minute passed as they awaited the boy's return. Soon enough, he dropped out of the lower branches, nodding his head. Audolf thought he looked a bit queasy. "Did you get a good look at it?" Thane Brandulfr asked. The boy nodded again and paled further. "Well?"

The young man swallowed and gathered his courage. "It was big," he said, indicating a height of about six and a half feet and a width of maybe three. "And covered in fur. And its legs were bent backwards, like a dog's. It stood upright like a man and had two arms and a head. Its hands—paws—whatever—had some wicked-looking claws." He shuddered, then continued. "Might've had some on its feet, too. I'd not recommend getting close to it."

"Did you see Sigund's man?" the thane demanded.

Gulping again, the boy nodded. He didn't meet Thane Brandulfr's eyes.

Steel flashed in the thane's gaze as he nodded in return. "Good work, son." He patted the boy on the back, then gently pushed him toward one of the older men, who took him under an arm in a fatherly gesture. "Looks like we'll need the longbowmen, then," he mused. "I don't like the idea of lowering a man down to the cave mouth; it's too vulnerable a position for something that nasty-sounding. Let's see if we can find a vantage point to take it down from a distance." Heads nodded around the group and they began to cast about for a suitable angle. The outcropping next to them was an unusual formation and seemed to be unique in its area; there were no accessible locations that gave a clear view of the cave within bowshot.

"We could set a trap for it, then lure it down here," one of the men suggested.

Thane Brandulfr shook his head. "We don't know how intelligent it is. If it's at all smart it'll avoid any trap we set, and I don't want to chance it. How did it get up there, I wonder?" He regarded the cliff face for a while.

Meanwhile, Ambjorg consulted her second pair of eyes. As they cast about and talked the creature sat in the back of the cave, bent over…something; she couldn't quite make out what it was. Eventually it straightened and appeared to sniff the air wafting into the cave. Standing, it stalked slowly to the front of the cave, following its vaguely canine nose as it twitched to take in the scents on the wind. She got a good look at the creature for the first time as it emerged into the daylight. It was covered with gray and white fur and its legs were, indeed, reverse-joined and reminiscent of a dog's. Both its hands and its feet were tipped with knife-like talons the size of Ambjorg's hand, and it had yellow eyes with pupils that were slitted sideways. Besides its overall unnatural appearance there was something very wrong about it that she couldn't quite put her finger on.

She froze as she realized the creature had fully exited the cave and was leaning over the side of the outcropping, eyes closed as it inhaled the scents on the breeze. Eyes still closed, she reached for Audolf's arm, tapping it frantically, then opening her eyes and pointing toward the cave. His gaze followed her arm and his eyes grew wide.

"Thane Brandulfr, I think we have a problem," he said as calmly as he could manage. A dozen more sets of eyes followed his and came to the same realization, and as one they began to back slowly away from the base of the outcropping. Just as they cleared a space about thirty feet in diameter the thing let loose a cry that was half howl, half scream and started climbing down the cliff face by digging its talons into the bare rock.

"Longbows at the ready!" Thane Brandulfr called. "Weapons out! Keep your distance unless you have no other choice." He strung his longbow in one fluid motion and nocked an arrow. Three other men with longbows followed suit, and the hiss of drawn steel rang through the woods. Ambjorg and Audolf drew their own swords and faced the outcropping just as the creature dropped to the forest floor.

The next few seconds were a blur. Bowstrings twanged and four shafts flew toward the creature. Three hit, but only one caught it center mass; the other two lodged in an arm and a leg. It howled again, an unearthly scream of pain and anger, and swung its head about, looking for a target. Three bow strings sang once more and two more shafts found marks in the thing's abdomen. It doubled over at the force of the impact, exhaling sharply and whining in pain. Thane Brandulfr had dropped his bow and unsnapped his broadsword; by the time the third volley headed toward the creature, he was right on its heels. Only one of the arrows found a mark, but it was enough to distract the now-pitiful beast. It barely registered the thane's presence before he swung the great weapon in a wide arc and hewed its head from its shoulders in a single sweep. Twitching, the body fell backward as its reverse-jointed knees collapsed and black blood spewed from the severed neck, scorching the plants where it fell.

Thane Brandulfr reached down and picked up the creature's head by one ear. Its lifeless yellow eyes still registered the shock of the final blow, rendering it even more grotesque in death than it had been in life. Tossing it carelessly toward the rest of the body, Thane Brandulfr bent and cleaned his blade on a large-leafed plant, watching as the bloodstains ate holes in the leaves as soon as they made contact.

Ambjorg felt she should have been ill, at the very least, having never been witness to such violence. She'd seen many animals slaughtered, but there was something different about luring an unnatural and dangerous creature out of its lair and putting it down. Wasn't there?

Audolf, on the other hand, was transmitting what he saw to the wolf pack nearby. He sheathed his sword just as the pack started up a vengeful howl. They could hunt safely once again.

"We'll leave this thing where it fell," the thane was saying as they rejoined the group, "but we should do our best to retrieve Sigund's husband. Let's climb up to the top of the rise; I'll lower a few people down with a blanket, and they can tie it up for us to lift." The search party filed quietly past the creature's body. A few spat on it as they passed.

The recovery of the body was largely unsuccessful. Both of the men lowered to the cave entrance were ill as soon as they saw what remained of their neighbor. In the end, it was decided that a small pyre would be built in the cave and the remains burned in situ.

As Audolf had surmised, the trip back to town took twice as long and was far more arduous. Many of the obstacles they'd been able to half-slide down or bypass on the trip down required climbing and sometimes ropes to navigate back up. Ingvaror was instrumental in showing the siblings how to get around the worst of the obstacles, but they still lagged behind the main group of erstwhile rescuers. Almost two hours later they finally met back up with the main road and headed into town.

Sigund was waiting at the holding. When she saw the search party returning without her husband she collapsed onto the porch, where Ingr was waiting with open arms. Thane Brandulfr offered quiet condolences as he passed and laid a hand on her shoulder. She nodded, shaking. Without another word, Ingr helped her up and started down the lane toward Sigund's home.

Thane Brandulfr turned to address the downtrodden group plodding back into town. "Send out word that the festival will resume tomorrow; we will spend tonight remembering our dead." With that, he turned and entered his house. The small crowd with them dispersed quietly, each seeking peace and comfort in their own way.

Ambjorg and Audolf trudged up the stairs to their rooms. "I think I'm going to get another bath," Ambjorg said absently as they reached the second floor. "Do you mind?"

"No," Audolf replied. "I'll wait for you to finish. We both got pretty filthy." He looked out the window. "And it's not even noon yet." With that, he turned and closed the door to his room.

Ambjorg collected her clothing and went to draw a bath.

The noon meal at the holding was served by Agvarr. "Ingr's down at Sigund's," he said as they joined him in the informal dining room. "Poor woman. They'd only been married a season or so." He shook his head, then took another bite of his cold cut sandwich. Ambjorg took a few small bites of hers, then set it back down on her plate. Even her breakfast wasn't sitting well. Audolf looked similarly inclined.

"Isn't there anything we can do?" Ambjorg asked, sipping cool water from a plain glass.

"Dunno, milady," Agvarr replied around a mouthful of sandwich. "You could always head over and check with Ingr. Though I'd recommend going by yourself, begging your lordship's pardon; Sigund's like to be wanting a woman's company more than a man's right now."

Ambjorg carefully pushed her plate away from her. "I think

I'll do that," she said as she rose from the table. "Thank you for lunch—it tastes wonderful, but I'm afraid I'm just not up to eating right now." She walked slowly from the room and out the front door.

Audolf pushed his plate over to his sister's now-empty spot at table. "Same here," he said. "Is there anything I can do?"

"Don't believe so, milord, but you could always check with Bran." Agvarr, having finished his sandwich, stood and collected the plates. "He's like to be in the stables or in town, at the inn." Nodding, he disappeared into the kitchen with the dirty dishes.

Audolf headed out the front door. By the time he rounded the corner Ambjorg was already out of sight, lost around a street corner. He thought he remembered the inn facing the town square, so he followed the road until he ran into the abandoned festival grounds, his feet moving of their own volition as his mind turned in on itself. Sure enough, there stood the inn, facing the south side of the square. As he approached Audolf realized that the common room was completely packed with townsfolk and that someone was speaking. He recognized Thane Brandulfr's quiet baritone over the hushed sounds of the crowd.

"We will start closing the gates every day at nightfall. They will not be opened for any but honest travelers until dawn. All the holders outside of town should find lodgings with family or friends in town until we can find out where these things are coming from. You may tend your fields and your herds, but always go out in pairs or threes, and never unarmed. We've learned that shortbows are often too small to pierce the hides of these creatures, but longbows generally find their mark and a good, sharp blade is always effective, though it's best to keep your distance.

"In light of this morning's events, let us spend the rest of our day mourning our dead. Gunnraor was a good man. He will be missed." Heads nodded around the common room. The thane bowed his head in a moment of silence, then made his way out of the inn, leaving the crowd to converse in hushed tones.

Audolf caught up with him as he headed toward the smithy. "Is there anything I can do to help, Thane?" he asked.

Thane Brandulfr shook his head. "Ingr is with Sigund; I know she'll take care of things there. Sigund has family in town–

it's likely she'll stay with them for a while. Meanwhile, I have work waiting for me in the smithy." He looked around briefly. "Where is your sister, my lord?"

"She went to see if she could do anything for the widow," Audolf replied.

The thane nodded, his furrowed brow softening. "If I think of anything you can do to help, I'll let you know. Otherwise I shall see you at dinner, my lord." With that he turned and donned his leather smithing apron.

Audolf, seeing no immediate opportunities to be of service, wandered somberly back to the holding.

It was twilight before Ambjorg returned. Audolf was waiting for her on the front porch, the beginnings of a small deer carving in his hand. He stood and regarded his bedraggled sister. "How is Sigund?" he asked.

"Better than she was this morning," Ambjorg replied, pulling open the door. "Her mother came as soon as she heard. She's taken Sigund back to her home to stay for a while. Gods, I'm tired." Despite her dislike for the sitting room, she collapsed into one of its chairs out of exhaustion and expediency. "I spent the afternoon helping get their farm in order so that one of the neighbors could look in on it every so often until she's able to manage it herself. Gunnraor and Sigund kept a few head of cattle and a horse or two, plus chickens." She closed her eyes. "How did you spend your afternoon?"

Audolf snorted. "Helping Agvarr around the holding, when he'd let me. I groomed the horses for a while, even exercised mine a bit. He's looking much better after some rest." He flopped down into the chair across from Ambjorg. She cracked an eye open to look at him, then closed it again as she began to melt into the softness of the chair. Despite the decor, she had to admit it was a comfortable place to relax.

"What about our host?" she asked sleepily.

"He's spent the entire day at the smithy–said he had work to do." Audolf propped his feet on the low table between the chairs. "If you ask me, it sounds like he's taken this pretty hard."

"I'd imagine so," Ambjorg sighed, eyes still closed and face upturned as her head lolled onto the chair back. "He cares a lot about his people."

"That's not all he cares about."

Ambjorg lifted her head to look at her brother. "What do you mean?"

"You know perfectly well what I mean."

"I'm sure I don't." She let her head fall back onto the chair and closed her eyes again.

"Ambi, Thane Brandulfr has hardly taken his eyes off of you since we arrived." Audolf set his feet on the floor and leaned his elbows on his knees.

"So we're playing the protective brother, now?" She didn't bother to look at him this time.

"Pfft. He's better equipped to protect you than I'll ever be. Did you see what he did to that thing?"

Ambjorg shuddered. "I'd rather not think about it, if you don't mind."

"At any rate, if I'm any judge of your behavior, you're just as interested as he is. Don't try to deny it!" He held up a hand to forestall her rejoinder. "We're siblings, remember?"

"And what if I am? Hmm?" she asked drowsily from her chair.

Audolf chuckled. "Well, you could do much worse than Thane Brandulfr, that's for sure." He settled back into his own chair.

"You know, that's exactly what Father said," Ambjorg replied sleepily.

"Just goes to show that I'm right."

"Mmm."

A few quiet minutes later, the front door opened and closed. Thane Brandulfr entered the sitting room to find both of his guests sound asleep in the chairs by the hearth. He roused Audolf long enough to get him walking toward the stairs, then spent a moment watching Ambjorg sleep, her head resting carelessly on the back of the chair and hands folded primly in her lap. He noticed for the first time that her hair was braided back out of her face with colored ribbons that had somehow survived the day's arduous journey through the woods.

Very slowly, he slid one arm under her knees and the other under her shoulders. She stirred, but did not wake as he picked her up and carried her up the stairs as if she weighed nothing. As he reached the second floor she mumbled in her sleep and slid one arm around his neck. He froze for a moment, then carried her into her room and set her softly onto her bed. She mumbled again, then went still as he covered her with a light blanket and crept out the door, closing it softly behind him.

Ambjorg woke before dawn the following morning with a growling stomach. Blearily, she realized she'd fallen asleep before dinner. *I wonder if Dolf missed the evening meal, too.* Looking around, she noticed that someone had carried her upstairs and covered her up with a blanket. *Probably Dolf. He really is a good brother—when he's not a complete nuisance.*

Since she was awake, she decided to see what she could forage from the kitchen. The stone stairs were cool on her bare feet as she tiptoed past Audolf's room and down toward the first floor. It seemed the rest of the house still slumbered; the kitchen was quiet and empty. Some thoughtful soul had left half a loaf of bread and some dried fruit on the counter in case anyone was up before breakfast, so she helped herself to a piece of bread and a dried apple or two, then snuck through the downstairs rooms to the back door.

It creaked slightly as she opened it, startling the figure sitting on the steps in the predawn light. "May I join you?" she asked as she looked around the door frame.

"As you will, my lady," Thane Brandulfr replied. She slipped through the doorway, closing it behind her, and took a seat on the step. They ate their breakfast in silence; she noticed he'd also poached his fare from the kitchen counter before coming out to watch the dawn.

"You have quite a view here," she said as she finished the last of her dried apples.

"That's why the old thane built the holding on these grounds," he replied. "We used to greet the dawn every day sitting right here." He rested his hands on his knees and gazed out at the brightening eastern horizon.

They sat in pregnant silence for a few moments before Ambjorg spoke up. "Are you angry with me, Thane Brandulfr?" she asked. When he did not reply, she continued. "I spoke rather harshly to you yesterday morning." He continued to stare out at the mountains ahead of them.

"Did you expect me to stay behind while you searched for your missing holder?" she asked in response to his silence. "Your people are also my people, if you remember. It is also my brother's and my duty to make sure they are safe. Might I remind you that it was Audolf who found the beast's lair?"

"It was not your brother I spent the morning worrying about, my lady."

"And why is that? Is it because I am a woman?" She turned to watch the sun peek above the mountains to the east. "Do you think me weak?"

"No, my lady," he replied hesitantly, shifting uncomfortably on the step.

"Then why?" Ambjorg rounded on him from across the step, staring him full in the face.

The thane blinked at her for a moment. "Is it not obvious?" he asked softly. He held Ambjorg's gaze for a moment, then looked away. She shifted back into her previous position to watch the sun climb the rest of the way above the mountaintops, wondering what she should do next. After a long moment she reached out to Thane Brandulfr, who had resumed his earlier position with his arms resting on his knees, and placed her hand on top of his, curling her fingers into his palm. He stared at his hand as if seeing it for the first time, then turned it so that he could twine his fingers with Ambjorg's. Their eyes met briefly before they turned as one to watch the sun rise.

The festival continued that day despite its inauspicious start the day before. The townsfolk were a bit more subdued, but still set up their booths to sell or trade some of the items and crafts they'd worked on over the year. Many of the townspeople and tradesfolk had hobbies that produced a wide variety of small luxury items. Crocheted shawls of dyed lambswool and intricately-carved wooden sculptures could be found next to handmade journals bound in leather and burned with knotted motifs. There were even a few who dabbled in jewel crafting and produced some handsome pieces made of wrought silver and gemstones found in the mountain mines. These last went largely untouched, as few of the townsfolk could afford such items, but many of the patrons slowed as they passed the jewelcrafters' booths.

Audolf, Ambjorg, and Thane Brandulfr walked the town for most of the day. The latter had announced his work at the smithy postponed until the end of the festival and had offered to show the siblings around Thorsbrand. For the most part, it was much like any other town its size—it had a town square, an inn, a smithy, an apothecary, a butcher's shop, a cooperage, and a chandlery. There were a few other shops along the roads, but none looked well-used as most of the trade goods coming out of the mountains were stone for building and mined ores, along with the occasional gemstone trade. These items helped pay for some of the life essentials that were difficult to cultivate in the mountains, such as grains for bread and flour.

Nor was Thorsbrand the only town in the thanedom; a few days' ride south was another town of near-equal size, and a similar distance north was a hamlet on the border of Thane Brandulfr's lands. Many of the townspeople in Thorsbrand had relatives in either or both towns and had sent out the word that the midsummer festival would be larger this year, which had swelled the number of people in Thorsbrand almost double. The added congestion did not appear to be of concern to the residents; if anything, the mood seemed lighter for all the visiting family and friends.

By lunchtime the siblings were already growing tired, so they stopped at the inn to take their meal with some of the holders, speaking with them as they ate. At first the townsfolk seemed rather in awe of Ambjorg and Audolf, but after a few minutes of conversation, during which it was made evident that neither of the pair was a stranger to hard work, the holders warmed to their presence. Before long they were inundated with chatter about farms, livestock, hunting, and mining.

The afternoon was spent perusing the wares for sale and listening to the traveling skald who'd heard about the festival plans and capitalized on the opportunity for an audience. He was good; not the best, but the feeling behind the music he played was genuine, and he had a large repertoire of music at his disposal. Audolf found his thoughts turning to their erstwhile teacher, Snorri, who had recently retired to the southlands with his wife and two young children. He sent a silent prayer to the gods for their safety.

Just before sundown they made their way back to the holding for dinner. Ingr was still cooking when they arrived, so they took seats in the sitting room and talked over the day's events, finding the conversation much easier than the prior day's. Audolf, who had spent some of his time speaking with the holders individually, asked if the previous day's events were a regular occurrence, seeing as how the townsfolk didn't seem terribly shocked at Sigund's story or the way events had transpired.

"Unfortunately, it's been happening once a month or so for the past half a year," Thane Brandulfr replied. "I don't recall it ever happening previously."

"What are those things, anyway?" Audolf asked.

"We're not sure. They're not all the same, which makes them hard to define. The one you saw yesterday was typical of the type—large, furry, and equipped with large talons and teeth—but no two are completely alike. I don't know if you noticed, but the creature was outwardly sexless, as they all have been. In short, we have no idea where they're coming from, what they are, or how they reproduce; all we know is that they're all deadly and they all think humans are food."

Audolf ruminated on this information for a while. Eventually he was also unable to come up with an explanation and gave up, slumping in his chair and staring at the stag's head mounted over the mantelpiece as if it held enlightenment. Ambjorg had pulled her hair over her shoulder and was toying thoughtfully with the ends of her braids.

All three had sunk so far into their own personal reveries that they jumped when Ingr announced from the doorway that dinner was served. They filed into the small dining room and took their seats in silence, still ruminating on their own thoughts. Dinner was roasted venison with a mild gravy, potatoes, and a salad of summer greens. For dessert, Ingr had prepared a cobbler out of wild blueberries from a large bush growing at the corner of the house. She sat with the group and chattered cheerfully about the bonfire planned for the evening as they poured chilled cream over the cobbler and ate as much as they could hold.

By the time they'd finished their meal it was dusk. In light of recent events, the bonfire, which was usually held just outside the town, was being held in the city square, one side of which had been cleared of booths and other easily-combustible materials. A large stack of dry, seasoned wood and logs was piled high in the middle of the road. When they arrived in the square a cheer went up from the villagers and one of them handed the thane a lit torch made of bundled sap-wood. He nodded and thanked the man, then held the torch to the base of the bonfire, lighting it from the bottom. It took slowly, but once the loosely-built structure was burning the light and heat from the blaze extended fifteen feet from the source. Hewn logs had been placed around the fire to be used as seats.

Audolf, Ambjorg, and Thane Brandulfr seated themselves close to the fire. The night was already growing chilly and the heat from the fire warmed their faces and hands as they conversed, the warmth melting some of the day's worries from their minds. A few townspeople also took seats near the fire, warming their bones and talking of events beyond the past few days. The rest took up places as the skald began to play a lively tune and they started to dance around the bonfire. Audolf noticed a beautiful young woman eyeing him as she passed and excused himself from the conversation to join her, leaving Ambjorg and Thane Brandulfr to fend for themselves.

"So, have your views on dancing changed, my lady?" asked Thane Brandulfr, cocking an eyebrow.

"Whether they have or not, my feet are still tired from walking today. I might be persuaded at a later hour, though," Ambjorg replied demurely. She watched as a group of children approached the fire carrying small leather bags. "What are they doing?" she asked.

"Salting the fire," the thane responded. "We've found in our mining that certain salts and minerals burn different colors." As he spoke, the oldest child opened his bag and tossed a handful of powder on the fire. It flared red where the powder landed, and the children squealed in delight. A second child pulled a small handful of another substance out of his bag and tossed it on the fire. Green light flared from the blaze next to the red. "The children like to make games of it. We have yet to find a better use for it, though."

Ambjorg absently watched the children toss handfuls of minerals on the fire as they tried to create different colors out of combinations of salts and powders. Once they managed to get a soft lilac hue for their efforts, causing them to shriek in triumph as it reflected on their upturned faces. She smiled at their apparent victory, remembering younger and more innocent times with her brothers.

Suddenly, Ambjorg realized they were the only ones making use of the seating by the fire; everyone else had joined the dance ringing the log seats. "Does your offer of a dance still stand?" she inquired.

"Of course, my lady," the thane replied, standing and offering her his hand. "For you, always."

She took his hand and they joined the whirling revelers circling the bonfire.

Some time later—hours, perhaps—Ambjorg and Thane Brandulfr made their way out of the ring of dancers and back to their seats by the fire. A few other couples who had grown tired of the dance were spread out among the log seats, each discreetly out of earshot of the rest. Ambjorg looked around and realized she could not find her brother. "I wonder where Audolf has gone?" she mused aloud.

"I last saw him with a rather pretty young blond," Thane Brandulfr said, chuckling.

"Hmph. Then it's likely we won't be seeing him until the morrow," Ambjorg replied with a smirk.

"Oh?" the thane replied.

"He tends to stay out extremely late when he finds company," she explained. "It's not unusual for him to wander in about dawn, if the company's attractive enough. Exactly how attractive was she?" Ambjorg asked, raising an eyebrow.

The thane appeared to think for a moment. "I'd say she was the third-best-looking woman in attendance," he replied.

"Is that so? At least he's done well for himself, though it appears you feel there was better to be had."

"Of course. But Ingr's a bit old for him, and you're his sister." The thane smiled as he studied the bonfire, casting a sidelong glance at Ambjorg.

"I see," Ambjorg replied archly. "Then I suppose I shouldn't feel he isn't living up to his potential." She regarded the fire as well. "Though I must admit to some jealousy of his stamina. I'm afraid I'm not accustomed to staying out this late."

"Do you wish to retire for the evening, my lady? I will escort you back to the holding."

"Not yet," she replied, "but I could do with a bit of refreshment. Is the inn still serving?"

"I'm sure it is," Thane Brandulfr replied. "The inn stays open until the last patron leaves during festivals. What would you like?"

"Mead is fine," she answered. "Would you like for me to accompany you?"

"Only if you wish to; I'll just be a moment, my lady." Thane Brandulfr bowed playfully and strode through the line of dancers toward the common room of the inn, which blazed with light.

Ambjorg didn't wait long; within minutes the thane returned bearing two large steins of mead. She thanked him as he resumed his seat and sipped from hers. It was good, if a bit heavier than what she was accustomed to, and she said as much.

"We brew ours heavier to last out the winters here," he explained. "We've found over time that the heavier meads tend to separate less and retain their integrity through the coldest days." He took a deep draught of his mead. "It takes getting used to if you're not raised to it, or so I hear."

"I like it," she replied, sipping at her mead a bit more discreetly. They enjoyed their drinks in silence for a while as they watched the bonfire begin to burn down. Some of the townsfolk had fed it a few more logs earlier in the evening, but now that people were drifting off in ones and twos back to their homes, the fire was left to die on its own. The light from the embers didn't quite reach the last two rows of seating, making them a popular spot for some of the more familiar couples; as it was, Ambjorg was perfectly happy to keep her seat in the first row.

Soon enough, she looked down and realized her mug was empty. So was Thane Brandulfr's. Reaching out, she took his mug from him. "Would you like a refill?" she asked as she stood.

"I can fetch it, my lady," he replied, half-standing. She switched both mugs to one hand and laid the other on his shoulder, pushing him gently back down onto the log.

"I need to stretch my legs a bit," she replied. "I'll be back in a moment." Following the thane's path from earlier in the evening, she entered the inn, found a place at the bar, and hailed the innkeeper. The townsfolk propped on the bar did a double take as they recognized her, then made more room, and one got the innkeeper's attention over the din. The barkeep's face lit up as he recognized Ambjorg and he made his way quickly over to where she leaned on the bar top.

"My lady! What can my humble inn offer you?" he asked, bowing theatrically. Ambjorg wondered if he might have been sampling a bit of the mead himself.

"Mead, if you will," she replied, extending the mugs. He nodded, taking the mugs from her, and hurried to refill them from one of the casks behind the bar. They sloshed slightly as he set them down before her. "How much?" she asked over the roar of the crowd.

"I could no sooner charge the goddess Freyja," he replied.

She fished a few coins out of one of the pockets sewn into her dress and pressed them into the barkeep's hand. "You run a good inn," she said, "but any businessman knows that giving away his wares isn't good for business." She winked and thanked him, smiling, then swept back outside.

Thane Brandulfr was watching for her to return. His expression, lit by the glow of the dying fire as he watched her approach, was more relaxed than she'd ever seen it, his gray eyes soft beneath his strong, dark brow. She smiled and handed him his mug, then seated herself next to him on the log once again. He thanked her, to which she nodded, then gazed up at the stars. "The sky is beautiful tonight," she remarked, gesturing with her mug.

"It always is this time of year," the thane replied. "It seldom rains during the summer festival, so the view is completely unobscured." He took another pull of his mead. "You should see the mountains on a cold, clear winter night; the starlight reflects off the snow so brightly you'd almost think it was midday."

"I'll bet it's gorgeous." Ambjorg pondered her drink for a while before continuing. "You truly love your home, don't you?" It was more a statement than a question, and it held a hint of sadness she couldn't quite banish.

"I do." He stared into the fire without seeing it.

Ambjorg nodded and stood, wavering as she drained her mug. "I believe it is time for me to retire," she stated deliberately. She set the mug on the bench where she'd been sitting and almost missed the log. "It's been a long time since I last had such strong mead, and I fear it's gone to my head and made me sleepy."

Thane Brandulfr drained his own tankard and stood with enviable steadiness. "I shall escort you back to the holding, my lady," he said as he offered her his arm. Ambjorg blinked at it for a moment, then slid her hand into the crook of his arm and smiled up at him. Arm in arm, they wandered back to the holding in companionable silence.

# CHAPTER 5

By the time Ambjorg awoke the next day the house was already awake and bustling. The sun was higher than she'd have liked; it seemed the mead combined with the late night had made for a late morning. Audolf had already packed and was heading downstairs in his riding leathers as Ambjorg emerged from her room. "Heya, sis," he said cheerily as she brushed past him on her way to the privy. She held up a finger and continued to the upstairs jakes.

When she emerged her brother was leaning against the wall beside the door, waiting for her. "Didn't you get in late?" she half mumbled.

"Yep," he responded, far more chipper than he should have given how little rest he must have had.

"Right," she replied when he didn't seem to be forthcoming with details. Her head was fuzzy, and her mouth felt as if a family of field mice had nested in it the night before.

Audolf followed her back to her room. "Ambi, we don't have to leave today if you don't want to. I know we'd planned to leave the day after the festival, but I'm sure one more day won't be a problem."

"No, it's important we get home, especially after everything that's happened," she replied as she began to pack the few things she'd brought.

"You sure?" Audolf gazed at her, concerned. "I mean, you and Brandulfr…" He trailed off meaningfully.

"Whatever may or may not be happening, we both have our responsibilities, and those come first. We need to get back to Asbjorn and tell him what's happened. Now go get breakfast; I have to change." She gently shooed him out of her room. Audolf shrugged and let himself be removed without protest.

Ambjorg sat heavily on the bed. What was happening between them? Did she love him? Was there room for such things in either of their lives? She shook her head to clear it. For now it didn't matter; they were already late and had a long journey ahead. She hastily changed clothes, packed the shift she'd slept in, and followed her brother downstairs.

Audolf was already eating by the time Ambjorg and her pack made it downstairs. "There's hot oatmeal on the stove if ye'd like, m'lady, or I can make you some eggs if that's more your taste," Agvarr rumbled from the far corner of the kitchen as he searched for something in the pantry. "Cursed shelves… can't find a thing…ah ha!" He triumphantly held aloft a small jar of indeterminate substance. "Found it! Last year's preserves." Setting it on the small table, he wandered off on another task.

"Don't mind if I do," Audolf said as he cracked open the preserves, adding a generous dollop to his oats. Ambjorg served herself from the pot, finding a clean dish and spoon by the sink, and did likewise. The sweet preserves–some mixture of berries– rounded out the earthy tone of the hearty oatmeal, making for a pleasant and filling meal.

When they'd both finished they enlisted Agvarr's help in saddling their horses, who were happy to see them after a few days in a new place. Audolf's stallion gave him a bit of attitude, but one stern look and a warning from Agvarr put him in his place quickly. It seemed the two of them had already had words.

Once they were saddled and ready they took their leave, stopping to say goodbye to Ingr and Sigund on their way to the town square. Both were sorry to see them go, but were glad they were able to join the festivities. As an afterthought Ambjorg asked if Ingr needed her ribbons back, fingering the braids still in her hair. Ingr told her to keep them "to remember her by an' as a talisman 'gainst peril on their journey." She thanked both women and they were on their way.

The thane was at the smithy again this morning, though he wasn't working; instead he was talking to an older man with silver hair and massive arms. "That must be the regular smith," Audolf surmised as they approached. "I'm glad he's back at work, though I have a feeling Brandulfr will miss the distraction." They walked their horses halfway across the square before the thane nodded in greeting and extricated himself from the conversation. He paced calmly to meet them.

"I had hoped you might stay another day, given the circumstances," he said as soon as he was close enough to speak. "We'd be more than happy to have you, and the weather is likely to hold at least until then."

"Thank you, Thane, but we really must get back to our brother," Ambjorg replied, regret tingeing her reply. "Especially under the circumstances. We must tell him of the dangers your people—our people—are facing so that we might help however we can."

Brandulfr nodded. "I understand, my lady." He met her gaze and held it for a moment. "I have a request of you, if I may be so bold."

"Of course," Ambjorg replied. "What do you wish of us?"

"May I have your permission to write to you, and you alone? Outside of my regular correspondence to the capital, of course," he added, turning his gaze to Audolf briefly, who nodded toward his sister.

Ambjorg smiled, her cheeks reddening slightly despite the coolness of the morning. "I would like that...Brandulfr." She said his name carefully, as if it was a foreign word she was determined not to mispronounce.

He smiled back at her, his expression a mixture of relief and triumph, with a hint of fire around the edges. "As would I, Lady Ambjorg." She started a bit at the sound of her own name in his voice. Somehow it contained more than just her name; it held everything she was in its syllables. Since it left her speechless for a moment and there were people watching, she extended her hand from atop her horse, expecting him to take it. He did, but instead of shaking it he kissed the back of it very gently before releasing it back to its owner.

"In that case I bid you both farewell with all the town's wishes for a safe and pleasant journey," Brandulfr said, stepping back to a polite distance as Ambjorg collected herself.

"Thank you, Thane," Audolf replied. "We've enjoyed your hospitality and hope to share it again sometime." He glanced at

his sister, who glared back at him before adding her own pleas-
antries to her brother's, then shared a last glance with Thane
Brandulfr before waving to the onlookers and bidding farewell.

It took everything she had not to look back.

The road home was much faster and easier going with the
paths Agvarr had marked on their maps. They were able to make
it further the first day than they'd hoped, even with a late start,
and were almost out of the foothills before nightfall. Setting up
camp, they set their respective watches in their usual way and fell
fast asleep, still exhausted from the previous evening.

Each day was largely the same: avoid a few brigands by day,
make steady progress shadowing the roads, do reconnaissance,
then find safe camping or an inn at night. By the end of the third
day they were staring at the gently rolling hills on the outskirts
of their home.

"Bet you there's a letter already waiting by the time we get
home," Audolf teased for at least the thirteenth time. Ambjorg
huffed at him and urged her mount into a trot, eager to be home
and away from her brother's endless needling remarks.

Someone must have seen them coming, for by the time they
arrived at the great hall there were stable hands waiting to take
their horses for them. Asbjorn came out to meet them, as well,
stretching and scratching his back on one of the large posts that
made up the door frame. "You don't have to act like a bear, you
know," Ambjorg teased as she embraced her brother. He responded by shifting his weight and gathering Audolf in with his other
arm, nearly crushing them both in a fierce hug.

"I'm glad you're back!" Asbjorn rumbled. "I've been managing on my own, but barely." He let them go to take a few deep
breaths. "So, what news from the east?" They walked into the
great hall in search of dinner. Luckily the tables had just been set
and the workers were just sitting down to the evening meal. The
three took their places at the head of the room and sat without
ceremony, not expecting or requiring anyone else to wait for them
to begin the meal.

Audolf started into a piece of meat, speaking around a

mouthful. "You wouldn't believe what we saw! The first day of the festival–"

"–Was wonderful," Ambjorg interjected with a significant look at her brother. Audolf swallowed hard and nodded. Asbjorn picked up that there were things they needed to discuss and turned the conversation elsewhere. Apparently there hadn't been much unusual going on while they were gone. There were the usual complaints between local holders and a few problems with fishing boats out on one of the fjords nearby, but nothing out of the ordinary. They finished their meal and retired to their father's study, as they had come to think of the rooms he'd once occupied. It had become their private meeting place of choice when there was something to discuss.

Ambjorg loosened her riding leathers, which were still covered in dust and sweat from the journey, then took a seat in her usual chair, taking care to perch on the edge so as not to soil the cushions. Audolf sprawled in his customary way in the chair opposite her, uncaring of his current filthiness, while Asbjorn took up the seat to her right. Their father's chair they left open as if extending an invitation to his spirit to join them and share its wisdom.

"So, how was the festival?" Asbjorn opened the conversation once they were all comfortably ensconced.

"The festival was great, but we ran into something we didn't expect," Audolf replied, kicking off his boots. "You remember those reports we've read of creatures that were part dog, part large cat, and part who knows what else?" Asbjorn nodded with a quizzical expression. "Well, we saw one. Snatched a man right off his farm and carried him off to its lair in the woods to eat him." From there he launched into the story of their search party and its eventual findings. Since he was telling the tale among his siblings he didn't omit the portion describing how he found the creature–or what else it had been hunting.

When he'd finished Ambjorg shared the extra information Thane Brandulfr had given them after the failed rescue mission. Asbjorn frowned at the rug for a moment as he processed everything he'd just heard. He was always the slowest of the three to think through a problem, but the most thorough by far, so the other two patiently waited for him to finish his assessment before prodding him for his thoughts. With a grunt and a distracted excuse, Asbjorn rose and left the room, only to return a moment later with a sheaf of mail, which he dropped carelessly onto the table between them.

"What is this?" Ambjorg asked as she sifted absently through the messages, some opened, some not.

"Quarterly reports," Asbjorn replied as he pawed through them himself. "Looking for one in particular...ah ha!" He pulled one from the middle of the stack. "Report from the southern holders from this past quarter. There's something…" He scanned the document, mumbling its contents as he skimmed them. "... Logs traded to…salted fish…brigands…there–'...reports of a creature standing on two legs, not four, but covered in the fur of a fox, with large, bushy tail and sharp talons. Small livestock and pets taken and eaten. One child mauled before adults hunted the creature to its den and killed it. No apparent gender or method of reproduction and no den mates.' This sounds familiar, if smaller and less deadly to humans." He lowered the report and studied his siblings. "I thought they were only legends."

"Old wives' tales, at best, but it seems we were wrong," Audolf replied. "We've seen one. It sounds like their form is determined by the local wildlife, if the reports are correct; they don't have many large predators in the southern woods besides bears…" He trailed off as he envisioned what a bear-creature might be capable of. "Gods above. We have to stop this."

"How?" Ambjorg threw up her hands. "We know nothing of where they come from or how they've come to be. Old wives' tales and legends aren't enough to go by, so what's our starting point?"

Asbjorn thought for a moment. "If the animals they're made of are local to the area, the source must be local, too. Let's send the packs out and watch from the skies. We already know our correspondence is watched, so word of this must go by trusted messenger only. We send three messages, one each direction, to speak with the thanes."

The other siblings nodded in agreement. "I don't know a pack directly that reaches that far south, but I can ask the ones nearby to pass word," Audolf replied.

"I can watch east almost to the mountains, but not quite," said Ambjorg. "I cultivated a few friendships out there while we traveled."

"And I can take the north until the winter," Asbjorn finished. "Once the snows begin I'll be useless, but until then I can find ways to keep an eye out. And a nose, too." Plan decided, the three adjourned to their own quarters to snatch what rest they could before the morrow dawned on their newest set of worries.

"That was close," said the figure cloaked in black from beneath his expansive hood. Only the end of his nose and bottom of his weak jaw were visible in the dim firelight.

"Close, yes, but nothing to give cause for alarm," the völva replied, waving a gnarled, arthritic hand in dismissal of the man's concerns. "You wanted to strike fear into men's hearts. This will begin the reign of terror. *Your* reign," she said as she dug through a densely packed closet in the hovel she called home.

Her guest shifted closer to the fire, careful to stay far enough that his face was still obscured. "I have your word it can't be traced back to me? Any of it?" His nerves were obvious in the tense tremor of his voice.

"Bah," the woman replied. "How can it? I don't even know who you are." She selected a box from the depths of her storage and extricated herself, closing the door carefully behind her. The man swore he heard a rustling from behind the door after it closed.

"What will you do next?" he asked, not without trepidation.

The old woman set the box down next to a small cauldron and regarded the man. Her eyes, dim with the films of age and blindness, still seemed fixed on his somehow. "I need a human. None of the animals you've brought me are smart enough to use for soldiers, no matter how much you train them. But if I could mix them with men..." She trailed off significantly.

Shuddering slightly inside his cloak, the man nodded. "I'll get you what you need." Satisfied, the völva went back to her work as he turned and left the hovel.

*Dear Thane*–Ambjorg scratched out the honorific and tried again. *Dear Brandulfr*–that still felt odd. Personal letters to anyone but Eyildr were a new phenomenon to her. She wasn't sure if "dear" was the right word to lead with. He was dear to her, yes, but was it presumptuous? Too sappy? Or would he appreciate it? The man was as inscrutable as she, so there was no telling. Might as well pick something that sounded good and stop overthinking it. *Brandulfr*, there–simple, but an acknowledgment of their familiarity, whatever shape it currently took. *I trust this finds you and your people well. Our return trip was just as pleasant as our*–wait, that sounded like she'd been happy to leave. *Our return trip was pleasant, though it came too soon.* Better. *My brother was glad to see us. He was, of course, perfectly capable of keeping things running without us, but we're not much used to being apart for long.* She paused again, unsure of what to say. There had been so much left unsaid, and letters weren't at all secure, so what else could she include that wasn't a risk to disclose? *While it's good to be home, I miss your company, and look forward to the next time we may talk in person instead of through a pen.* Forward, yet honest. Ambjorg found her thoughts frequently straying to the thane, wondering what business he might be about at any given moment. She wondered if he did the same. *Warm regards, Ambjorg.* There; short, but prompt. In fact, if it left with the post today it might arrive before his first letter to her.

She copied it carefully onto a new parchment, blotted it, folded it, and was about to seal it when she remembered an old tale she'd heard as a child. It was probably false, but given everything they'd seen lately, it was worth a try. Closing her eyes, she spoke quietly so as not to draw attention from outside the room. "Odin Allfather, I call upon your wisdom and protection and ask that you seal this letter, that it may not be read by any but the one to whom it is addressed. To this purpose I seal it with my own hand and symbol–" she tipped hot wax onto the folded parchment and pressed her own eagle-shaped signet into the soft wax. "I thank you for your gifts, and go directly to the library, where I will spend one hour this day gaining wisdom through the books I find there." She rose, took the parchment from her desk, and started toward the library, which was on the way to where she was headed to post the letter.

As she stepped into the library a soft rustling sound stopped her progress. When she looked down at the letter in her hand, she realized the edges of the parchment had fused together, leaving no way for the seal to be broken and the letter read without tearing the whole thing in half.

Stunned, Ambjorg stared at the parchment as if it were alien to her before sinking into a chair and placing it on a small table. Before long a servant passed through on her way to some other part of the building and Ambjorg stopped the woman briefly, asking her to summon her brothers and stating that she would be reading in the library. The bewildered woman nodded and went about her requested business. Ambjorg left the letter on the table and headed straight for the section on folklore.

Asbjorn found her teetering on her toes to reach a slim volume on the top shelf. He reached over her head and slid it from its dusty home. "The Eddas?" he asked as he handed her the volume. "Haven't you read those many times over?"

Ambjorg took the volume from him perfunctorily. "Of course," she replied, "but it seemed a fitting starting point. I might have found a way to secure our correspondence." She glided over to the small table, book in hand, and held up the letter for Asbjorn to study. He took it, then blinked and turned it over in his giant hands.

"How did you…?" he asked, staring at the letter as if it might grow teeth at any moment. He tugged at the seal, attempting to dislodge it with no effect. It wouldn't budge. Taking a corner of the paper he tried tearing it, but it was as if the parchment was made of rubber; it resisted every attempt to tear. "This is incredible!" He handed his sister the letter almost reverently.

"Another old wives' tale," Ambjorg replied. "Remember our nurse used to pray to the Allfather for protection? Apparently he's listening." She opened the book and started leafing through it, searching for something.

"Odin sealed your letter?" her brother asked, almost skeptically.

"I didn't do that with my own hand," she replied without looking up from her book. "I did promise him that I would spend an hour in the library gaining wisdom in return, and it didn't seal until I crossed the threshold of the room. So I'm making good on my promise." Finding the page she was looking for, she began to study it intently.

A few minutes later Audolf sauntered in. "So, what'd you find?" he asked. Asbjorn simply handed him the letter. He'd begun reading over Ambjorg's shoulder and was engrossed in the edda they were perusing. When Audolf realized how the letter was sealed he started, stared at his sister for a moment, and then began to attempt to find ways to open it. He even held it over a candle flame for a moment to see if it would burn, but it stayed cool to the touch no matter how long it was exposed to the fire. "I don't know how you did it, sis, but this is amazing. How do you open it?"

"You have to be the intended recipient of the letter," she replied. "Those were the terms I gave." Ambjorg explained again how she'd come across the sealing to Audolf.

"So let me make sure I understand: you prayed to the Allfather and promised to study–which you do every day anyway–and he sealed this to everyone but its intended recipient for you? That sounds way too simple." He tossed the letter back onto the small table before them.

"Agreed, but it works," Asbjorn said from behind the chair Ambjorg occupied. "If this works every time we might have solved our correspondence problems."

Audolf eyed the letter suspiciously. "Won't people think it strange to get letters like this? It's pretty unusual, to say the least, and while most folk respect the old ways they're likely to be suspicious of something like this."

"What choice do we have, Dolf?" Ambjorg leveled a stare at him. "We can't have all our missives read by everyone from here to the border and beyond, and we can't spare the people to send a runner every time we need a message to get through. Plus the roads are getting more dangerous by the day. We don't have a standing army; all we have to call upon is the citizenry to defend their land if things get rough enough for that. In those cases we need to know we can send communications securely to those who are helping us. I feel the ends justify the means in this case.

"Besides," she added as she flipped through the pages of the Eddas, "it will mean you get more reading done."

Audolf stuck out his tongue petulantly.

Glaring at his brother, Asbjorn stood and stretched. "Perhaps this isn't the only thing we can try that will work," he suggested. "Dolf, why don't you collect some more old legends and superstitions for us to test?"

Audolf snorted. "Chasing children's stories…next thing you know I'll be writing fairy tales." But he wandered off toward the kitchens nonetheless in search of rumors and superstitions. *At least it will give me something to do.*

"Why don't you go try this with your next letter to Eyildr, Asbi?" Ambjorg asked. "We should find out if this is something only I can do."

Never one to put off writing a letter to his betrothed, Asbjorn assented, moving off to his own quarters to test out the theory.

Ambjorg finished her study of the Eddas through her promised hour, then stood, stretched, and posted her letter, pausing only to give a silent thanks to whoever might be listening.

Later that evening they reconvened around the hearth in Ambjorg's rooms to compare notes. Asbjorn's letter had indeed sealed in much the same way as hers, but Audolf had found no further options for unexpected help. What he had found mostly involved strange combinations of foods and farm substances that were said to have properties to aid one in various endeavors, none of which had panned out in a bout of rather messy testing. So they resolved to let their allies know of their new method of securing missives and move on with their plans. And since there was word from the south of more strange, dangerous creatures, they agreed to send Asbjorn to investigate as soon as possible.

The next morning Asbjorn rumbled about the kitchens near dawn in search of breakfast. Ambi and Dolf had had their trip; it was his turn to spend some time outside the capital. After all, someone needed to look in on whatever was happening to the south, and he was getting cabin fever cooped up in his stuffy rooms with the eastward-facing windows and no breeze any time of year. Nevermind that he was missing Eyildr terribly and needed something to keep his mind from constant worry over her safety.

Last night's leftovers were easily acquired from the head cook as she arrived for her morning's work, and just like that there was nothing left to prepare. Asbjorn preferred to travel light and unaccompanied; he made better time that way. Plus his first destination was much closer than that of his siblings, a mere day's walk from home. *Closer than I like for these reports to come,* he thought as he trundled through the back door, sword on his hip and leathers on his back.

He stopped at the grove to commune with the ever-present chain of consciousness that connected him to the biggest of the predators hunting the forests. One answered immediately, as if she had been waiting for his call. Her response to his wordless query was a clear series of images and impressions of safety along a given route that paralleled the main road, crossing over it once or twice as game trails do. The animals always avoided using the paths as a thoroughfare, ever mistrustful of humans. *As am I.* Path determined, Asbjorn thanked the bear for her wisdom and started south.

The sun crested the horizon just as he entered the trees. *Not a moment too soon—it's going to be a late-season scorcher.* True to form, the days were getting thicker and warmer as they hurtled toward autumn. Sweat ran down Asbjorn's back between his shoulder blades, itching terribly until he stopped to scratch it on a tree. He realized idly that the particular specimen he'd chosen was a popular scratching post for deer, which gave it the most lovely rough bark. Sighing with contentment, he moved on.

Midday found Asbjorn seated in the midst of a wild blueberry patch, picking and eating his fill. They'd had just enough rain for the fruit to be sweet and plump, but not waterlogged, and he almost didn't leave any for the next creature to come along. But discretion won out and he continued on his journey under the stifling humidity beneath the forest canopy.

It was nearing twilight when he first sensed danger. The forest around him grew quiet and still as a cat waiting to pounce, and Asbjorn found himself setting his back against a tree to scan his surroundings.

There—a flutter of movement in a thicket. Had he imagined it? No, there it was again, but across the clearing. A streak of reddish fur flew past him at knee height and headed down the game trail back the direction he'd come. Turning faster than his bulk should allow, he lumbered down the path after the creature, more certain with every moment that it wasn't natural. Smaller animals darted left and right as they were nearly run down in the chase. Try as he might, Asbjorn had trouble gaining ground on the smaller creature, and before long he became winded. *Think, nimrod—what would Dolf do?* The answer came in a bolt of adrenaline-fueled clarity as he ran.

Skidding to a halt, he cast his thoughts in an expanding circle until he heard an answering roar. His quarry, now some ways ahead, froze to assess this new threat, giving Asbjorn time to slip closer. A great crashing to their right sent the smaller creature into a headlong dash straight toward his new hiding spot. Timing carefully, he darted a hand into the path and scooped up the strangest being he'd ever beheld. It was the size of a large dog and had a red body like a fox, though the resemblance ended there; its paws were much too large for the rest of it and were shaped like those of the large cats that cleared smaller game from the outskirts of the mountains to the east. Sharp claws retracted and flexed as it scrabbled for purchase against Asbjorn's viselike grip on the scruff of its neck to no avail. Dog-like ears laid flat against its misshapen skull, and it hissed its impotent displeasure at being captured.

Asbjorn regarded the creature for a moment. It was pitiful, this strange amalgam of features nature had separated all shoved under one skin. Before long it tired itself out and hung, limp, from his grip. *What exactly is your plan, Asbjorn?* It was unlike him to not think through his actions until after the fact. He didn't like feeling constricted by a smaller set of options due to a lack of foresight. Sighing, he resigned himself to carrying his catch as far as the outskirts of town and acquiring help restraining it for further study.

Half an hour and a few bloody scratches later he and a stout forester carried the creature between them trussed up on a large branch. The man who'd come to his aid led them straight up to the doors of the largest building in town, the great hall. He swung one large door inward on protesting hinges and strode confidently into the building. By the time Asbjorn's eyes adjusted to the relative gloom he was aware that many sets of eyes rested on him.

"We come bearing a gift," the forester announced. Silence answered, unbroken until a plump man in his mid-fifties stood from beside the room's fire pit.

"And you are…?" Derision dripped silvery barbs from the man's voice as he spoke.

"Ivar Arvidsson, at your service." Somehow the forester sketched a bow without dropping the load over one shoulder. "We wish to see the lady."

"No one sees the mayor except through me." The man who'd spoken shifted to bar further entry.

"Let them pass, Birger." A melodic contralto floated past their erstwhile roadblock, which moved grudgingly aside. Its owner was a woman of solid build with thick braids of dark, silver-gilt hair draped over one broad shoulder. She reclined in a skin-covered chair that had seen too many seasons to maintain its comfort. After a brief pause she rose to meet the newcomers, squinting at them across the fire's smoke column as it ascended, her eyes finally alighting on Asbjorn.

The woman's fist shot out and caught a glancing blow to the side of Birger's face as she passed, then crossed her chest as she bowed before her king. "My sincerest apologies, your majesty. Bergljot, mayor of Eikthwaite, at your service."

Asbjorn nodded, still holding the branch with the strange creature. "My thanks, mayor. Where might we put this?" He gestured vaguely at the furry mass before him. "I thought you might wish to study it, or perhaps use it to find more of its kin, though the reports made it sound as if they do not live in groups."

Straightening, Bergljot narrowed her eyes at their catch, considering. "Let me check with the head of the trappers," she said at last, motioning for them to set down their burden. "He's been keeping track of the ones we've found and may have a use for it. If not, we'll kill it and have done." She swept from the room, leaving the newcomers alone with a passel of unfamiliar faces.

The one named Birger bowed in an almost insolent fashion before strutting over to their quarry to inspect it. "So, how'd you manage to catch this, your majesty? Looks pretty fast–sneaky, too." There was a stifled chuckle somewhere in the small crowd that had accumulated during their conversation with the mayor.

*I see what's going on here.* But before Asbjorn could speak, the forester stepped forward barrel-chest first. "Do you have a quarrel with our king of which I am not aware?" he asked point-edly. "Or is needling outsiders simply your favorite pastime since you know the rest of us won't tolerate it?"

"Gods, no," Birger replied offhand as he turned away from the man. "Nor do I envy him his position, not with everything going on in the country right now."

Asbjorn laid a hand on the shoulder of his unexpected ally, who deflated. "I am lucky to have the support of my siblings," he began, stopping as a derisive snort emanated from somewhere in front of him. Birger smiled almost imperceptibly and met Asbjorn's gaze like a cat waiting to see if the mouse would play. In the blink of an eye he closed the space between Birger and himself and set a large, tanned hand on the older man's shoulder, his grip tighter than friendliness allowed. Blue eyes met hazel as Asbjorn leaned down to stare directly into the man's face as he spoke. "I understand your kind," he rumbled calmly. "All you respect is strength and speed. You are like these–" he gestured at the small predator they'd caught "–feeding on the small and weak and bowing only to those who best you. What you forget is that without a head and a heart, even the strongest arm will fail." Let-ting Birger go he addressed the rest of the group. "We are facing many challenges, that is true. But we will face them together or not at all. Anyone who disagrees is welcome to take their leave, though I recommend the south pass; it's safer right now than the north or the east." He turned on his heel, back to the crowd, and strode through the main doors to await the mayor, followed close-ly by the forester.

Both men sat heavily on the soft grass outside. "Begging

your pardon, majesty, but that was a damned fine show you gave in there. Birger's been completely unmanageable ever since the first of those things showed up."

Asbjorn's ears pricked at this last comment. "You mean to say he was reasonable beforehand?"

"Not exactly, but at least you could count on him in a pinch. Anymore I wouldn't trust him any further than I could throw him, and you've seen his size."

"Hmm." Asbjorn pondered as they sat in the gathering twilight. *There is more to this than it seems, but I cannot fathom it yet. I need more information.* "My apologies; I didn't catch your name," he said, turning to his unexpected ally.

"Ivar Arvidsson," the man repeated, this time with a respectful bow.

"Are you good with a bow, then?"

"One of the best–at least around here." Ivar leaned into his knees, which were propped before him on the sward. They waited a few minutes more in companionable silence before Bergljot reappeared through the door to the main hall.

"The trappers are going to take the beast you've brought us. They hope to use it to find the rest of its kin, or perhaps its master." She joined them on the grass with a hefty *thump*.

"You believe it has a master?" Asbjorn raised his eyebrows at this last comment.

"Aye." Bergljot spat and traced a rune of protection over her chest. "These things certainly aren't natural, so what other explanation is there besides dark powers?"

Asbjorn grunted in response as Ivar made a similar gesture to Bergljot's. "Which direction have they been coming from?"

"The east, as best we can tell." Bergljot pointed toward the far mountains, obscured by the trees in the fading light. Asbjorn frowned, silently piecing together what his siblings had seen. "At least, that's what we think. A couple villages south of here have seen them, too, so you might check there to get their stories."

"That is my plan," Asbjorn agreed, standing. "Does your town have an inn or a spare bed I could beg for the night? A skin in the hall is fine if there's none to be had."

Bergljot hesitated, but Ivar stepped into the side between

them. "I have room in my home–have plans for a family one day, but none yet. You're welcome to the spare room, such as it is."

"Many thanks, and I'll take it," Asbjorn replied, clapping the man on the shoulder. He turned to the mayor, who looked relieved. "Thank you for your assistance," he began, but she waved him off.

"It is I who will be thankful if you can help rid us of these creatures. And I am in your debt for the lack of hospitality shown by my kinsman today. If there is anything I can do, please ask."

"I believe Birger and I have come to an understanding," Asbjorn replied with a dangerous glint in his eye. "Though he may disagree, in which case I am happy to reiterate. In the meantime, I'll let you know if there is aught you can do, and be thankful for it besides." Nodding respectfully, he turned and followed Ivar out of town to the man's home. It was a decent walk, and with every step both men breathed more freely. They spoke of lighter subjects, of the upcoming harvest and hunting and how much of the forest must regrow before it could be harvested for timber. Asbjorn made mental note of Ivar's knowledge of regional husbandry and resolved to invite the man to the next quarterly gathering as an advisor.

He left at dawn, well rested and fed, and thanked Ivar for his hospitality as they parted ways. The following week bore much of the same for Asbjorn, and though his welcome was warmer in the rest of the southern towns, each held an undercurrent of unrest. Parents worried for their children, farmers worried for their livestock, and some few blamed the new monarchy for their troubles. By the time he returned to the capital Asbjorn carried the cares of nearly half the population with him. It must have shown as he trudged back into the main hall to report to Audolf and Ambjorg, who met him at the door with their brows knitted in concern and insisted he have dinner before giving his report.

A half-eaten plate of food later he finished describing what he'd found. "Every town has seen these things, and most of them have killed more than their share," he explained as he finished a mouthful of potatoes. "I had nothing to tell them, no assistance to render besides hunting the ones I found. I put the local bears on alert, but in a few months they will find their dens for the winter."

"They came from the east, you said?" Ambjorg pushed a sweet bun toward him as she clarified.

"So it seemed." Asbjorn tore a corner off the bun and returned it to her, unable to stomach much of the treat in his current mood. It was unusual for him to lose his appetite, but after the mental trials of the last few days he found his interest in food severely lacking.

"How can they all be coming from the east?" Audolf asked, exasperated, as he ran a hand through his unruly hair. "There's nothing to the east but mountains!"

"And roads that run south." Ambjorg added quietly. They pondered in stillness for a moment, then Asbjorn pushed his plate away entirely.

"I'm writing to Eyildr." The three nodded to each other and took their leave.

Eyildr stared blankly out the window of her room, hands folded on her desk. She'd finished her latest letter to Asbjorn some time ago, but hadn't been able to muster the energy to stir from where she sat. The last few weeks weighed heavily on her; preparations for storing the harvest were mingling with training and the setting of watches and perimeters around settlements across their lands. To her knowledge Eyildr's people had never needed to stay vigilant against attack, and even now it seemed surreal to be discussing watch rotations and training schedules in the same breath as preparations for the end of harvest season. But despite the oddity, she was more certain than ever that their planning was necessary. There was an unsettled feeling in the pit of her stomach that had grown more and more pronounced as the weather cooled, and she was sure that winter would bring the subject of her current dread.

Shaking off the mental cobwebs she'd been building, Eyildr stood, stretched, and kneaded her lower back to release the knots she felt there. Her eyes drifted out the window, dancing across the tree line that obscured her view beyond the small garden they kept, and for a moment she thought she saw movement. *Probably a bird*, she thought, *stopping on its way south*. Even she was dubious of her own thoughts, and as she stooped to fold her letter, she kept a surreptitious eye on the bushes. There it was again–a flash of green that didn't quite fit in with the late season. Narrowing her eyes, Eyildr moved toward the window, watching the trees for movement.

There it was again–a shifting of the bushes around...the hem of an emerald green dress? Who would be stalking the fringes of their property, much less in finery? Setting down her letter, Eyildr took up the shortsword she kept by the door and stalked toward the tree line, bare blade in hand. Her gaze swept across the bushes, scanning for signs of inhabitants as the forest stilled around her. Exposed as she was, she searched for a more secure approach until her eyes lit upon a large-boled oak directly in her path. She ducked behind it, peeking past the knot of a long-lost branch to see what awaited her.

A pair of sparkling green eyes met hers and she abruptly lost all sense of space and time.

"Eyildr!" Her father's voice rang out through the woods, concern deepening its rich tone. Blinking, she sat up, staring at the unfamiliar forest floor around her. She was in a clearing, with no recollection of how she'd gotten there or why she'd left the yard. Her shortsword was stuck in the ground next to the bed of soft leaves on which she'd awoken, and she grasped the hilt to haul herself up, yanking it from the ground as she stood. Suddenly she recognized her surroundings–she wasn't far from the house at all. In fact, she could almost see the outer walls through the brush.

"Coming!" Eyildr replied as she took off toward the sound of her father's voice, which was slightly left of the house from where she was. Before long she burst onto the path he strode, sword in hand and leaves in her hair.

"Eyildr!" Her father took in her appearance with a shocked expression. "Are you well? What has happened?"

"We must gather the villagers and raise the militia," she replied, her answer surprising them both as she spoke. "They are coming."

Brandulfr wiped sweat from his brow for the third time in as many minutes. Looking up from the hole he'd dug he cast about for the sharpened log to go in it, finding a new stack behind him and to the left. He grabbed the closest one and jammed it into the hole, adding to the nearly-finished stockade that had gone up almost overnight. It had been two months since midsummer, and villagers had been disappearing under increasingly familiar circumstances weekly, causing the village council to recommend the abandonment of the outlying farms and holdings. The village proper had swelled to capacity in order to accommodate the holders and their families, who were currently employed in building the stockade. Soon enough there would be idle hands and unrest, and the thane tapped a foot on the newly-laid stockade pole as he considered the effect the current late-season heat wave would have on the already crowded town. They needed more options, and fast.

Setting down his shovel, Brandulfr took a long swig from the waterskin he carried on his hip, then strode toward his house on the edge of the village, patting shoulders and giving encouragement along the way. His words were met with grim smiles and renewed effort that he hoped would be enough to protect them all from what lay outside the walls.

Agvarr met him at the door to the house with a spare handkerchief and the day's mail. "Stockade's lookin' stout," he remarked as Brandulfr followed him into the house, mopping at the worst of the sweat so that it wouldn't drip through the house. "By my reckoning it'll be done by end of week. 'S a good thing we've had as much help as we have," he said, nodding, as he continued on into the kitchen. Brandulfr followed him, retrieving the mail from where the man dropped it unceremoniously on the table. He sifted through it to the background noise of Agvarr's good-natured mumbling over the midday meal, stopping abruptly as he reached an oddly-sealed letter addressed in a familiar, spindly hand. Setting the rest aside, he flipped over the missive, inspecting the eagle seal affixed unnecessarily to the back. He waited expectantly as lines appeared where there previously had been none before breaking the seal and opening the letter to devour its contents.

> *Brandulfr,*
>
> *Forgive me for dispensing with pleasantries in this letter; I find myself increasingly disturbed with each day that passes, and my concern for our kingdom weighs heavily on me. More reports have poured in from the south of creatures attacking villagers, pillaging food stores, and besetting travelers on the roads. In the north Eyildr and her father are preparing to defend their own lands, though it has as yet been eerily quiet. I trust it not, given their proximity to Thane Alfgrimr's domain, but we have yet to hear word of anything disturbing. How fare your people? Your last report indicated a similar turn of events in the mountains.*
>
> *More importantly, how fare you? I know the safety of your people weighs as heavily on your shoulders as it does on mine. Know that you and your people have a place here should the worst occur. We have been making plans for our people to retreat to the capital if their homes become untenable. In the meantime, if there is anything we can do from our position of safety, please let me know.*
>
> *It is when times are hardest that I miss your company the most.*
>
> *Yours,*
> *Ambjorg*

His eyes lingered over the signature as if they could conjure its owner through sheer force of will while his mind turned over her message. Something more was afoot than any of them knew, and he would bet his life that Alfgrimr was behind it.

Without turning from the stove, Agvarr grumbled, "Letter from her ladyship, sir?"

Brandulfr chuckled. "How did you know?"

"Nought else commands your attention so," Agvarr replied in a knowing tone. "How're things in the capital, then?"

"Could be better," Brandulfr replied. "It seems we're not the only ones having trouble with...wildlife." Sighing, he set down the letter, which resealed itself as it left his hand.

"Unnatural, that is," Agvarr said, shivering. He flipped an oat cake in the pan on the stove before continuing. "Y'know, me mum used to tell stories of a wise woman in her village with strange powers. She knew things afore they happened, like when the harvest wouldn't be sufficient to last the winter and who would die in childbirth. Said she could do other things, too, like give people the pox, or take their luck when they hunted." He shunted an oat cake onto a plate and set it in front of Brandulfr, who'd taken a seat at the table. "Hinted she could do worse if she chose." Returning to the stove, Agvarr spooned more batter into the pan.

"Hmm." Brandulfr pensively spooned preserves onto his oat cake, then bit into it, too deep in thought to notice the taste. A year ago he'd have dismissed Agvarr's comments as superstitious, but he found them taking root as he turned them over in his mind. The creatures they'd encountered could not have been the product of any natural phenomenon; they seemed to be a physical combination of the most deadly traits of the animals living in a given area, and they had no way to interbreed or adapt in the ways their traits manifested. He had to admit the idea had some merit. *Perhaps I'll add that to my response.*

Looking down at his empty plate, Brandulfr realized he'd finished the oat cake as Agvarr added another. "Buildin' be hungry work," the man said as he slid two more cakes onto Brandulfr's plate. "Eat up, and there be more where that came from if ye like." He sat down across from the thane with his own plate of oat cakes, slathering them liberally with preserves before tucking in with a will. Brandulfr shook himself out of his reverie and applied himself to his own lunch as he sorted through the rest of the mail. None of it appeared to be of much consequence; he could delay responding until after he'd returned Ambjorg's letter. He still wasn't sure how she sealed them the way she did.

At the rate they were being attacked, he might get the chance to ask her sooner rather than later.

Ambjorg stared out from the watchtower as the last rays of sunset cast themselves over the plains. The fields shone red and gold as the sun's beams trickled over them toward the harbor in the west. This year's harvest would be abundant–possibly even enough to feed their people through the winter if they were forced to pull back to the capital and its more defensible location. The thought tempered Ambjorg's pleasant reflections as she left a chunk of leftover meat from her dinner on the edge of the tower.

A cry from overhead caught her attention as a familiar winged shadow descended toward her. Ambjorg raised an arm to catch the eagle as it pumped its wings, looking for a safe spot to land, then helped it onto the ledge for its dinner. It whistled at her as it bolted the meat, then waited as Ambjorg scratched the back of its head fondly. She leaned toward the bird and closed her eyes. "What have you seen?" she whispered.

Flashes of terrain flew through her thoughts as she saw as the eagle saw. Plains, then trees passed beneath her until she recognized the edge of Eyildr's family lands. A clearing stood out deep in the forest itself and she focused on it, inexplicably intent on its contents. But before she could see what it contained, a pair of green eyes flashed before her vision and her mind was ejected from the eagle's recollections.

*That's never happened before*, she thought as she shook her head to clear it. With another cry the eagle leaped from the watchtower, gliding back toward the northern woodlands. *Good hunting*, Ambjorg sent as a benediction, watching it until it was out of sight.

Her brow furrowed, she descended the stone watchtower stairs without seeing them, heading straight for the hall and her brothers. Perhaps they had seen something similar.

She found them sitting in Dolf's rooms, arguing. "It makes no sense," Audolf was saying as he paced the room restlessly. "The attacks have come from the south and east. What does the north have to do with anything?"

"It's been too quiet," Asbjorn rumbled from his chair by the small table in the study attached to Audolf's room. It creaked as he shifted uneasily. "We all know Alfgrimr was never friendly with Father, and we suspect worse. It's just like him to try to distract us from whatever he's planning so that we don't see it coming."

Audolf's pacing stopped abruptly as Ambjorg entered the room. "You may be right, brother," he ventured after nodding a greeting to his sister, who closed the door quietly behind herself. "We shouldn't underestimate his craftiness." His gaze shifted to Ambjorg as she seated herself in another chair next to their brother. "What do you think, Ambi? Is Alfgrimr behind all this?"

She frowned for a moment. "He's definitely the obvious culprit," she replied after a moment's consideration, "but the obvious one is not always the responsible party." Shifting her skirts into a more comfortable position, she regarded each of her brothers in turn. "Any word from the packs? Or the bears?"

Asbjorn shook his head. "Most are doing their best to fatten up for the winter. Few have seen anything of use beyond what we already know from our reports."

"Same with the packs," Audolf replied as he resumed his pacing. "Though they're restless; something has them spooked, a scent on the wind they say reeks of things that are unnatural." He shivered as he recalled the feeling they'd passed on to him. There were no human words to describe it.

"The eagle to the north has seen something in the forest," Ambjorg began uncertainly, "but before I could see what it was I got dumped out of her thoughts, as if someone didn't want me to see what was there. It's never happened before, but the feeling I got from it was not malicious; if anything, it felt…calm." She wrung her hands nervously in her lap.

The three of them sat in contemplative silence, each mulling over the information unsuccessfully. After a few moments Asbjorn stood, his chair creaking as he vacated it, and proclaimed he would check with the bear that lived closest to the hall in the morning. Audolf mumbled something about reviewing some reports, and Ambjorg took the hint, retreating to her own rooms in the knowledge that sleep would be slow to come.

The next day dawned red. Audolf was up with the sun, loping toward the nearby grove; he'd been awakened twice during the night by howls from the pack and was concerned. He'd skipped breakfast entirely in order to allay his fears–or face them on an empty stomach and save himself from sickness. His ground-eating strides hastened him to the grove, and before long he was face to face with the pack's leader, who turned silently and lead him deeper into the gloomy woodland. The sun's rays were just peeking through enough gaps in the trees for him to make out the form of an animal lying motionless in the first clearing they reached.

Recognizing the shape, Audolf hurried forward–only for the alpha wolf to bar his way, snarling. He crouched down to meet its gaze for a moment. *Caution*, he seemed to be telling Audolf. Nodding, he stood and moved past the alpha, who turned his attention to the figure on the forest floor. It was still breathing; rapid, light movements of its ribcage spoke of a tenuous grasp on life that would soon flee, but Audolf edged closer from the side regardless to get a better look.

It had once been a wolf, that much was certain, but something had elongated its body and exchanged its front feet for those of a wildcat. The face was mauled and damaged almost beyond recognition, but seemed to be a combination of rounded ears and a long snout through which the creature huffed out its final breaths. The pack had been merciful in its kill, tearing at the creature's neck until it was a shredded mass of flesh pumping lifeblood onto the grass, and just as it started to snarl at Audolf its eyes glazed over in death, its shallow breath stilled.

With the threat past and their pack mate notified, the alpha huffed once toward the corpse and melted back into the brush, the rest of the pack following close behind. Audolf thanked them silently and wondered if the creature had once been one of their own as he watched the last tail disappear on silent footpads.

Looking to the grass beneath him, Audolf began to track the creature's path to the clearing, discovering to his surprise that it had been headed toward the hall when the pack caught it. He spent the next half hour tracking its original course southward and slightly east, noting that the pack had run it a good distance before they'd caught it. *It must've been fast, whatever it is*, he thought as he turned back toward the hall at a jog.

Asbjorn was still asleep when he arrived, but Ambjorg met him in the kitchens as he searched for breakfast. "Good morrow," she said, nodding to her brother as she carried a lightly laden plate from the preparation table in the kitchen. Audolf nodded, but said nothing as he loaded a second plate with fruit, cheese, nuts, and pastry, then steered his sister toward their rooms. "What's all this?" she asked as he propelled her through the door to her own suite.

"We need to talk. I'm going to wake up the bear." Audolf pulled the door to as he rushed down the hall, shoving pastry into his mouth as he went. Asbjorn was in his bed, snoring, with one arm thrown over his face against the daylight streaming through his curtains, and Audolf had to prod him multiple times in the ribs to elicit a grumbled response. "Meeting in Ambi's rooms," he said, shoving a piece of cheese at his brother, whose eyes cracked open at the smell of food. "It's important." Seeing Asbjorn throw a leg over the bed and grab at the cheese in his face, Audolf popped another morsel in his own mouth and strode back down the hall.

Half a minute later Asbjorn joined them, closing the door behind himself. With a stretch and a yawn, he mumbled, "What's this all about, now?"

Audolf swallowed another hurried bite of his breakfast as Ambjorg picked daintily at her own. "I've seen another one," Audolf blurted around the remnants of some fruit. "Another creature, like the one we saw in the mountains this summer, only different." Ambjorg started, staring at him quizzically as he continued. "This one looked to be half wolf and half cat." He paused to shove more fruit into his mouth and Ambjorg took the proffered opportunity to interject.

"Where?" she demanded. "Is anyone in danger? Did anyone else see it?"

"The grove, no, and no," Audolf replied around another bite. "It's dead; the pack found it and led me to it. I can take you there."

Asbjorn stuffed his entire piece of cheese in his mouth at once. "What are we waiting for?" he rumbled, opening the door for his siblings. Ambjorg abandoned her breakfast, but Audolf grabbed a few tidbits off his plate before following his sister out the door.

It didn't take long for them to reach the clearing with the creature's corpse. Having already encountered one of the creatures–and a more grotesque one, at that–Ambjorg was circumspect in her inspection of the carcass, but Asbjorn's eyes grew round as he took in its features. "Gods of the realms," he said as he knelt near its feet. "What is this? It's much larger than the ones I saw in the southlands."

"It's unlike the one we saw in the mountains, that's for sure," Ambjorg said as she considered its features in as clinical a fashion as possible. "This one is smaller, for one, and there was nothing catlike about the other. Still no visible means of reproduction, which is similar." She cocked her head to one side, looking for all the world like one of her eagles for a moment. "Nothing in nature could have done this. Thane Brandulfr has reported an increase in sightings in his area, mostly when villagers have been snatched, and now one has made it this far inland…"

"It reminds me of the ones I saw to the south some weeks ago," Asbjorn added. "If they were headed westward, it seems they've grown much bolder to be this close to home."

The siblings considered in silence for a moment before Audolf asked the question they were all pondering. "When do we pull in the holders?"

"If we can make it through the harvest, we can be sure to be able to feed them all," Ambjorg said as she stood. "We should make provisions to defend them while they work."

"I'll speak to Geirvarr," Asbjorn volunteered as they turned to leave. "He'll have a feel for how many able-bodied folk we have to mount a watch." With one last look at the carcass, he made a beeline for the weapons hall.

The rest of the day became a blur. The carcass was retrieved from the grove for use as evidence and a teaching tool, the armsmaster spent half the day setting up watches around the clock, and missives were sent with all speed to the rest of the kingdom, warning them of the imminent threat. It would be a few days before they reached the outlying thanedoms, but the siblings felt it was important they let their people know they were aware of the situation. The holders near the capital were notified of the danger and chose to stay the course through the harvest, provided they were furnished with ways to defend themselves. Each of the siblings volunteered for a watch around the capital, but were denied on the basis that they needed rest to coordinate the defense effort.

For once, Audolf was in his element. All the time he'd spent studying tactics and warfare suddenly paid off, and as soon as it became apparent he had a flair for planning defenses and organizing troops, his brother and sister were happy to delegate all such duties to him. They even declared him lord marshall of the militia for the duration. Geirvarr heartily approved of his student's appointment to the position. Asbjorn buried himself in logistical preparations for storing and rationing supplies to support bivouacked troops and civilians alike through an entire season, finding it amusing that he was helping his people think like the bears he favored. Ambjorg was left with the communication and coordination of both efforts across the thanedoms so that her brothers could concentrate on local concerns. Given her standing relationships with many of the thanes and their children she was the natural choice even when her brothers were idle, so she embraced her duties willingly.

By sunset all three siblings were exhausted. They took their evening meal in the great hall in an effort to be visible and give their people heart, but as soon as they'd finished eating they retired to their rooms, falling asleep even before removing their clothing.

# CHAPTER 6

Eyildr watched as the line of carts trundled past, carrying the fruits of their holders' labors–and any valuables they might own–further south. The northernmost holdings had been under duress for the last two weeks, fending off strange creatures while attempting to bring in as much of the harvest as they could. Given their higher latitude, the lands they farmed ripened earlier than their southern counterparts, so they'd been able to reap most of what they'd sown before it had become too dangerous to keep to their lands. Eyildr had included these details in her reports to the capital, but given the time frame she knew there was no way help could arrive before the harvest was in.

Sighing, Eyildr joined her father at the door of their house. Before long they, too, would have to venture southward, the line drawn by the attacks moving ever toward their home. She found herself thinking of her mother, who had died of sickness nearly a decade earlier. Their home was one of the last bastions of the time they'd shared as a family, and it would grieve her to leave it. She forced herself to acknowledge that her living family was more important than memories that would follow her wherever her feet took her, finding that the thought brought her a measure of peace.

She fought off a shudder and turned to her father. "Have you packed?" she asked, ducking inside the low lintel.

"Aye," her father replied, "though I don't believe your brother has. He's still holding out hope we won't have to leave."

Eyildr snorted. "Hope he's admitted it by the morning, else he'll find himself without a pack," she said as she trudged to her own room to gather her things.

They traveled with the next day's dawn, carrying only what they must. A few stragglers from the outer holdings joined them, offering rides on carts and company as they abandoned the homes they'd known for decades. Eyildr found a seat on the last cart in sight in order to keep watch as they made their way south.

The first few miles were quiet due to the early hour and somber mood, and Eyildr found herself nodding on the back of the cart. She tucked her feet beneath her and settled into the packed belongings behind her in case she fell asleep, her eyelids growing heavier as the swaying of the wagon lulled her into a sense of warmth and security. Her gaze slowed as she swept across the forest behind them and she took a few long blinks. The day had dawned an angry orange, but not a cloud showed in the cracks between the foliage as they trundled along. Golds, browns, umbers, and reds had started to creep into the canopy, and the occasional leaf floated to the ground in their wake, settling lightly onto the packed dirt of the path as furry gray paws kicked up tiny clouds of dust…

Gray paws?

Shaking herself fully awake, Eyildr shuddered as she surveyed the creatures following their carts. They eschewed the cover of the brush in favor of the ease of travel afforded by the path and the opportunity to frighten their prey as they cantered a scant few lengths behind the cart.

"'Ware behind!" Eyildr cried as she drew her shortsword, leveling it at the closest creature. "We're being followed!"

Cries went up along the column behind her and the wagon lurched as its driver pushed the horses to a trot despite the loaded wagon. Eyildr almost lost her balance, but righted herself with her free hand just before she tumbled to the packed earth passing beneath her at a goodly pace. Answering howls unlike anything she'd ever heard went up from the pack of creatures behind them and they picked up the pace as more appeared on the path. Their gangly, reverse-jointed legs gained ground steadily against the loaded wagons, and before long Eyildr found herself fending off fangs and talons, too engaged in the fight to even cry out for assistance. She thought she heard a shout from the driver's seat of the wagon she occupied, but it faded into the background as training and instinct took over and she swung, parried, and riposted, her efforts rewarded with the demise of first one of the creatures, then another. Two more took their place and attacked together, learning from the mistakes of their predecessors, and she found herself hard pressed to keep the teeth and nails from scoring her skin. A triumphant snarl tore from one creature's throat as its claws sank into her forearm, latching on and yanking her from the wagon. The ground rose up to meet her–and was the last thing her eyes registered before darkness overtook her.

As suddenly as it began, the attack ceased as the creatures fell back and melted into the woods on either side of the path. Eyildr's father drove the wagons on for another few minutes before calling a halt to regroup. The last wagon had trouble catching up, and by the time it reached the main group the horses were badly in need of a rest. The driver was gesticulating madly and yelling something unintelligible as he approached.

"Out with it, man!" one of the farmers cried as soon as they were within earshot.

"It's Eyildr," the man panted, slowing his horses to a walk. Lowering his eyes to avoid the thane's gaze, he continued. "They took her. There was nothing I could do; she fell from the wagon, and as fast as we were going I could never have stopped in time. I'm sorry, my lord."

The thane's face went slack for a moment. "You did all you could," he said woodenly. "We must go on." Handing the reins of his horse to his son, he said, "Lead the people on to the capital. Don't stop unless there is no other choice."

"But Father, where are you going?" his son cried, taking a few steps toward his father.

"I am thane no longer; that responsibility falls to you now, Davyn." He turned long enough to put a hand on his bare-ly-grown son's shoulder. "Today I am but a father seeking his daughter's safety. Lead well, my son." They embraced briefly, the younger man holding back tears before watching his father disappear into the woods of their homeland in the knowledge they may never see each other again.

A hush fell over the assembled holders as they watched their leader go, then looked to his son for guidance. Dashing his arm across his eyes, Davyn squared his shoulders and took up the reins of his father's horse, swinging himself into the saddle. "You all heard," he said as his mount sidestepped against his sudden weight. "We ride for the plains. No unnecessary stops, no sparing of beasts except in dire circumstances. Set a watch on the last two carts." Turning his mount, he started down the path.

Midmorning of the sixth day after their departure saw the ragged group of northern holders deposited onto the outer plains to the south. They were fewer in number than they had been to start with, having been set upon at every stop and harried through the daylight hours, and many were ready to collapse with exhaustion. The edge of the plains brought watchers from the capital, who were quick to send word of their arrival and lend a hand. Once they were beyond the tree line the attacks stopped, at least for the time being, and they were able to make camp within two days of the capital in a more secure location than they had in a week.

Davyn met with the head of the northern watch contingent over supper and briefed her on what they'd encountered. Concern etched her brow, and she excused herself early to pen an update to her leadership, dispatching her fastest rider to relay the message with all haste. A young boy, barely twelve years old, hopped onto a sleek chestnut mare and sped south, promising to stop for the night in the next town. Davyn watched him go with trepidation, praying the message and the boy would reach their destination.

The stockades around Thorsbrand weren't enough. The creatures were just too big, too strong, too fast; they could leap over any barrier the townsfolk could erect. There were more of them now, enough to push through the town's defenses if they desired, but they seemed to be waiting, biding their time.

Thane Brandulfr cursed beneath his breath. Thorsbrand was his home, and he'd planned to defend it to the last, but his people were looking to him for leadership with fear in their eyes. They knew they were defeated, and it showed. Yet they fought on, their wills bolstered by their love of the land and the leadership of their thane. Brandulfr's heart swelled with pride in his people as he surveyed their determined faces. *I cannot condemn them to death when there is another option*, he thought. None would be happy to leave their home, but they had a better chance at survival if they abandoned the town and headed for the plains to join the rest of their people. There was safety in numbers.

The thane crouched along the wall they'd hastily constructed on the eastern edge of town, passing word to the defenders posted there. Come dawn, they would leave their posts as quietly as possible and join the throngs already winding their way down the mountain paths. These would be the last of the defenders to leave, being the furthest out, and he vowed to stay with them until it was time. His things were already packed and heading down the mountain with Agvarr and Ingr; there was nothing left to do but lend his support to his people.

They slept in shifts so that they wouldn't be too tired to make the journey the next day. The night was blessedly quiet, as if the gods had seen fit to give them a brief respite before ejecting them from their mountain homes, and they took full advantage of the lull to make sure their packs were properly taken care of. Come dawn, the wall was empty, and the town of Thorsbrand was left to the will of the wild.

The next three days saw the mountain folk beset at every pass as they wound their way down the mountain, even with a vanguard of volunteer guardsmen and women and the thane taking up the rear with more. As the ground leveled out and they exited the switchbacks that had protected their flank Brandulfr called a halt so they could regroup and leave fewer of their number exposed. Every able-bodied person in the caravan was armed with something, whether they owned a proper weapon or not, and the hunters kept their bows strung at all times. When the attacks came there was never any warning, and now that they had more angles of attack the creatures had redoubled their efforts.

The village that normally served as a waypoint between the capital and the hills was deserted except for a single pig that roamed the streets. Homes had been hastily abandoned and left unsecured, so the ragged group of villagers took advantage of the relative safety and comfortable beds they found. The thane chose the room in the inn that was closest to the outer door and laid down to rest with his scabbard by his side.

Sleep was a long time coming. He found his mind wandering back over the creatures they'd seen in the last few days and realized they had changed as the villagers moved westward; instead of huge, hulking wolf or bear-like creatures, they saw more large cat aberrations and smaller predators. *It seems they're drawn from the wildlife around them,* he pondered muzzily as his eyes finally closed. He slept fitfully, his rest punctuated by dreams of fearsome creatures and bloodied eagles, so that when the sun finally kissed the horizon he was well awake and ready to move on.

Most of the houses in the village had come through the night unscathed, though two on the outskirts had been attempted by smaller creatures that were fended off with ease. Taking it as a sign their luck was turning, the villagers reformed, set their watches, checked their bowstrings, and headed west toward the plains. By midday the first outriders from the capital found them, followed shortly by a small contingent of militia. It was led by the armsmaster himself. Geirvarr saluted Thane Brandulfr smartly as he approached. "Seems you've had a rough time of it," he remarked, looking over the ragtag bunch of villagers. "Their majesties sent us to make certain you made it to bivouac." Gesturing to another of the soldiers, he gave orders that they should join the exhausted watchmen and women of Thorsbrand as the group made its way into camp.

Whether it was the additional numbers or proximity to the capital they sustained no more casualties between the edge of the plains and their allotted camp site. Materials were piled nearby for the erection of temporary shelters, but no efforts had yet been made toward that end, and the villagers were too exhausted to begin until the morrow. Besides, the sun had almost set, and there was a meal to be had in the great hall. They were inside the guarded perimeter now, so the villagers felt comfortable leaving the carts and wagons containing what was left of their worldly possessions out in the field while they trudged to the hall for their first hot meal in days.

Brandulfr found himself at the front of the group despite being one of the last to arrive. He stepped lightly, his eyes on the dais as they adjusted to the dimmer interior of the building. It was empty. Deflating slightly, he held the door as the rest of his people filed in, filled plates, and found seats. The prospect of good food lifted their spirits, and before long the hall was filled with the buzz of comfortable conversation as the villagers were joined by the hall's staff and holders. Some chose to take their plates outside to ease the crowding as the hall filled nearly to bursting, but the thane merely relinquished his seat to lean against the back wall of the building. It warmed his heart to see his people finally safe and well fed, and he began mental preparations for starting to build out a temporary settlement the next day as he finished his own meal.

At last the crowd thinned as people filtered out by ones and twos, and Brandulfr was able to cast about for one of the hall's staff, catching the woman lightly by the arm as she hurried out the door with a tray of food. "Forgive me," he began as she startled, nearly dropping the tray, "but I was hoping to speak with their majesties tonight. We've only just arrived, and I would like to make a report." He dropped his hand from her arm as she straightened, nodding.

"They've taken to eating in their rooms of late," she replied, setting off toward the adjacent building that contained the meeting rooms and sleeping accommodations for those who lived at the capital year round. "Follow me and I'll take you there. This tray's for them." She swept through a side door and down hallways Brandulfr hadn't even known existed before leading him into a familiar hallway. She knocked on the door to        Ambjorg's rooms, calling out, "Thane Brandulfr to see the kings and queen." A muffled acknowledgment followed, and Brandulfr found his hands sweating as the serving woman opened the door, tray in hand, and ushered him through.

Ambjorg sat at the small table in her sitting room, flanked by her brothers on each side. They looked up from where they'd been poring over a map, all three sagging with relief as the thane entered. Dinner was laid on a side table and the woman bustled out of the room, closing the door behind her. Brandulfr bowed low, then straightened. "Thank you all for your hospitality," he began.

Asbjorn stood and clasped the thane's large hand in his even larger one. "We're glad you made it," he said, sounding genuinely relieved. "The reports we've gotten have been dire, and we feared the worst."

Audolf cleared his throat as he stood. "What my brother means is, we hope your journey went as well as could be expected," he said as he also shook hands with the thane.

Ambjorg stood slowly, smoothing the wrinkles out of her dress as she slid from behind the table. She nodded in greeting, extending a hand, and Thane Brandulfr took it slowly, leaning over it just long enough to brush his lips against the back before letting it go. "I'm glad you're here," she said simply as her cheeks colored. "Forgive us–how are your people? The journey must've been difficult."

"They are tired, but as well as can be expected," Brandulfr replied as the siblings resumed their seats at the table. Asbjorn found a fourth chair and offered it to the thane, who sank into it gratefully when he realized he'd been standing for hours. "We lost some along the way."

Ambjorg's mouth pressed into a thin line. "I'm sorry to hear that," she said. "We sent an escort as soon as we s–as soon as we knew you were coming." A look passed between Audolf and his sister, and she raised her chin as she broke his gaze.

"Watches have been set around the plains," Audolf continued, "and we've been able to secure the areas designated for overflow residence both north and east of the hilltop. Word is that Eyildr's people are heading south through the woodlands and should be here in the next day or two. We have yet to hear from the south."

"Last we knew they'd had more success defending their own homes and farms," Asbjorn replied as he rose to make a plate from the tray on the sideboard. "I'm sure Ambi has sent word."

"Of course," she replied, standing to make her own plate. "Multiple times. I'm fairly certain the messengers got through, so they're aware of the situation and can act according to their own best interests. We've reserved space to the south of the hill for them in case it's needed." She picked at the assortment of meats and vegetables on the tray, selecting a few seemingly at random before seating herself again at the table. Audolf followed suit, heaping his own plate with most of the remaining foodstuffs.

"Are you hungry?" he asked the thane, who shook his head and explained he'd already partaken. "Would you mind giving us a full account of your travels, or would you rather wait until tomorrow? You must be exhausted."

"I would prefer to give it now, if it please you," the thane replied, settling into his chair to tell the tale while the rest ate. He left nothing out of his retelling, and by the time he was finished all three had cleared their plates and were listening in stillness. Ambjorg reached for a quill and parchment and began to take notes around her empty plate.

"I will add this to the reports we've already had," she said as she hurriedly noted the major details. "Did you happen to see where any of the creatures might have staged their attacks? Or were they directed in any way? Were there any strange folk on the roads as you traveled?"

"No, no and we saw no one but ourselves," Brandulfr replied. "Have you any clue as to where they've been coming from? We did notice that they seem to consist of creatures native to the areas in which they're found; the ones in the mountains were larger and more deadly than the ones we saw out here on the plains." He shifted uncomfortably in his seat as his thoughts drifted back over some of the more grotesque combinations they'd seen.

"No ideas yet," Audolf acknowledged. "But each day brings more information on the creatures themselves, and we're hopeful that information will lead to a breakthrough on that front." Stretching his arms out in front of him, he stood. "It's been a long day, and I'm for bed. Will you be staying in the hall or camping outdoors?"

"I would prefer to be near my people," the thane answered, and both Audolf and Asbjorn nodded.

"In that case I will bid you goodnight as well," Asbjorn said as he rose, yawning. Brandulfr couldn't be sure, but he thought he caught a wink aimed at Ambjorg as the huge man rose, then ambled to the door behind his brother, closing it deliberately behind him.

Ambjorg was still busily scribbling notes on the parchment before her when she heard the chair Asbjorn had vacated creak. Looking up, she found Brandulfr peeking at her notes. He was close enough to touch, and it distracted her from her writing as she studied the face she'd held closely in her mind's eye for months. It wore more cares than it had the last time she saw it, and her chest tightened as she noted the added lines were not from laughing.

"Are you well? Truly?" she asked, setting down her quill.

Brandulfr looked up, meeting her steel-gray gaze with his own. "I am now," he replied, reaching out a hand to touch the side of her face. "I've worried about you."

Ambjorg smiled and placed a hand atop his on the table. "And I you." She leaned into the palm against her face, closing her eyes for a moment and allowing herself to relax more than she had in weeks. Their letters had been personal enough that she'd dared hope for constancy in his regard for her, and she felt the last of her fears and apprehensions over it unwind as she breathed in deeply. Opening her eyes, she reached a tentative hand across the space between them and laid her free hand on Brandulfr's own cheek. "I'm glad you've come."

He dropped his hand and turned the other to engulf Amb-jorg's. "As am I, both for my people's sake and my own." He looked down at their joined hands, then covered her hand with both of his as he raised his eyes to hers.

She pulled her other hand back from his face, laying it atop the other three and running a thumb over his knuckles. "The coming months will be hard, and busy," she began. "I rarely see anyone but my brothers as it is, and with more holders joining us from the north things are only likely to get busier."

"Then we shall make the most of what time we can steal," Brandulfr replied, one corner of his mouth turning up in a small smile.

A rider appeared on the northern horizon around midnight,

his horse lathered and shaking. It almost streaked past the capital picket before the watch cried out a halt. The horse reared, throwing its surprisingly diminutive rider, before collapsing onto its side, completely spent. Two watchmen approached cautiously as a boy stood slowly, dazed by the fall. As soon as he was able to speak words tumbled out of his mouth in a steady stream, and it was difficult to make sense of them beyond "monsters" and "northern farms."

"Whoa, son, slow down," said one of the watch, reaching out to lay a hand on the lad's shoulder. "You're safe. We're here to help. What have you seen?"

Still breathing as if he'd run the last few miles, the boy's words slowed as his eyes stopped darting through the shadows. "Monsters," he panted, "not a league behind. Followed me from the last village. My horse…" He shuddered as his wandering eyes took in the now-still form of the horse that had saved him from his doom. "She bolted. I couldn't stop her, and I couldn't get off. They're coming–behind me–" He struggled against the watchman's grip, looking over his shoulder as if expecting something to burst from the tall grass at any moment.

"Where did you come from?" the second man asked as he knelt to the boy's level to meet his eyes.

"The northern villagers," the boy replied, calming as he focused on the man before him and not the fears behind. "The captain sent me to bring word. They're coming to the capital, and they're being followed."

"By what?" the first man asked, his brows drawn together.

"Those," answered the second, drawing his sword and pointing it toward the snarling creature that parted the grass north of them. He shoved the boy behind him and stood ready as the creature pounced on reverse-jointed legs, just managing to get his sword between its claws and his face as the second man hacked at its side with an axe. It screamed in pain, jerking toward the new attacker just as the first watchman slid his sword into its neck, spilling its lifeblood onto the fields. It shuddered twice and was still.

Taking up a horn at his belt the first man blew a long call, then waited. It was answered to the west and he nodded. "Stay with us, boy," he said, "and keep your eyes peeled for more. We'll get you to the capital and get the message through."

A few minutes later footsteps pounded the earth to their west and a voice called "'Ware the watch!"

"Here!" the first watchman called, sheathing his weapon. Two more figures appeared in the gloom, weapons drawn, and took in the scene before them.

"More, eh?" one asked, a woman by the sound of it; it was too dark to make out many features.

"Aye, following this one," the second watchman said as he patted the boy on the back. "He's come with a message for the capital. Northern holders are coming and dragging more of these." He indicated the carcass on the ground at his feet.

"Arild," the woman turned to the other figure with her, "go. Take him the rest of the way. Use the horse at camp—it can carry double with one this small." The figure nodded and knelt before the boy.

"What's your name?" he asked in a pleasant, light tenor voice.

"Arngeir," the boy replied in a shaky voice.

"All right, Arngeir, we're going to get you safely to the capital. Right up to the great hall," said Arild as he placed an arm carefully around the boy's shoulders and led him off into the night. "Have you ever been there?"

"No," the boy answered shyly.

"Let me tell you about it on the way."

Asbjorn awoke to the sounds of construction to the east. The sun was just clearing the horizon, and the day had once again dawned red, heralding a potential for storms later in the day. Rolling himself out of bed, he stretched, yawned, availed himself of the jakes, then dressed and trundled off to find breakfast.

Just as he left the main building a guard skittered up to him, breathing hard. "Majesty," he said, saluting as he gulped air. "Report from the northern perimeter."

Asbjorn returned his salute. "What news?" he asked, all thoughts of breakfast forgotten.

"It's the villagers, sir. They've come, but they're being chased." The messenger was finally able to breathe well enough to speak in more than short bursts, and he elaborated. "They reached the outer perimeter about an hour ago, but they need reinforcements."

"Wake my brother," Asbjorn growled and set off toward the weapons hall at a jog. "I'll get the weaponsmaster and gather a party." The man nodded and sprinted for the hall as Asbjorn went in search of Geirvarr.

Ten minutes later a sizable group was assembled on the practice field, clad in armor and weapons bristling. The weaponsmaster himself stood at the front, leading his horse while another two, a man and a woman, led theirs forward. Nodding to the assemblage, Geirvarr raised his voice to address them, noting in passing that Asbjorn had joined the party. "We stick together, no matter what," he instructed. "Remember your training. Remember the faces of those around you. Defend each other with your own lives and you'll see the sunset this day. To war!" he cried, mounting his horse and setting off at a walk. A cry went up from the crowd as they took their first steps northward to help their kinsmen.

At the back of the group Asbjorn munched on a loaf of bread he'd filched from the kitchens on his way out the door. It settled some of the roiling in his stomach every time he thought of Eyildr and wondered how she fared. Her letters had stopped coming weeks ago; now he knew why, and it unnerved him that no word had been sent of his beloved. His fears deepened as they neared the spot where they would lie in wait for the caravan and its pursuers.

Just before they crested a hillock Geirvarr called a halt, dismounting and peeking over the top. He motioned for the group to stay low as he checked their position, then scooted back down the hill and took back the reins of his horse. "We stand here," he said, gesturing across the hillock. "Spread out and wait for my signal. The caravan will pass just to our right and we'll fall on the creatures' flank as they pass." Heads turned to the barely-visible dirt road to their east and the impromptu soldiers settled themselves into the tall grass.

They didn't have long to wait; after a few scant minutes

the creaking of wagons and pounding of hooves could be heard over the sighing of the wind across the plains. Weapons cleared sheaths with whispers of menace as the war party crouched, waiting for the signal to pounce.

The first wagon passed, followed quickly by a second and third, then three more almost abreast. A cart or two followed, then four riders on horseback looking much the worse for wear. One was just kicking a strange-looking creature to the ground as they passed the hillock and he looked up, startled, before meeting Asbjorn's eyes. The king recognized Eyildr's brother and took a half step forward before Geirvarr shot out a hand to stop him. "Wait for it," he warned, his eyes still on the road.

A pack of mismatched creatures swarmed past, too intent on the riders on the road to notice the opponents flanking them. Glancing over the hill once more, Geirvarr shouted "Now!" before leaping into the saddle, his mount surging forward at his command. With a yell the group charged down the hill and took the creatures from behind as they turned to meet their new foes. The battle joined with deadly fervor as the mounted troops charged deep into the pack, hooves flying and trampling a swath of destruction in their wake. Asbjorn and the others were close behind and fell upon the remaining creatures with horror-fueled fury, hacking, stabbing, and clubbing through an unnatural number of limbs and claws as they slaughtered the monsters wholesale. A few all-too-human cries of pain bubbled up through the snarling madness of the melee and Asbjorn glanced up just in time to see one of the mounted troops tackled from her horse by a catlike creature. He waded his way to where she'd fallen, but was too late; the creature had already sunk its teeth into her throat and her life's blood pumped into the hard-packed dirt beneath her. Anger lent Asbjorn strength as he raised the sword he'd brought and severed the beast's head from its shoulders, bellowing his triumph. The dead woman's horse kicked savagely and caught another of the monsters under its jaw, sending it sprawling to the dirt where it sprawled unmoving, its head twisted at a strange angle.

As suddenly as it began, the battle ended. A few of the creatures fled, tails between their legs, but most of them lay bleeding and broken on the road with a scattering of wounded and dead guards between them. Geirvarr dismounted and began dispatching the creatures that hadn't yet expired while Asbjorn and a few others looked to the wounded. Many of the injuries were gruesome, but not life-threatening, and those who were sound of body moved from person to person to find those most in need of attention. One man, a holder from near the capital, held his arm over a gash in his chest that was seeping blood around visible bone, his face a rictus of pain. Asbjorn recognized the man and called him by name as he helped him stand before moving on to the next grievous wound, a woman he didn't recognize. She sat propped against a large rock, cradling her arm around her stomach, and he sickened as he realized the squirming mass she held behind her arm was her punctured intestines. Geirvarr passed by, took one look at the woman, and met Asbjorn's gaze, shaking his head to confirm what the man already knew. She wouldn't last the day.

"Please, milord" she said through gritted teeth. "My knife. I can't reach it." Her free hand groped across her body awkwardly, seeking the dagger secured to the opposite side of her belt. Kneeling down, Asbjorn pulled the weapon from its sheath and wrapped her fingers around the hilt. "Thank you," she said, smiling faintly as she laid the razor-keen edge of the knife across first one wrist, then the other. "I will see you in Valhalla, my king." Asbjorn held her blood-slick hand in both of his as she crossed over into death, his mind unable to fully process what he'd seen.

"We must get them up." Geirvarr's voice cut through the groans of the wounded as he scanned the horizon. "They'll be back, and in greater numbers. The carts should be here soon."

"Carts?" Asbjorn asked, standing in a pool of the unknown woman's blood.

"Battles always have casualties," Geirvarr responded gently. "I arranged for wagons to follow us to carry the wounded and dead back to the capital. They should be here soon—ah, there they are." On the horizon appeared three hay wagons that had been repurposed for human transport by adding fresh straw and pallets to the bottom. Baskets of bandages and ointments bounced next to the drivers as they approached the field of battle and pulled the wagons around to face the way they'd come, then climbed down to help. The shock of battle had begun to wear off and many of the defenders were flagging despite the relatively early hour, but they managed to get the wounded onto two wagons and the dead onto the third before the creatures returned. Asbjorn took the reins of the horse that had lost its rider in battle and mounted up to join the rearguard, which consisted of the other three cavalry they'd brought with them. The rest of the troop followed the wagons on foot as they trundled back home, eager to put the morning's horrors behind them.

The northern holders had arrived at the capital half an hour before the remnants of their guard and had begun to settle in as the wagons returned. As they passed the northern campsite an older woman detached herself from a group that was raising a temporary shelter and made a beeline for the wounded, hopping on the back of the wagon as it passed. She immediately began moving around the wagon, triaging the injuries she saw as they continued on toward the great hall. Asbjorn slowed his horse and dismounted, handing the reins to the closest page he could find and instructing the boy to make sure she was well cared for before casting about for signs of Eyildr. He hadn't seen her as they'd passed the main group that morning, but was still hopeful she was near. His eyes lighted on her brother and he strode directly toward the younger man, who was speaking with a few of his folk. The conversation floated across the field to Asbjorn's ears as he neared.

"...the great hall for something to eat," Davyn was saying to one of the men. "We will need our strength to get shelters built before nightfall."

"Thank you, thane," the man replied, relief at even a brief respite evident in his voice. Asbjorn started; where was Eyildr's father? She hadn't mentioned anything in her letters, and he'd seemed quite hale at the last gathering; he should have years yet before he passed on his title. His brow creased in worry as the holders noticed him approach and took a collective step back, and he realized dimly that he must look a sight; covered in blood and sweat and striding toward them with a purpose. There was no help for it, though, and his concern for his betrothed overrode his desire for propriety. Davyn looked up, starting as he recognized his king through the gore, and his expression caused Asbjorn's blood to run cold as he voiced the question closest to his heart.

"Where is Eyildr?"

"...told you to be careful," an acidic male voice was saying as consciousness seeped awareness into Eyildr's mind. "Now we'll have to delay our plans by days as she recovers." She cracked one eye open just enough to take in her most immediate surroundings. A dirt floor surrounded by hides indicated she was in a tent of some sort, and the rough tension against her wrists told her she was bound to one of its poles. Light seeped through the entrance, which was peeled back and secured to allow ease of traffic into and out of her makeshift cell.

There was an animal hiss in response to the words she'd registered, and she flicked her eyes briefly to the left to see what had produced the noise. Immediately part of her wished she hadn't. One of the creatures responsible for her capture sat on awkward haunches at the far edge of the tent, by the closed back. It was short and built for speed instead of power, with feline legs and tail and a fox-like head. Its midsection was unrecognizable, with patchworked fur that didn't seem to match either its head or posterior regions. A rust-colored substance had dried on its face and front paws, and her gradually sharpening powers of observation informed her it was her own blood. This was the creature that had torn her from the wagon.

A sigh escaped the other human in the tent, about whom she'd completely forgotten while she engrossed herself in studying the creature responsible for her capture. She was barely able to see the man from this angle, though it looked like he wore a deeply hooded cloak despite the warmth of the day.

"Go, lick your wounds," he spat derisively at the animal before him. It hissed once more as it strode past the man and out of the tent. "I swear, once we can get humans to work things will be so much easier..." He trailed off, raising a hand to his forehead, and Eyildr cast about in her mind for the owner of that voice. She'd heard it before, she was certain, if she could only recall to whom it belonged...

The sound of the man standing abruptly and walking toward her shocked Eyildr out of her rumination. She closed both eyes again, feigning sleep, until the man drew close enough to touch her arm. Fire seared the raw nerve endings as he poked a finger into the large gash she'd gained defending her people, and she cried out despite herself.

"Ahh, I thought you were awake," the hooded man drawled. "Good." He seemed to consider the seriousness of the cut on her arm, then nodded as if he'd made a decision. "We'll need to see to that. It needs stitches." To her horror, he removed a small sewing kit from within the folds of his cloak, along with a skin of something that smelled like a strong wine or mead. Keeping his hood folded as far over as possible, he uncorked the skin with his teeth and poured a liberal measure of it down Eyildr's bound arm. Everywhere the liquid touched her flesh it felt as if it were molten. She whimpered, earning a low, throaty chuckle from her captor as he re-corked the skin and turned to the sewing kit. "This is going to hurt," he said with very little inflection as he threaded a needle with some sort of twine that appeared to be made of dried gut. He pressed the needle to her skin at the top of the wound and she heard the smile in his voice as he started to sew.

"And I'm going to love every minute of it."

Eyildr woke from a nap brought about by exhaustion and prolonged pain. Her throat was dry, her voice more hoarse than it had ever been; she'd screamed as her captor had sewn up her arm, and then afterward as he poured more of the liquid down it. To prevent infection, he'd said, but from the little she could see of his face he'd smiled as he poured it. His smile was a cruel smirk, thin lips pulling back just far enough to see the tops of bone-white teeth, and it struck her as familiar, though she still couldn't place it; her thoughts were still muddled from both the blow to her head when she'd fallen from the wagon and the pain in her arm. Doing her best to sit upright around her bonds, she realized she needed to answer a pressing call of nature, but saw no chamber pot in the tent.

"Hey!" she called, hoping her captors were near enough to

hear. "I need to use the bathroom!" She was rewarded with the sound of footsteps approaching the tent, and the hooded figure who had treated her arm entered. By the dim light floating through the entrance she could tell it was twilight, almost full dark. *Perhaps that bodes well*, she thought as she studied her surroundings once again.

A long, thin hand shot out as the man approached and grabbed her by her wounded arm, hauling her upright as she nearly blacked out. Her wrists jerked cruelly against their bonds, blood seeping down one palm where the rough ropes had abraded her skin. She was finally standing, but that wasn't enough for her captor; he kept pulling at her arm until her stiff joints screamed, then let go suddenly, leaving her arms to fall jarringly back into place. Only then did he untie one of her wrists, keeping the other bound and holding the rope. "Can't have you soiling yourself," he said as he bound the rope to his own wrist, "but can't have you running, either." Giving the line a jerk to test its hold, he nodded and dragged her out of the tent.

Not much was visible past the light of the campfire, but Eyildr could see that they were in a small clearing of some sort. All was dark beyond the ring of firelight. Her captor dragged her to the edge of the woods and bade her relieve herself, turning his back in a surprising show of politeness—or disgust. It was impossible to tell which with his hood covering his face. Eyildr took her time, scanning the surrounding woods for any sign of familiarity, but found none. Unwilling to provoke her jailer further just yet she finished, stood, and tugged on the makeshift leash to signal she was done.

The man turned around and seemed to stare at her for a moment. At least, that was what it felt like; she could discern no portion of the man's expression, but could feel the cold of his regard from a few feet away. Then a muffled sound from a nearby tent broke the spell and he looked away, dragging his charge behind him, back toward her prison. She let herself be led, wishing to lull her jailers into a false sense of security and desiring a few moments to process what she'd heard.

She was almost certain it had been a bear.

Rough hands on her arms dragged Eyildr from her contemplation as she was tied once again to the post inside her tent. Once she was bound her captor produced some dried meat from a pocket on his cloak and held it out in front of her. It smelled like deer, but she couldn't be sure, and he held it just out of reach. "Don't eat it all in one go; this is all you'll get until morning," he teased as he moved the morsel back and forth. She stopped straining at her bonds once she recognized the game for what it was and he seemed to frown before stuffing the entire piece of jerky in her mouth. Eyildr gagged for a moment before chewing carefully, eyeing the man with every bit of dislike she could muster as she swallowed.

Within moments the world began to spin. The sound of her own vomiting sounded distant as she slid sideways, unable to control her body. Boots swam into view as her vision dimmed and a cackling laugh sent her off into fevered oblivion.

Alflakr emerged from the prison tent and removed his hood. A manic grin split his otherwise handsome face as he turned to his father and the völva, who stood at a hastily-erected table by the campfire. "She is ready," he said as he joined them, staring down at the strange and terrifying instruments laid before them.

"And she ate the meat?" the völva asked without looking up from her preparations.

"She chewed and swallowed it, but vomited just before she fainted," Alflakr replied, the grin fading from his expression.

The völva spat a curse, then looked up. "It will have to be enough," she said as she stepped back, the small sack of bones at her waist clinking softly. She wore leather breeches and a cloth tunic with a leather apron over it and the sleeves tied up to her gnarled elbows in preparation for her messy work. A larger chunk of dried meat sat before her from the same deer that had provided the jerky Eyildr had eaten, and she coated it liberally with a viscous, black substance from a thick pot at one end of the table. "Give this to the bear," she ordered, holding the meat out toward Alflakr. "Then clean your hands before you eat again or you will be caught up in the spell." The völva turned and washed her hands in a small basin of water on the table as if to illustrate her point.

Alflakr hesitated only a moment before approaching the tent across from Eyildr's. Peeling back the flap cautiously, he peered in and was met with a deep-throated growl. He decided discretion was the better part of valor and tossed the meat into the tent, watching as the beast snapped it out of the air and swallowed it in a single motion. Before long its eyes rolled back into its head and it sunk to the ground, snoring loudly. Alflakr closed the flap and nodded to his father, who threw back his own hood.

"Let us begin." Thane Alfgrimr looked to the völva, who handed him a large ceremonial knife.

"Pierce the beast's paws, back, and legs with this. I will do the same with the woman." She illustrated where they were to use the knife and drew a matching blade of her own from a sheath at her waist. "The wound must not be fatal, but should bleed. Then wait for me by the fire." Without waiting for an answer she moved to the tent where Eyildr slept and disappeared inside.

Thane Alfgrimr did not hesitate as he approached the sleeping animal. His son watched from a cautious distance as his father pierced the bear's extremities as precisely as possible, just enough for a trickle of blood to flow. Alflakr's expression was an amalgamation of excitement and fear as his father strode out of the tent and back toward the campfire, where the völva already waited in utter stillness. She held before her the knife she'd used, still stained with the blood of her subject, and held out her other hand for the knife Alfgrimr had used. He handed her the weapon, careful not to touch her skin, then took up a place behind the table where his son joined him. "And now we watch," he murmured, crossing his arms and setting his gaze on the witch and her work. Alflakr stood beside his father and focused his own attention on the völva and the strange chant she'd begun. It was guttural, spoken in a dialect that hadn't been used in generations, and as her voice wound its way into the woods something answered. Tendrils of darkness snaked into the clearing, unafraid of the campfire and its light, and pushed open the tent flaps on both sides of the fire. Out floated the two subjects of the spell, carried aloft on deft, shadowy fingers as the völva brought the dripping knives closer together. She began to sweat under the strain; the

weapons fought her as she forced them to meet. Ever so slowly the knives inched closer while the bear and the woman did
likewise, until at last with a triumphant yell the witch touched the
blades together, mingling the blood on their edges, and a whirling storm of darkness engulfed them. For a full minute even the
campfire was blotted out, and then just as suddenly as it began
the whirlwind died, leaving everything as it was before–with one
exception.

The völva, panting and drenched with sweat, smiled grim-
ly as she surveyed her work through milky eyes. Turning to
the thane, she pointed a veined, shaking hand at what she had
wrought. 'There is your experiment," she said, trudging past him
toward another tent on the edge of the snap encampment. "Do
with it what you will." Her tent flap slapped closed with a finality
that suggested she would not be emerging for some time.

Thane Alfgrimr looked on impassively. "Check it," he ordered his son, who inched around the table toward the campfire.
"I wish to know if the witch succeeded."

Alflakr kept his distance, finding a large stick with which to
poke the mass of fur before him. It shifted and grumbled as he
did and he shuffled further away in case it awoke. "Looks plenty
alive to me," he replied as he scooted back to the fireside.

"Good." The thane turned on his heel and headed for his
own tent. "We leave in the morning. It is time we took what is
rightfully ours." Alflakr followed him, finding a creature to set
a watch and telling it to wake them if anything happened before
finding his own bedroll and turning in for the night.

Outside, the hulking new creature slept on.

# CHAPTER 7

Thane Vidar stalked through the underbrush, following the trail of blood left by the rearmost of his daughter's victims. His mottled green cloak masked his soundless passage down the game trail his quarry had used as he stopped briefly to consult the signs before him. There—a bloodstained leaf on the forest floor next to a set of broken twigs. The signs became easier to follow as the creature's strength failed until finally he came upon it, lying broken and bleeding under a thicket. Its breath rasped through punctured lungs that sent bubbles of froth up to its coat along the lines of a clean stab wound between its ribs as it labored to fill them with air.

The thane could almost pity the beast; it had not asked for this fate. Something—or someone—had turned it into this abomination. He could see bits and pieces of the creatures it had once been: the rear legs of a wolf, the forepaws of a bobcat, and the ears of something like a stoat. It regarded him in the resigned way of an animal that sees the hand of death reaching for it, and as he considered whether or not to show it mercy, it shuddered and surrendered to its wounds. Vidar's lip curled slightly as he considered the once-animal, wondering again who could perform such atrocities, then cast about for the rest of the trail.

He was able to pick it up by backtracking to the bloodstained leaf and finding an offshoot trail, less clear, but recently traveled, and followed it until the sky began to darken. Not wishing to be caught out among the trees with no shelter or defense, he decided to make camp for the night under an overhang at the base of a small hill. At least there was stone at his back, even if he didn't dare light a campfire.

The next day dawned cold and clear. Vidar shook himself out from beneath the dried leaves he'd heaped below and above himself for warmth and picked back up the trail he'd followed the previous day. It had been many years since he'd made such rough camp, and his joints protested as he worked his way through the forest, stomach rumbling. *You can't sneak up on anything if your stomach is loud,* he told himself as he veered off in search of late-season berries and other edibles. By the time he'd eaten enough to get by and drunk from the waterskin he'd brought with him his joints were looser, and he was able to make his way through the woods with nearly the same stealth as the previous day. The signs were fresher this deep in the forest, meaning he was closer to whatever source housed these aberrations. He would need to proceed with all caution.

It was midmorning before Vidar heard the first stirrings ahead of him. Crouching low into the brush, he watched as some sort of pig-goat combination snuffled its way across the forest floor, searching for truffles and other edibles. It was oblivious to his presence and seemed less of a threat than the creatures he'd seen the prior day, so he skirted around it and moved on. Less than half an hour later he caught sight of gray fur passing between two trees to his left. A twig cracked to his right and another flash of fur, brown this time, danced along the top of the brush. He squatted with his back to a tree, still as the bole behind him, breathing shallowly for what seemed like an eternity. When a quarter hour had passed and he heard no more sounds he stood with painful slowness, eyes darting about for signs he was not alone. A bird flitted from bush to bush and he heard the call of a hawk above him, but there were no indications that he was being followed. He allowed himself to relax just enough to loosen up his muscles before pushing on.

Midday found Vidar on a hill overlooking a small encampment. Three hide tents were situated around a large campfire with a makeshift table full of strange instruments to one side. As he watched, a woman emerged from the largest tent carrying a sack, which she deposited on the table full of instruments. She cast about, then opened the bag with a knife she produced from her belt and dumped its contents onto the table, spreading them out before her. Vidar couldn't tell what the sack contained from such a distance, so he set about watching for other signs of habitation. Before long a figure strode into the clearing, seeking out the woman. His dark hair and mode of attire were instantly familiar to Vidar, and his eyes narrowed. *Alfgrimr. I should have known.* The thane of the north had been a thorn in his side for as long as they had known each other. Even as children they had never gotten along; Alfgrimr was more interested in courting the favor of his friends and manipulating his enemies while Vidar preferred open dialog and, where that failed, an honorable fight to sort things out. As they'd grown older and taken up the leadership of their respective thanedoms Vidar had noticed a change in Alfgrimr. He was no longer playful in his machinations; in fact, with his father's passing and his own son's growth into a man he had become increasingly paranoid, seeking ever more power and influence and trusting no one but himself. Now it seemed he'd found a new way to achieve whatever his goals may be.

A lone gray creature loped up to the woman at the bench, panting. She gazed at it for a moment, then exchanged a few words with Alfgrimr that were carried away by the wind. Both figures turned their heads to look directly at Vidar's hiding spot.

He'd been discovered.

Turning on his heel, he took off down the back side of the hill, a sharp shout ringing out behind him as the baying of the creature he'd seen began in earnest. He ran aimlessly for a moment as he gathered his thoughts, then stopped to listen for sounds of his pursuer. Surely it could follow his scent, and running on four legs would make it faster than his two were capable of; he couldn't outrun it. But could he outsmart it?

He doubled back on his own trail just far enough to find a tree he'd spotted in his rush that had a low-hanging branch he could clamber onto and swung himself up into the branches just as the howling creature broke through the brush at the bottom of the hill. Drawing his belt dagger, he waited until it streaked directly under his hiding spot, then dropped out of the tree, latching onto its tail as it went past. Surprised, the creature snapped its head around and reached backward to bite at Vidar, who yanked on its tail hard enough to make it yowl, then dragged it closer to him. It fought for freedom, teeth flashing as its paws scrabbled in the damp autumn leaves covering the forest floor. But Vidar managed a well-timed strike to the ribs that carried the point of his dagger between the beast's bones and into its heart. It yelped, then fell to the ground.

Vidar ducked past the spasming body of the creature, seeking to put more distance between himself and any pursuit that might be coming.

"Who is it?" Thane Alfgrimr snarled at his son, who cowered behind a tent stave. "Who has found the camp?"

"I didn't see him, Father," Alflakr sniveled from behind his scant cover. "Probably some local hunter out after game."

"Find him," Alfgrimr demanded, pointing at the hill where Vidar's swift retreat could no longer be heard. "And kill him." Alflakr nodded, grabbing two creatures as he turned toward the hillside.

Vidar crested the hill cautiously, ears pricked for signs of pursuit. He spared a glance at the clearing below and behind him, noticing an increase in activity among the few rudimentary shelters, then turned quickly to disappear over the hilltop, mind churning. Certainly his daughter was at the camp below, but he hadn't had time to do a proper reconnaissance to determine where she might be kept—if she was even still alive.

Shoving aside the unproductive thought, he stepped lightly through the forest, doubling back on his trail periodically to confuse his scent and taking a meandering path generally away from the camp. He would lose his pursuers, then circle around to the lee side of the clearing under cover of darkness.

A tumult of animal noises shattered Vidar's mental planning. His instincts told him what his reasoning mind could not—that somehow they had already found his trail and even now were giving chase. He began to run doggedly through the forest in a straighter line than before as the sounds of the wild hunt behind him intensified. He heard them crest the hill faster than he'd have thought possible, then veer off in various directions as his doubling back paid off, confusing the creatures scenting his trail as he took advantage of the precious extra moments it bought him to find a tree to climb.

Moments after he managed to pull himself upward far enough to hide behind the trunk of a large oak Vidar heard his pursuers pick up his true scent, crashing through the brush heedless of noise. Soon two creatures appeared, long of leg and sharp of talon. Both cast about for his trail, noses in the air, while a third figure appeared behind them. Vidar immediately recognized the silhouette of Thane Alfgrimr's only son, Alflakr. *I should have known he'd send his child to do his bidding*, Vidar thought bitterly. He recalculated his chances of slipping past the creatures, deeming them lower than he'd previously thought. Steeling himself, he waited until the small group stopped at the base of the tree he'd climbed before loosing the arrow he'd nocked directly at one of the creatures' heads. It barely grunted before falling to the ground. Before it fell he had another nocked, but the second creature was not to be caught unawares; it dodged his shot and barked awkwardly up at him just as Alflakr caught up

"Taken to hiding in trees, I see?" Alflakr called up toward Vidar from behind the bole of a large marine close by "Very unthane-like behavior of you. I expected more of a chase, if we're being honest."

"I am no longer thane," Vidar called in response. "My son has taken up my duties. Now I am simply a father out to save my child." Vidar's mind spun as he puzzled through why Alflakr would stop to bandy words. It had never been his style. Then it struck him: he was stalling. Vidar needed to move, and fast.

"Your child is beyond saving," Alflakr spat from his hiding place. "We have bound her to our cause–permanently."

For a moment Vidar's heart sank. Then he realized that whatever Alflakr had meant, he had still let slip that Eyildr was alive. *Then there is still hope.* "Nothing is permanent short of death," he retorted, preparing to make his next move. There was a branch that he thought he could just reach that would take him toward the maple Alflakr had chosen for cover, and he quietly worked his way toward it. The branch was smaller than he liked, but might hold his weight long enough to spring across the gap beneath. Steadying himself, Vidar transferred his weight–

–and the world tumbled around him as the branch gave way,

dropping him painfully to earth. The last thing he saw was Alflakr's grinning face before everything went dark.

Vidar regained consciousness to the sensation of being dragged by the collar through the sodden leaves on the forest floor. He cracked one eyelid long enough to see that the clearing drew near, earning a low growl from the strange beast that followed in his wake. "Hush," soothed a reedy tenor voice from above. He recognized it as Alflakr's. "We'll be home soon." Closing his eyes again, Vidar stayed limp and took in the sounds and smells around him. There was a fire nearby and he heard the snuffling and grunting of beasts on every side of him. None of them were anything he could identify, though many were on the edge of familiar, and it sent an involuntary chill up his spine. The roughness of the terrain hid his shudder as the air opened around him. They must have entered the camp.

He was dumped unceremoniously onto his back and rolled over, his hands pulled roughly behind him and tied with coarse rope or heavy vine; he couldn't tell which. Thus secured, his captor dragged cruelly at his bound wrists, pulling him upward from behind with no way to steady himself as his shoulders tugged at unnatural angles. Unable to maintain the charade of unconsciousness, Vidar cried out and lifted himself to his knees. "Good, I thought you were awake," Alflakr purred as he studied his captive. "Father! I found our visitor, as you asked, and have brought him back to enjoy our hospitality." Vidar could hear the grin on the young man's face as the flap of the tent directly before them opened and Thane Alfgrimr strode from inside. He was drying his hands on a soft cloth as if he'd just washed them. Ignoring the captive for the moment, he eyed his son.

"Good work," he began, then shifted his regard to Vidar, still on his knees. "Long have I wished to see this one on his knees before me." Striding forward, he leaned down an arm's length away and studied his rival. His direct gaze held no emotion; it was unsettlingly reminiscent of the eagles that hunted the high reaches of the north. *Or a carrion-bird,* Vidar thought as he met Alfgrimr's stare. *He even cocks his head like one when he's curious.* After a few uncomfortable moments the northern thane stood, having evidently discovered whatever it was he was looking for. "Pity he no longer represents his people." Alfgrimr dusted his hands on his pants as if to remove something distasteful despite having not touched anything since washing them, then nodded to someone inside the tent he'd just left. "Make the preparations," he announced. "We move now. We can wait no longer." Without another glance at Vidar he re-entered the tent, closing the flap behind him.

Alflakr reminded Vidar of his presence by dragging on his bonds until he was upright. "You get to follow along behind my wagon," the youth said, a grin splitting his face. "Backwards." To illustrate, he tied a rope to the bindings on Vidar's wrists and pulled him backward across the camp to where a tent was being struck. As they passed the campfire, Vidar noticed a large, blood-stained table that had recently been used for what had to have been cleaning kills–*What else would leave that much blood? And why would they do it inside the camp?* Looking around him, Vidar realized that no predator would be tempted to steal from the horrific things that wove in and out of the camp, carrying items and keeping watch. His gaze stilled on the sleeping form of a bear on the opposite side of the dying fire; it looked surprisingly normal, but there was still something not quite right about it…

"Come!" His bonds were jerked and he fell onto his backside, scrambling to get his legs under him. "No time to gawk! You'll meet her soon enough," Alflakr cackled knowingly. The bear stirred, but Vidar was dragged past a tent and lost sight of it. A one-horse cart sat before them with a large mountain-cat-crossed-with-elk type of beast in the traces. Its front feet were padded and bore retractable claws, but its hind feet were longer and sleeker and bore wide hooves at the bottom. Tying his charge to one side of the wagon with a lead about his height, Alflakr mounted the driver's seat and pulled a whip from beneath the bench seat. He cracked it experimentally and the creature before him voiced a bone-chilling scream somewhere between a mountain cat's call and the bugle of an elk that Vidar's mind could neither accept nor make sense of, and the wagon lurched forward.

Vidar was left with a choice: walk or be dragged. Knowing there would come a time he could no longer choose, he kept his feet under him and his mind racing as he searched for a means of escape.

Sounds filtered through the bear's unconscious state, lighting gently on portions of its mind that recognized them. The packing of barrels. Wagons creaking under increasing loads. Human voices drifting across the campfire.

Smells came next. The fire still smoked, but had died beyond rekindling. The humans had eaten recently and the remains of their fish and dried fruit made its stomach rumble with hunger. At least three beings had recently marked the camp as territory.

Blinking, the bear opened her eyes. The camp buzzed like a hive of bees as the humans prepared to leave. She stood slowly, stretching out kinked limbs unprepared for the long sleep she'd had, yet starting to desire the longer sleep of the winter, and moved away from the fire to relieve herself and mark territory.

A long chain stopped her not two lengths from the fire. She had grown somewhat accustomed to her captivity, but it chafed, and she found new anger rising from within. It came from a strange new source buried in her psyche and it screamed at her to use her strength to rise up against her captors and flay them alive as she was wont to do. She decided there might be merit in that–but first, nature called.

Territory marked, she cast about for food. It took considerable amounts of sustenance to maintain her bulk, and it felt like it had been at least a day since she'd eaten. The voice in her mind became more insistent, telling her she must forgo scavenging long enough to win her freedom so that she might hunt the forest as she pleased, but she knew there was easy forage within the camp. Her captors had not been so cruel as to starve her, so she snuffled her way to the closest tent and poked her large, wet nose inside the flap. She was rewarded with the scent of provisions seeping out of a barrel at the back, just outside of her reach.

Shrugging unconcernedly–though she wasn't sure where she'd learned to make such an odd  gesture–she pulled at the stake anchoring her chain and felt a gratifying *pop* as the last link snapped, leaving her free to rummage in the barrel. It was packed with salted fish and dried berries, and she ate until she could fit no more in her bulging stomach. The barrel, now empty, became a toy to bat around the tent.

Absently, she recalled that she had freed herself and decided to wander out into the camp. Most of the barrels and supplies were aboard the wagons lined up on the south side of the clearing, and she wondered how many more had food in them. She trundled toward the rearmost wagon, testing the air to see what she found. A new scent wafted to her from further up the column–human, but different; he smelled of the forest nearby, and of blood. Curiosity got the best of her and she started around the carts only to be met by the witch-woman who had captured her in the first place.

*Völva.* The word leaped into her mind as she struggled to remember the sounds the humans used when they spoke of her. Knowledge of human speech–and the ability to interpret it–flooded her consciousness, stunning her as she stood before her captor, unable to move. The woman mistook her stillness for obedience, beckoning for her to follow as she walked beside the column of wagons. And the bear followed, head swinging side to side, as she reveled in her newfound knowledge. Before long she overtook the völva, who reached out to run a hand down her side. The bear shivered, twitching her large form with uncanny precision to remove the woman's touch, and continued past to find the source of the new human smell.

Three wagons up–she could count them now–there was a man tied to the back of a wagon. He walked backwards, bound at the wrists, but held his head high as he also searched for a way free of his captivity.

*Father!* The word had no meaning for the bear; she recalled her mother and siblings, but had never known other family. Yet it held so much meaning and purpose for the other she began to acknowledge, the one who passed her knowledge beyond the ken of her kind. She ruminated on the concept and noticed as she did that her form began to change; her fur receded over parts of her body, and she began to walk upright as the humans did. She still towered over them, but she had arms instead of forelegs, though she kept the clawed feet at the ends in case she needed them for defense. Even her head began to change, her nose shrinking and drawing in to flatten her face and dull her sense of smell. She felt awkward and ungainly and almost went back to being a bear, but the voice inside her head gently encouraged her, offering assistance with balance and movement. Hesitantly, she let the voice have more control over the body they shared and watched as her movements grew confident and graceful.

The bear decided she needed time to watch and learn. So she slipped into the background of her own mind and let the other take the lead, content to observe until she could make more sense of what she saw.

A blink and a heartbeat later Eyildr ran to catch up with the wagons.

At first, Vidar kept up with the wagon's steady pace with ease, falling into an awkward, but effective backwards gait. But soon his legs tired, unused to the odd step. He stumbled every so often, managing to stay upright through sheer force of will, and kept his head on a swivel in case he found an opportunity to escape. This was also how he first spotted the bear. It looked perfectly normal to start with, one of the large, brown variety commonly found in the forests throughout the summer and into the autumn, when they put on as much weight as possible in preparation for their long winter's sleep. It appeared to have started its late-year gluttony, but wasn't quite as fat as it needed to be this late in the season—or was it thinner than it had been a moment ago? He blinked the dust and grit out of his eyes to see if they deceived him.

No, it had shrunk. It walked on two legs as they did when they fought one another for territory, though it had no rivals here, and as he watched it seemed to diminish further, its fur retracting and limbs refining until it looked to be half-human. Before long it had relinquished its long nose for a recognizable face, though much of it was still covered in fur and it bore claw-tipped paws instead of hands. He couldn't be sure, but the eyes looked familiar…

"Father!" The hoarse cry ripped from the throat of the creature as it bore down on Vidar, and his mind reeled as his instincts drew him toward it–he would know that voice anywhere. As it drew near more fur retreated from its face and confirmed what his heart had already told him.

"Eyildr!" he cried, tears springing unbidden to his eyes. "Gods, what have they done to you?"

She reached her father just as Alflakr turned in his seat and cracked the horse whip he held. It bit painfully into Eyildr's shoulder as she reached for the line connecting Vidar to the cart and she felt the bear stir within her, asking to be freed. *He has my father. Wait. We will strike when he is safe.* Grumbling, the bear settled, watching. A small rivulet of blood trickled down the fur still covering her shoulder, and she let more of it grow in to help protect her from Alflakr's cruelty.

"Let him go!" she shouted from an arm's length away. The wagon stopped and Alflakr brandished the whip again.

"We will do no such thing," a voice said from behind Eyildr. Thane Alfgrimr appeared with the völva, who carried a bear-tooth charm before her. It felt wrong, somehow, as if it twisted the very essence of the natural things it touched, and Eyildr shied away from it involuntarily. "And you, my dear, will cooperate with us fully–or she will force your cooperation." He gestured toward the witch, who held the charm before her like a talisman.

Eyildr reached out a paw and batted the offensive thing out of the woman's grasp. Shrieking, the völva dove into the underbrush beside the path after the item, distracting Eyildr long enough for Alflakr to scramble across the bed of the wagon and wrap the whip around her father's throat. By the time she'd turned and started toward his bonds, he was already trapped.

"Any closer and I tighten my grip," Alflakr snarled. Eyildr sagged, defeated.

"What do you want of me?" she growled through grated teeth that didn't seem to all be the right shape.

"As I stated, we want your full cooperation." Alfgrimr strode back into view, taking up a place next to his son. "You will help us direct these creatures–" he gestured at the throng of beasts that had gathered at the smell of blood, "–so that we may breach the capital's defenses. You will fight for us against the defenders, and you will help install me on the throne." He paused to let his words sink in. "If you do not do this, I will let my son practice his favorite pastimes on your father. He can be very creative."

A low rumble sounded from Eyildr's throat, but she lowered her eyes, unable to meet Alfgrimr's dead gaze. Vidar tried to speak, but Alflakr tightened the whip until he gasped for air and began to turn blue before relaxing his grip. Again the bear questioned Eyildr, not fully understanding what was happening, but desiring the blood of these men. *No. We must wait.* "Do not hurt him," she replied, staring at the ground before her.

"I knew you would see reason." Alfgrimr climbed into the driver's seat of the wagon his son had occupied, instructing Alflakr to secure their prisoner hand and foot inside the wagon and guard him at all times. As soon as Vidar was trussed up properly and in the back of the wagon they started off once again, Eyildr trailing behind her father's wagon in varying states of being as she conferred with the bear.

It was strange sharing her mind and body with another creature. The bear agreed, having less context on the world in general and finding it very hard to adjust. Neither felt animosity toward the other, simply curiosity and a desire to understand their current state of being. It seemed they could change their outward appearance from bear to part-bear as it suited them; Eyildr wasn't interested in trying to turn fully human due to her lack of clothing and the unknown effect that would have on Alflakr, who had a reputation for rapaciousness, but guessed it was possible. The trick was that they both had to be of one mind to have full control over their shared limbs and transformations. This was difficult, as Eyildr was new to being a bear and the bear was entirely new to being human. So they practiced, and learned, and bided their time. Eyildr's best guess was that they would have to wait until they reached the site of whatever battle was brewing so that they could use the confusion as a cover to free her father and make a break for it, but she realized her plan had a fatal flaw: none of their allies would know who she was underneath her newfound form, and she was better protected as a bear. She would have to hope her father could explain before things went poorly.

Eyildr felt better with a plan, and she agreed to let the bear have some time at the helm of their new body so that she could learn its ways while they waited for their opportunity. It would come, she knew, and as soon as it did they would be ready.

They camped overnight in the foothills at the edge of the northern territory, within sight of the fields surrounding the capital. The trees gave them cover to scout their enemy's encampment and plan their assault, which would take place just after midnight when the defenders would be at their weakest. They had the advantages of high ground, better night vision, and faster movement; they should be past the first line of defense before the humans knew what hit them.

Eyildr was, of course, part of the planning, as it was her task to keep the rest of the creatures from straying off course. She watched silently as Alfgrimr outlined his plans in the dirt floor of his tent, memorizing them as he spoke so that she could analyze them for any signs of weakness or flaw. Her father and Alflakr were housed in a tent across the camp where she had been assured he was comfortable and sleeping. The bear lent her its hearing long enough to determine that this was, in fact, the case, and she settled in to focus on her own part in this plan.

She couldn't let them go through with it. Asbjorn and his siblings would be among the defenders, she knew, and she couldn't bring herself to cause them harm. The townspeople and farmers defending the capital did not deserve any of what was happening to them. But how could she stop it without costing her father his health—or his life? Both options split her heart in two. There had to be a better way forward, one that didn't come with such great loss.

"Am I clear?" Alfgrimr's words crackled with command, and Eyildr found herself nodding along with the völva, who was the only other human party to the proceedings. "Good. We leave in ten minutes. Ready yourselves." Alfgrimr opened the tent flap, gesturing for Eyildr to precede him.

"I wish to see my father before we leave." She refused to meet her captor's eyes as she made her demand in the hope he would see it as a sign of submission. Alfgrimr pondered for a moment, then nodded.

"You may see him just before the battle. No sooner." Brooking no argument, he strode to his own tent and closed the flap, leaving Eyildr with the völva.

"How is the bear?" the witch asked with surprising gentleness. The question startled Eyildr.

"She is well, though we both are adjusting," she replied as politely as possible. *Certainly she cannot care for either of us.*

"I'm sure you are; I wasn't even sure fusing you would be possible. There was a very real chance neither of you would survive, or that one of you would go completely mad." The woman's piercing stare bit into Eyildr as she studied what she'd wrought. "Of course, there is still time." Without another word she went about the camp, speaking softly to the creatures she'd made.

*:I don't like her.:* The voice belonged to the bear, but the sentiment echoed her own as if it had pulled the phrase from her mind. She supposed that was exactly what it had done.

*Neither do I, bear. Neither do I.*

The minutes passed quickly as Eyildr and the bear planned their next move, and before they knew it Thane Alfgrimr emerged from his tent wearing a full suit of hide armor. Much of it still bore the fur of its original owners as an extra layer of warmth and protection. Had she not known the depths of the man's depravity she might have mistaken him for a great general; instead he looked more like a bully.

At the sound of the camp's waking Alflakr appeared with Vidar held before him, a long knife to his throat. His hands were still bound and multiple new bruises shone on his face in the light of the campfire. Anger rose again in Eyildr's chest, threatening to loose the bear before they remembered what that might cost. Vidar shook his head almost imperceptibly and turned his attention to Alfgrimr, who stood ready to address the group. A throng of beasts gathered around the camp just outside the fire's light, shuffling and grunting their discomposure at the close quarters and itching to be let free and given their heads. No rousing speech was necessary; no inspirational song was sung; Alfgrimr simply gave the word and the creatures flowed down the hill toward the first defensive line.

"You! Follow them, and make sure they stay on track," he snapped at Eyildr. She hesitated, holding onto her human form long enough to meet her father's eyes. They seemed to glow with an inner light as he smiled–her favorite smile, the one she remembered from her childhood when he would come home at the end of a long day and throw his arms around his wife and children–and his mouth moved just enough to form three words: "protect our people." Then he threw himself forward into the razor-sharp blade of Alflakr's knife, slicing his throat and pouring his life out onto the ground before them.

Eyildr was aware of her own screaming in a detached, background sort of way as the bear rose up, fur covering their body and skin thickening to protect against attack. Their snout lengthened and smells flooded into their consciousness, merging with the sounds they could now hear, but holding onto their human sight to aid with vision at a distance. Eyildr's scream merged with the bear's challenging roar as they stood on hind feet and swung one great paw, knocking Alflakr to the ground and opening one side of his face in three huge gashes.

Suddenly the völva stood between them and their quarry, swinging a small satchel back and forth and chanting in a low voice. The metered movement calmed them, drawing them in, making them feel safe and warm and ready to sleep for the winter.

Bright green eyes flashed before Eyildr and she blinked. The völva was still chanting but it no longer had an effect on them. Roaring their rage at her attempt to control them, they lashed out again, knocking her through the campfire and across the clearing to slam into the trunk of an oak tree. She slid to the ground and did not stir.

Alfgrimr took advantage of the distraction his son and cohort provided and ran for the tree line in hopes of winning free and directing the battle from elsewhere. He had reached the edge of the clearing when the bear caught up with him. It was the work of but a moment to snap his fragile neck and leave him in a pile on the ground.

They turned once toward the fire, torn between seeing to Vidar and joining the battle, but his final words turned them toward the tree line and the mounting battle beyond.

"'Ware the north! An attack comes!" The cry went up along the line of defenders keeping watch in the dark hours. It passed backward toward the cantonment where the refugees and volunteers were housed and rang through the capital, calling everyone to arms. Audolf strode out of the hall at Geirvarr's side, the two deep in conversation about how best to repel the offensive. Asbjorn, who had fallen asleep propped up on a cart near the northern holders' tents, roused himself and shook off sleep like the bear of his namesake before going to find his kin. Ambjorg found herself the last to join the planning, having been sleeping in the hall when the cry went up.

Audolf wasted no time. "Creatures are attacking our northern defenses," he began, sketching lines in the dirt to illustrate. "Their numbers are far greater than we've yet seen, even in the eastern mountains, and we believe they've massed their main force here." He drove a stick into the ground due north of their perimeter.

"What about the east and south?" Asbjorn asked. "Certainly they won't pass up an opportunity to flank us when we're effectively surrounded."

"Nothing yet," Geirvarr grated, his rough voice underscoring his doubt, "but I'll wager they'll see action before the night's through."

"Send me a runner to the tower," Ambjorg replied. "I will scout from there and send word when I find something." The rest nodded as she ran to her well-worn vantage point.

Even before she climbed its stairs she could hear the sounds of battle. Torches lit along the northern flank illuminated writhing masses of furred bodies rendered indistinct by distance. Given the sheer number of beasts throwing themselves at the defenses she could not help but feel they would not hold for long.

Ambjorg forced her eyes away from the battle and steeled herself to her purpose. Reaching out with her senses, she found an eagle nearby, as she always did, though this one had been disturbed by the fighting. She borrowed its sight and asked it to fly east, then south, then finally north once again to scout the full perimeter. By the time she returned to her own senses a girl of no more than ten stood at the top of the stairs, awaiting instructions.

"Send word to my brothers–the eastern and southern flanks will soon be attacked, and the outer defenses on the north are failing. They must meet me in the grove. They will know what to do." The girl nodded once, then sprinted down the steps and across the lawn toward their erstwhile command center to deliver her message. Ambjorg hurried after, angling south of the hall toward the stand of trees that had ever been their haven in troubled times, hoping it could again provide them with the wisdom and assistance they so desperately needed.

Five minutes later the siblings met once again by the chattering brook in the clearing, though its cheerful sound jarred their senses. Ambjorg took each of her brothers by the hand and nodded, then spoke. "We must ask the forest for aid. I have seen creatures–so many beasts, from every side but the fjord. It is too many for us to hope to defeat ourselves, but if the packs and the bears are with us, we may yet prevail."

"This is not their fight," Audolf began, but Asbjorn interjected.

"It will soon be their fight as these things take over their territories, eat their food, and attack their young," he rumbled. "Nature is out of balance. It will help right itself." He let go of his sister's hand and found a tree to scratch his back on, very much resembling the creatures he called. Shrugging, Audolf moved a short distance away and sat, closing his eyes and letting out a soft howl.

Ambjorg found herself without occupation and folded her hands together to keep from wringing them. She wandered over to the creek and sat down on a flat rock at its edge, intending to listen for sounds of battle to the east, when a white light flashed before her, blinding her utterly. Exclamations from behind her told her Audolf and Asbjorn had suffered similarly, and when her vision cleared a woman stood before them. She was clad in flowing green robes that contained every natural shade of the color, her auburn hair trailing in a breeze that none of the siblings felt. Her eyes, though gentle, pierced their innermost souls as she gazed at each in turn.

"You have come here in your direst need, seeking the help of the forest," she began, her voice an echoing amalgamation spanning the range of female tone and inflection, "as it was foretold you would do." She took a step toward them and turned toward Asbjorn. "You are correct; nature is out of balance here, and nature will restore equilibrium, but it needs your help. Come here, Asbjorn." Ducking his head, he approached cautiously, stopping just within arm's reach of their visitor. She smiled and reached out to brush a stray lock of hair out of his face. "You carry your father's strength and your mother's kindness. As you have proven yourself worthy of the gifts you were born with, I bestow upon you one more." Shifting her hand she touched a fingertip between his eyes and whispered a word–and removed her finger from the forehead of the large, brown bear now standing before her. "You may now choose to take the form of your companions at will or need. Change back and join your siblings." With a thought, Asbjorn returned to his normal self, holding his hands before him and staring at them in confusion.

"Audolf." He approached without instruction and submitted to the woman's touch. "You carry your father's cunning and your mother's wit. You have also proven yourself worthy." A gray wolf stood in his place for a moment before flashing back into Audolf, who grinned lopsidedly at his brother. Asbjorn still appeared to be absorbing what was happening as the woman stepped toward their sister.

"Ambjorg." She held her head high as her name was spoken. "You carry your mother's practicality and your father's sense of purpose." The woman paused, tilting her head. "Do you find yourself worthy?"

Taken aback by the question, Ambjorg considered, feeling the weight of many outcomes in her response. "Worthiness is not something that can be once earned and never sustained," she replied. "I hope to earn mine with each breath I take." She held her breath, hoping her response was enough.

The woman nodded. "You show wisdom beyond your

years." She touched Ambjorg's forehead and a great eagle, the largest they'd seen, took her place. "May it guide you and your people long past the days of your reign.

"Now, go and find your brethren and sistren. They will help you purge the land of this foulness." With one last look to each, she turned to go.

"My lady," Ambjorg called as she retook her human form, "whose name might we call on to thank for these gifts?"

The woman smiled. "I have many names, but among your people I am known as Freya." With that, she disappeared into the night.

The siblings shared a long look, then took to their tasks without another word between them.

"Where is the king?" the runner asked, a boy of about twelve. "I have news for him from the perimeter, and a request for orders, sir."

"He is tending to a task of utmost importance," Geirvarr replied. "What can I do for you meantimes?"

"The outer defenses aren't going to hold, sir," the runner began. "There's too many of them. They're requesting permission to fall back and regroup at the second line."

"Granted," the armsmaster grunted, and the boy nodded and ran off to deliver his message. They had known the outer defenses were too spread out to hold against a direct assault like they were seeing, and there was no sense in taking chances when they had a stronger redoubt to pull back to. It was alarming how quickly they'd breached the defenses, but it couldn't be helped.

Just then another runner approached, this time from the south. "Sir! Creatures attacking from the south–they're small enough to fit through the holes in the fences. Requesting permission to pull back." The boy, a lad of about fourteen, looked as if he itched to be on the battlefield. Geirvarr held his gaze long enough to consider their precious few options, then nodded.

"Granted," he replied, catching the boy's arm as he started back toward his post. "And stop by the eastern lines to warn them–they need to fall back as well or be cut off." Nodding, the boy took off at a dead run toward the eastern command before veering off to the south.

"Where could their majesties be?" the armsmaster grumbled beneath his breath. The longer they were absent, the greater the chances someone would notice and think the worst of them. He turned toward the grove they'd entered, watching as if it might suddenly eject them onto the night-dark plains before him. Instead he saw two shadowed forms burst from beneath the cover of the trees, one streaking to the south and across the fences before it could be stopped, the other lumbering with surprising speed toward the eastern flank. No fence could stand in its way as it crashed past the line of defenders and into the trees at the edge of the fields. A third figure appeared and strode north, directly toward Geirvarr and the command center. Her bearing made her instantly recognizable as Queen Ambjorg, and Geirvarr breathed a small sigh of relief.

"Your majesty," he nodded as she reached the area where they'd set up to command the field. The hall sat at the top of a small hill, lending it a superior view of the surrounding plains, so they'd set up a makeshift command near the hall itself in case they needed to fall back behind its walls. "We've just had word from the north and south—both sides are beset. The east will fall back with them to avoid being cut off." Geirvarr paused for a moment to let Ambjorg absorb the information, then looked about for eavesdroppers before continuing. "If I may speak freely, majesty, there are too many of these things. We'll never outlast a full-on assault from all sides."

Ambjorg nodded in agreement. "Hopefully we won't have to," she replied cryptically as her eyes roamed the plains beyond the reach of the torchlight. Geirvarr wondered briefly if she could discern more than the jumbled shapes he saw, then dismissed the thought as foolish; she was young, her eyes undimmed by years of sunlight and use. Of course she could see more than he. Nodding as if to reassure himself, he went about his business, leaving the queen to survey the battlefield.

Sounds of battle from the northern flank could be heard across the encampment as steel met claw and talon. The defenders' second redoubt was less hastily constructed than the first and consisted of mounded rocks and earth with trenches in front. Sharpened stakes and posts jutted out from the fronts of the mounds at odd angles to deter frontal assault, which seemed to work for the time being; the defenders were able to hold the line with minimal losses. But Ambjorg could see the writhing forms of more creatures massing in the foothills beyond the torches' light. Once they advanced in numbers even the earthworks would fall, and there would be fighting all the way to the hall.

She took a moment to survey her people. Many were still exhausted from their flight from their homes, but every able body not caring for the young or the infirm had a weapon and took a turn at the wall. There was a grim determination to the set of the defenders' jaws that said they would not easily give up this last bastion of their homeland. Ambjorg's heart swelled with pride and affection as she walked among those at rest, encouraging and supporting them in any way she could. She herself cut a dashing figure in her riding leathers, sword strapped to her hip and hair braided down her back, as she moved from torchlight to torchlight in the depth of night.

Soon she made her way to the group of defenders from the east who had shifted to reinforce the northern line while theirs stayed quiet. Chief among them was Thane Brandulfr, whose longsword was free of its sheath and stained red with the night's work. He wore an animal skin as a cloak and the leather sleeves he wore for smithing to protect his arms, plus a jerkin to protect his chest. All were spattered with gore, and Ambjorg swallowed her concern as she reached his position; they had no time for worry. "They will need you on the east soon," she said without preamble.

Brandulfr nodded. "I suspected it wouldn't be long," he replied. He turned to his group and gestured for them to follow. "Come—we are needed eastward!" To Ambjorg he cast a brief but meaningful glance containing everything that had passed between them. She returned it, unsure of the night's outcome, before he turned and led his people to their post. Steeling herself to her own duty, Ambjorg turned and marched back toward the command center to watch for signs of her brothers' success—or failure.

Before she reached the tables they'd laid out a cry went up

from the northern line. Ambjorg strained her eyes to see what caused the commotion, unable to discern what was happening past the torches' light, and caught a runner as she sprinted toward the eastern encampment. "What has happened?" she asked the girl.

"Something…outside the earthworks," the runner answered breathlessly. "Something big. We think…it's helping us, majesty." She gulped a cup of water that was handed to her, returning the empty cup with a grateful nod. "Got to take a message to the eastern flank, ma'am." At Ambjorg's nod away she flew on her errand.

"Get light on that field," Ambjorg ordered, pointing at the grassy knolls past the northern line. "I want to see what's out there." Turning on her heel she ran around the dark side of the building until she found a spot so deeply shadowed she was certain not to be seen. Moments later a great eagle soared over the hall, spiraling upward before drifting north. She found her night vision to be dimmer than she'd hoped, but the extra torches the defenders had lit created a nearly contiguous line of visibility at the edge of the breastworks, enabling her to see the piles of carcasses littering the trenches. These she perceived in excruciating detail every speck of blood and gore as clear to her eyes as if it sat at her feet. Wrenching her attention away, she swept the field from a safe height, seeking any sign of irregularity in the attackers.

There—a flash of brown fur caught her eye at the edge of the torchlight. Swooping closer she could see that it was a bear; not a bear and something else, but a proper, fully-grown brown bear, like the ones found in the northern woods. It held in its massive paws a squealing creature that was half bobcat, half wild boar, and as she watched the bear snapped its neck cleanly, almost severing the head. Dropping the carcass it moved on to the next closest beast, ripping it off the ground and slinging it into three more of its fellows before crushing its skull beneath its feet.

Having seen enough, Ambjorg wheeled back home, landing in the same shadows she'd vacated, then ran back to the northern defenses. "'Ware the brown bear—it fights against our foe," she shouted, and heard the instruction passed down the line. "Leave it be unless it threatens." *Asbjorn, I hope that's not you,* she thought as she turned her attention eastward.

Fighting had begun in earnest on the eastern flank. It was beset by raw-boned mountain creatures, mostly part-wolves and part-mountain-cats. The citizens of Thorsbrand held the front of the line, having already fought these creatures longer than the rest of the folk, but the onslaught was relentless. Already the line was weakening in a few places as carcasses piled up beyond the earthworks such that the creatures could bound to the top of the hillocks. Ambjorg sent up a quick prayer to Freya that her promised aid would arrive soon.

The southern defenses were a mess. Small predator hybrids threaded their way through the pikes in the breastworks and over the hill to harass the defenders. Few of them were large enough to be deadly on their own, but soon their sheer number would overwhelm the defenses. Ambjorg saw no good way to assist beyond picking off the few creatures that made it past the line and into the camp. She despaired of timely aid as the slow trickle of creatures increased from the south.

A howl split the night, cold and clear and full voiced. It cut across the strange rumbling and chittering of the beasts on the field and drew the attention of attackers and defenders both. In the ensuing lull a second howl joined the first, then a third, until the whole southern woods rang with the song of the pack.

The hunt had begun.

The bear continued to rage across the rolling hills north of the capital, barely aware of the defenders. It vented Eyildr's rage and grief and its own frustration at this disruption of the natural order of things on the unnatural creatures before it, killing quickly and indiscriminately. In this Eyildr and the bear were of one mind, and they worked seamlessly to achieve their ends. Some portion of Eyildr's mind realized they would eventually need to be wary of the humans defending her people, but for now there were targets aplenty, and that was enough.

On the eastern flank the defenders took advantage of a lull in the fighting to peek over the earthworks and onto the field of battle. From what they could see their enemy now fought a battle on two sides: one against the capital's defenses, the other at their backs. Many were turning to face a new foe emerging from the woods nearby at a ground-eating pace. Just before the two lines of creatures clashed a challenging roar went up from the new-comers as they crashed into the creatures, leaving swaths of tram-pled and broken carcasses in their wake. Soon the battle became a rout as the defenders picked off the last stragglers still attacking the breastworks and the mysterious beasts that had aided them split to chase down the main force.

The defenders to the south continued to hack at the steady flow of smaller creatures trickling through the defenses until they realized the flow had all but stopped. Across the field past the trenches they could see little besides white teeth and yellow eyes as the packs fell upon their prey. Before long the southern field was a jumble of carcasses and sleek, well-fed wolves, who padded silently back into the forest.

Asbjorn ran down another misshapen creature, snapping its neck as he trod over it, then looked around at the carnage sur-rounding him. At least fifteen bears of all shapes and sizes lum-bered about, swatting at the unnatural beasts in their midst with sharp claws and heavy paws. Few of the enemy were left now, and the bears began to mill about, unsure of their purpose, until Asbjorn looked to the northern flank of the battlefield. Unaware of the rout to their south, the creatures there continued to attack the defenses, though something seemed to be distracting them from the treeline to their rear.

He turned and belted out a mighty roar as he wheeled toward the north, intending to flank the attackers from the east. Most of the bears followed, though a few split off east, their part in the night's events played out. The remaining group gained speed then bowled into the beasts from the side, trampling any that didn't dodge out of the way. The already confused creatures broke in the face of this new onslaught and ran for the northern hills, tails tucked firmly between their mismatched legs.

As the bears gave chase Asbjorn passed a rogue group of creatures ganging up on a large brown bear. It stood its ground though its sides heaved with exertion and it oozed blood from a myriad of scratches and bite wounds. He turned from the chase to aid this new ally, registering that he hadn't seen this particular bear when he'd collected his initial group. Without warning he fell on the beasts, paws swinging and teeth snapping, and within moments the creatures were either dead or fleeing for the forest.

The injured bear swayed on its feet for a moment, then slumped onto its side, panting. It curled up in a most un-bearlike pose as its fur began to recede, giving way to what had to be human skin. Before long a woman with thick, dark hair lay curled up in the leaves, blood seeping from countless wounds. She faced away from Asbjorn, but he would have known her figure any-where. Shifting back into his human form he ran to where she lay and brushed her hair back from her face.

"Eyildr?" he called gently.

She stirred and opened one eye long enough to register where she was and who spoke, then curled into herself even tight-er. "Go away," she whispered.

"You know I won't," he answered, brushing a hand down the side of her dirt-smeared face. "Whatever they did to you I will do unto them a thousandfold, but for now we need to get you to safety; the battle is almost over, but I won't feel easy until dawn." He helped her off of the ground and saw that her leg was injured such that walking would be difficult. "Can you sit astride?" he asked. When she nodded, he placed both hands on her shoulders and looked into her eyes. "Then I need you to stay calm and trust in me. I cannot explain what I am about to do, but it will get us both home safely." He paused before adding, "And I think it might make you feel a bit less terrible." When Eyildr nodded, he stepped back and resumed his bear form. Her eyes went wide for a moment, then filled with tears–of relief, or fear, or of under-standing, he couldn't be sure, but when he lowered his shoulders for her to climb into his broad back she smiled a little and clam-bered aboard, wincing as she put weight on her injured leg.

And so they returned to camp, the thane's daughter and the

king, both unsure of what the dawn would bring, but trusting in each other.

# CHAPTER 8

Ambjorg had just finished checking with the defenders on the south when someone shouted, "His Majesty!" Whirling to face the field she saw Audolf's form emerge from the shadows, head bowed and arms hanging at his sides. Ambjorg ran to meet her brother despite cries of warning from the defenders, leaping over half-eaten carcasses to reach his side. He looked up at her call and grinned, throwing out one arm for a brief embrace before Ambjorg stepped back to take stock of his condition. He seemed whole, if battered and bruised, and she walked with him back to the encampment.

A cheer ran through the gathering crowd at Audolf's safe return. "Where is Asbjorn?" he asked, taking a proffered waterskin from one of the folk nearby.

"I had hoped you would know," Ambjorg replied, her brows creasing in worry.

"We split up to cover both flanks, and then he thought to head north and cut off the enemy," Audolf explained as they made their way to the command center by the hall. "Last I saw he was heading northeast to find…help." He cast his gaze about to see who might be listening, altering his speech as he realized how public their conversation was.

Ambjorg's frown deepened. "The eastern flank went quiet a while ago," she said, her eyes searching the eerie stillness of the battlefield for clues, "and the north followed shortly after. He should have returned by now, unless…" Their eyes met, neither wishing to voice aloud what both were thinking. Ambjorg started toward the lee of the building. "I'm going to look for him," she began, but a commotion to the north stalled her. Both siblings froze, ears straining, until they heard someone shout "Make way for His Majesty!"

A bedraggled Asbjorn strode over the earthworks, carrying the unconscious form of Eyildr. Ignoring his own state he immediately asked for a healer for his betrothed and was guided to one of the hospital tents set up for the wounded. Ambjorg and Audolf met him there and threw their arms around their brother, whose oversized embrace encompassed both.

"How is she?" Ambjorg asked as the healer began dressing Eyildr's wounds, starting with the ones requiring stitches since she was already unconscious.

"She will be well, I think, but it may take some time," Asbjorn replied, sinking to the dirt floor to take Eyildr's hand. "I'm not certain what they did to her. She was captured, you see." His expression darkened as his mind wandered through the possibilities.

Ambjorg laid a hand on her brother's shoulder. "They will face justice," she reassured him. "For now, she needs you. I will go and find her brother." She left her brothers in the healer's tent to fulfill her task. Audolf made his excuses awkwardly and almost managed to leave the tent before another healer took him by the arm and guided him to a stool under protest to treat his superficial wounds.

Dawn breathed a sigh of relief into the encampment. Most of the defenders had gotten little sleep before being roused to arms and were at the end of their endurance; only the fear of a second attack had kept them alert. As soon as the sun's rays touched the fields they began organizing a watch so that the people could rest. Audolf had fallen asleep an hour earlier in the healer's tent while they saw to his wounds and Asbjorn refused to leave Eyildr's side, but Ambjorg found herself uneasy, unable to rest despite the urging of everyone around her to do so. As soon as the light touched the tower she climbed its stairs and took off from the far side of the building to survey the fields.

Carrion crows and vultures had already begun their feast on the glut of carcasses below. Ambjorg had never seen so many of nature's undertakers in one place; it almost seemed unnatural. But she supposed it was reasonable given the amount of cleanup to be done, and it would save the exhausted defenders some work. She swept across the edge of the southern forests and heard the occasional wolf song–it seemed the hunt continued deeper into the woods. Turning east she passed over the stands of trees and groves that dotted the edge of the plains and saw the swaths of trampled beasts left behind. Very little moved as she passed overhead, though she saw a single creature run into a stand of trees, then disappear completely. It never emerged from the other side. She turned westward and north to search for signs of friends or foes and found little of either, but a trail of campfire smoke further up the hill caught her attention. Using an updraft to gain altitude she soared over the small clearing, her keen sight taking in a few tents–and three corpses. She circled lower until she made out the faces of Thane Alfgrimr and his son, but was unable to identify the third, which lay with its face in the mud. A bloody trail ran from beneath a nearby tree into the forest beyond, but no fourth corpse was visible.

Deciding she had enough assurance her people were safe, Ambjorg turned toward home, suddenly exhausted. She landed in the watchtower and wandered to the hall, where someone directed her toward her rooms and into bed. Before her head touched the pillow she was fast asleep.

She awoke to the sound of voices in her antechamber. It seemed both of her brothers were there, along with Thane Brandulfr and, most importantly, Eyildr. The sound of her childhood friend's voice flooded her with relief as she stood and dusted off her clothes, which were covered with a full day's worth of grime. Deciding she didn't care too much about her appearance Ambjorg rushed out to embrace her friend.

Eyildr smiled broadly as she returned Ambjorg's gesture, though a portion of it didn't quite reach her eyes. "It's good to see you, too," she said, relief evident in her voice. Pulling back, Ambjorg studied her friend. Her usually open demeanor carried a shadow Ambjorg couldn't quite identify.

"Are you well?" she asked quietly as her brothers began discussing watch rotations and planning sessions. Eyildr took a seat at the informal dining table nearby, gesturing for Ambjorg to join her.

"As well as I can be," she replied. "Much has happened in the last few days." She shuddered involuntarily, hugging her arms around her stomach, but plowed on. "There is much I wish to tell you, but I must speak with your brother first. He found me, and I believe he has first claim on my tale."

"I understand," Ambjorg replied. "I, too, have much to tell, but there is another I must speak to first." She glanced across the room to where Thane Brandulfr stood, half paying attention to Audolf, half studying her. His expression carried the collective burdens of both his people and his own heart, and she wished for nothing more than to relieve both.

Eyildr smiled more genuinely this time. "Go," she said as she stood, her eyes traveling to Asbjorn. "Speak to him, but do tell me when I can wish you joy." Winking at Ambjorg's blush, she rejoined the brothers, her hand twining into Asbjorn's.

Ambjorg stood and straightened her clothing unnecessarily; her leathers never showed much wear or wrinkle despite their relative comfort. Gathering her resolve, she strode over to the group and stood between Brandulfr and Audolf, who was presenting a plan to send raiding parties into the nearby woodlands to track down the last of the creatures. Ambjorg cleared her throat and words on his lips petered out.

"I believe that will be unnecessary," she began. "I took the liberty of doing some reconnaissance in all directions, and it seems there are still forces at work outside of our own that are… righting the imbalance." Her brothers nodded, satisfied, while Brandulfr and Eyildr shared a quizzical look. "I do suggest keeping a watch posted, and we should delay the return of our people to their homes for at least another week, perhaps two." This Brandulfr could agree to, though it was apparent he did not fully understand the justification. "Now, if you'll excuse me, I'd like to head up to the watchtower for a while to see what can be seen." With a significant look at Brandulfr, she turned and headed out the door. Audolf gave the bigger man a shove as she left.

"You're supposed to go with her," he said, guiding the thane out the door of his sister's rooms and toward the exit. "And I'm to make myself scarce so that my brother and Eyildr can also have a talk." He shook his head. "Good luck," he sent over his shoulder as they parted ways at the main door. Brandulfr could see the retreating figure out Ambjorg as she strode purposefully toward her usual retreat, never once looking back. He wondered for a moment at the endless reservoir of resolve she possessed, then followed.

Ambjorg stood in her accustomed spot looking out over the western fjord. It struck Brandulfr that mere months before they had met in this same place–the night they'd danced, and also the night she'd lost her father. So much had changed since then, and he could see in her bearing that she had become every inch the queen her mother was. She turned to face him as he exited the stairwell and he could read uncertainty in her posture and expression as he approached.

"There are things I need to tell you that I must have your word will never leave this tower," she began. "My brothers and Eyildr are the only others who will share this knowledge. I trust in your discretion, but if you do not wish to keep such secrets I will understand." She paused, unwilling to meet his eyes.

"There is no secret you could tell me that I would not gladly bear," he answered solemnly. "You have my word it goes no further than us." She blinked and looked up at him briefly before nodding and leaning against the parapet.

"Then I shall start at the beginning." She told him everything; about her father's affinity for ravens, her affinity for eagles, her brothers' affinities, and finally their most recent gifts from the lady Freya herself. Brandulfr nodded at each revelation and she could see wheels turning behind his eyes as words and actions that had previously seemed cryptic or odd clicked into place. When there was no more to explain, she fell silent, staring apprehensively at the waves that crashed against the rocks just beyond the coastline.

Brandulfr had listened silently, simply nodding as she spoke. He had a thousand questions, but none of them seemed to matter at that moment. What mattered was that Ambjorg–the most stoic woman he had ever met–had just shared with him a part of her life she had never shared with anyone but her family. He held onto that thought as it gave him the courage to take her hand as he moved to her side by the tower wall. She looked down, startled, then up at him, a strange, vulnerable hope in her eyes. It was an expression she was unaccustomed to wearing, but it made her all the more beautiful.

"I recall standing by this same wall some months ago, asking if you would come visit my home," he began. She blushed and smiled–actually smiled–as he continued. "And I was amazed when you and your brother accepted my invitation. It seemed too much to hope that you might think of me as often as I thought of you. Yet there you were, riding into my village for the midsummer festival, looking much as you do now." He gestured to her leathers, the same ones she'd worn months ago to travel, now dirtied and much the worse for wear, and she felt self-conscious for the first time in days. "Then this whole situation began and I saw not only the face you wear for your duties, but the strength of your spirit and your dedication to our people. I knew then that there could be no one else who would capture my attention and affection as you have, and I vowed to myself that when this was over I would make it known.

"And so I ask you, here where it all began, if you would allow me to bind myself to you, to be your husband, and to share all that I have and am with you for as long as I shall live." Tears sprang into Ambjorg's eyes as she smiled up at him, the midday sun giving a sheen to her honey-blonde hair. Then her expression turned somber.

"But I cannot go with you to the mountains," she replied, deflating. "My first duty is here, with our people, with my brothers."

He raised her chin with a finger. "I did not ask that of you," he answered gently. "I would never ask you to forsake your duty, only to share its burden with me. The capital would be my home, as well."

"But…your people need you," Ambjorg said, furrowing her brows. "You have a duty to them, as well."

"I am replaceable," he answered, his hand dropping from her chin as he turned toward the fjord. "To tell truth, there is much about my home I would fain leave behind. Many memories." He leaned on the parapet and fell silent.

Ambjorg sensed that she'd touched a nerve and thought back

through her words as she considered how to reply. Her answer came quickly: he had just declared his intention to marry her, if she would have him, and she had not given an answer. Her cheeks burned as she realized she had once again let her mind rule her heart, even when there was no reason for it to do so. Acting entirely on impulse, she turned toward Brandulfr and extended a hand to brush her fingertips across his cheek. He turned, his clouded expression clearing, and before she could second guess herself she raised up onto her toes and kissed him. For a moment he stood perfectly still, then he wrapped both arms around her waist and returned the kiss. When they parted, she left one hand on the side of his face for a moment.

"If you will have me, I am yours," she said, and he smiled with the same look in his eye she remembered from her trip to the mountains, when she'd agreed to write to him. He kissed her then, fiercely, before they returned to the hall, hand in hand, to face whatever lay ahead.

When they returned they found Eyildr and Asbjorn still deep in conversation in Ambjorg's rooms. Discretion seemed the best plan, so instead they found Audolf, who was consulting with Geirvarr on the watch schedule. He noticed their joined hands and gave a lopsided grin, but said nothing beyond asking their opinions on leaders for the watch patrols. Brandulfr named five of his own people, three men and two women, who had shown resilience and skill in the face of their trials. Audolf noted their names and promised to ask for their aid.

Before long Asbjorn and Eyildr appeared from within the hall. Eyildr had been weeping, and Asbjorn walked with one arm around his betrothed as they approached. "Let us take a walk in the grove," he said without preamble, and his siblings nodded in understanding. Brandulfr looked confused for a moment, but followed Ambjorg and her brothers to the stand of trees close to the hall. As they passed the large boles of the first set of trees the sounds of the camp fell away and were replaced only by the soft crushing of pine needles and leaves beneath their feet. Soon they could hear the rill of the stream that crossed the grove, and they stopped by its gentle waters, finding seats on moss-covered rocks. No one had spoken during the walk, and once they were settled Asbjorn addressed the group.

"Eyildr has asked me to help share her story," he began, and he launched into the tale of her capture. They listened raptly as he spoke of Thane Alfgrimr and his son and their involvement with the völva, along with their plan to use their army of unnatural creations to take control of the capital. He hesitated for a moment, looking to Eyildr before continuing. She nodded, then raised her head and told them how the völva had used her dark powers to experiment on her, combining her body and mind with that of a bear. Ambjorg reached out to her friend and laid a hand on her arm in sympathy. Covering it with her own, she continued to tell them what she'd heard and seen, including her father's death and her subsequent rampage through the camp. By the time she finished her tale her voice shook and tears flowed down her cheeks, and Ambjorg threw her arms around her friend as she vented her grief once more.

No one spoke for a few minutes as they processed what they had heard. When Eyildr wiped her eyes and sat up, Ambjorg sat back and studied the woman she'd grown up with. There was a rawness to Eyildr that spoke of recent tragedy and sacrifice, and it pained her. But when Asbjorn put an arm around her and held her to his shoulder the edges of that rawness dulled. Reassured that Eyildr was in the best of hands, Ambjorg gave her friend a tight-lipped smile and turned to face the group.

"I think our path is clear," she said as she met the gaze of each person in turn. "The greatest threat has passed, and our allies in the forests will aid us in ridding the land of this blight. However, I did not see the body of the völva in the clearing, and I think we all wish to be certain she never gets the chance to continue her experimentation." Grim nods met her statement, and she continued. "The trail may be cold by now, but with the aid of the pack–or at least Audolf–we should be able to pick it up and find where she's gone to ground. With the amount of blood I saw she cannot have gone far."

"I will go with him," Asbjorn volunteered, a dangerous glint to his eye.

"Do you wish to go with them?" Ambjorg asked Eyildr quietly.

Eyildr shook her head, closing her eyes. "I wish only to know that she will never harm another being."

"Then it is settled." Ambjorg gave her brothers directions to the clearing she'd seen and admonished them to take care, as they weren't sure what other feats the völva was capable of. "And may Freya watch over you," she added as they strode out of the grove. Eyildr, Ambjorg, and Brandulfr filtered out after them and wandered toward the hall, where Ambjorg threw herself into the necessary tasks of organizing the next steps for her people. Judging that Eyildr needed employment, she set her to the task of checking with the kitchens to be sure they were properly supplied for the next two weeks and organizing meal rotations for each set of holders. Brandulfr was charged with overseeing the disposal of carcasses within the earthworks to avoid sickness and disease. Ambjorg herself oversaw the designation of a span of ground to lay out the dead, who numbered more than she'd hoped, but fewer than there might have been had they not had aid. Once they had been counted they would find a boat large enough to hold all of them and give them a proper burial at sea, sending them off down the fjord to join their ancestors.

By the time Audolf and Asbjorn returned it was nearly sunset. Both were tired, but grim satisfaction showed on their faces. "We found her," Audolf said without preamble as they sat down at the dining table in Ambjorg's suite, which had become the de facto headquarters for the reconstruction efforts. "Or rather, what was left of her."

"It seems the local wildlife—or the creatures themselves, we can't be sure—made certain she was dead," Asbjorn continued as his brother got up to make a plate from the sideboard. "We found pieces in a trail leading away from the camp. Most of them had been gnawed, but were distinguishable. Especially the head." Asbjorn reached for Eyildr's hand. "She will never work her dark magic on another living being." Eyildr deflated visibly as if a weight had been lifted from her. She had been picking at the food on the plate Ambjorg had made her, but with this news and the safe return of her betrothed she began to eat in earnest.

"Thank you for easing that worry," Ambjorg said to her brothers, who waved off her gratitude.

"It needed doing and we were the best option," Audolf said around a mouthful of cheese. "Plus it kept us busy and out of your hair while you organized the next month of all our lives." He rolled his eyes theatrically in an attempt to look long-suffering and earned a punch on the arm.

"It's no fault of mine you cannot even organize your own socks," she replied with a sniff. "Besides, you know it's what I'm best at. Someone has to keep the country running while you all are off doing feats of derring-do." Audolf grinned and rubbed the shoulder she'd hit, popping some fruit into his mouth.

"Are they always like this?" Brandulfr asked Eyildr.

"They're often worse," she replied with a grin as she picked up a slice of cold meat. "Always have been. The stories I could tell you…" She trailed off meaningfully as she glanced sidelong at Asbjorn, who chuckled.

For the first time in weeks the group fell into relaxed conversation. They talked well beyond sunset, sharing stories of their childhood and generally keeping a jovial atmosphere. When Eyildr fell asleep on Asbjorn's shoulder he picked her up and carried her from the room, bidding the rest a quiet good night as he went.

"I seem to recall having to do the same to you once," Brandulfr said to Ambjorg with a mischievous grin. "You'd fallen asleep in my study after a long day of hard work."

Ambjorg's jaw dropped. "But…Audolf…I thought…" She looked to her brother, who shrugged.

"You're heavier than you look. Better him than me," Audolf replied as he stood. "And with that I bid you both a good night." Bowing theatrically, he wandered out the door and down the hall toward his own room.

Ambjorg punched Brandulfr on the shoulder. "You could've said something," she complained. He chuckled, a pleasant, deep sound that started in his chest.

"I thought I just did," he answered, earning another punch. This time he caught her hand and pulled it toward him to kiss her knuckles, and she blushed. "You are adorable when you're angry," he told her.

"Flattery will get you nowhere," she answered with a mischievous glint in her eye.

"You cannot blame me for trying."

# EPILOGUE

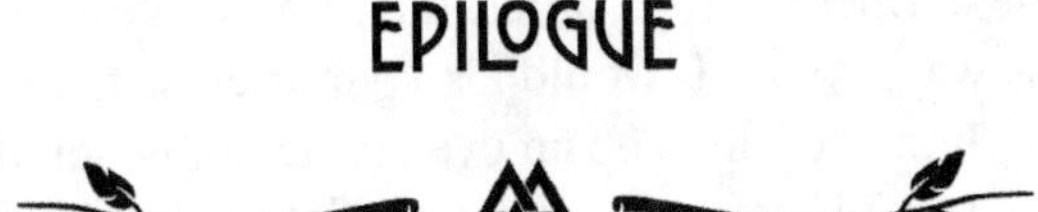

Early spring saw a double wedding. Eyildr and Asbjorn had postponed their own to give her enough time to fully understand her bond with the bear. They'd also wished to avoid having to plan separate events for both siblings, and since Brandulfr had duties to attend for his people he and Ambjorg had had to wait a few months. But as soon as the last snowfall melted both couples had given the all-clear and the wedding had been planned. Flowers festooned the great hall and bonfires were set up in the fields around the capital in preparation for the ceremony and subsequent celebration. People thronged the capital, camping on the fields and in the forests nearby so that they could participate in the momentous occasion.

Ambjorg and Eyildr had even chosen coordinating dresses for their wedding day, and both were happier than they could express. They looked radiant as they joined their betrothed on the outdoor dais raised for this distinct purpose and gave their hands to be fasted with their beloved. For three days the people feasted and danced to celebrate the royals' felicity.

Audolf took the opportunity the gathering afforded to dance with as many ladies as possible under the pretense that he thought it important for morale. No one was fooled.

After the celebration ended and people began to drift back to their homes Asbjorn called a conference of the siblings and their newly-made spouses. Once again they met in the chambers Ambjorg now shared with Brandulfr, sitting around the table as they were wont to do. Eyildr sat next to Asbjorn looking apprehensive.

"I'll get straight to the point," he started as he looked them each in the eye. "Eyildr and I wish to go on a leave of absence." He let the silence stretch before them for a moment before continuing. "It is difficult for her to live among others; the bear who shares her body also desires freedom, which she cannot give often living in a settlement. We wish to retire to her family's home on the northern border, at least until we can find a more harmonious way to live. It would also put us close to the northern thanedom, where we can keep an eye on the goings-on there with no one the wiser." He stopped to draw a deep breath. "What say you?"

Ambjorg sat back in her chair, deep in thought. Just before Audolf opened his mouth to make a flippant reply she said, "I think it is a very sensible idea, though I wish it did not take you both so far from us." She reached across the table to squeeze Eyildr's hand briefly. "It has been wonderful having you both so close by in the wake of last fall's events, but it is time you followed your own path." She smiled at her brother, who put his arm around his new wife and grinned. "My only question is how we will continue the rotation of duties Father set forth in his will."

"That's simple," Asbjorn replied. "I will abdicate. I see no other real option." Ambjorg's blood ran cold as his words sank in. "Besides, we all know you're the one running things here, Ambi. Neither Dolf nor I can manage our stint without you in the wings, keeping us afloat."

"He's right, you know," Audolf agreed. "In fact, we had been talking of appointing a general and setting up a militia, and I have to admit the idea of taking on that project sounds very enticing. Perhaps I shall do the same and leave the running of the country to the responsible party." He gestured to his sister, who was having trouble raising her jaw in the wake of her brothers' revelations. Finally she found her voice.

"But…what of the succession plan? I've never done this on my own. How will I manage everything without your help? Have you considered…" Her questions died on her tongue as Brandulfr laid a hand on her arm.

"It does solve the question of succession beyond your generation," he said quietly, "which is something your father trusted the three of you to sort out. And having seen you in action these past months, I have to agree that you would be the logical choice. You've been ruling almost single-handedly since the battle, though you haven't realized it." Thinking back she realized the truth in his words and exhaled sharply. It did make sense, although the prospect was strangely lonely.

"I've always had my brothers near me; what will I do without you?" she asked as tears pricked her eyes. Asbjorn blinked rapidly, wiping at the corner of one eye before responding.

"We'll be here when you need us, you can be sure of that."

"I should be at the capital most of the time after I get things running," Audolf added. Ambjorg nodded, realizing this truly was the best path for both of her brothers. Dolf had always had a brilliant mind for strategy, and Geirvarr was no spring chicken; soon he would wish to retire, not set up a militia. And Asbjorn was Eyildr's best hope for a full, happy life. Living in the forest they could be free to explore both sides of their personalities while also keeping the promises they'd made, both to each other and to their people.

"Then I suppose it is settled," she said heavily. "I'll draw up the papers tomorrow for us to sign." She stood and took both of her brothers' hands across the table. "But you must promise to visit, and to write whenever possible."

Audolf grinned. "You can bet on it."


*"And so the line of succession was secured," Magnus concluded, "though it is said to this day that the northern forests are protected by powerful brown bears who remember the great once-king.*

*"So it has been these six generations of peace and prosperity hard-won by our ancestors. May they all meet us in Valhalla at the end of our days." His epic complete, Magnus Sturlusson left the dais one final time on the arm of his daughter to thunderous applause.*

# ALSO BY
# EMILY BARLOW

SUNCHASER

STORMKINDLER

INVOLUNTARILY IMMORTAL

# SUNCHASER

**She can bend the weather to her will…but will it help her forge her own path?**

A small inland farm and a valley in the mountains are all Glorya has ever known. When she graduates from weatherworking school penniless, she must rely on her ingenuity and determination to make a name for herself. Her resourcefulness earns her a berth on a ship in exchange for protection against the foul weather that runs rampant off the coast.

But the coastal weather–and the people who sail through it–are unlike anything Glorya has ever experienced. Soon she finds herself navigating both extreme weather and new cultures as she struggles to make a place for herself in the world.

**Will it be enough? Or will the raw power of nature combine with deadly foes to defeat her before she has a chance to prove herself?**

*** Note: Sunchaser is a novella consisting of three short stories that introduce Glorya Sunchaser as she begins her adventures.

# STORMKINDLER

In the shadowy winds off the north coast of Midlands, a sinister plot brews on a ship poised to pounce, threatening the fates of thousands unaware of the danger lurking just beyond their shores.

Enter Glorya Sunchaser, a formidable name across the lands, as she returns to school after years in the field. She accompanies her niece Zayira, a gifted but unconventional student, whom she promises to protect as she attends the only weatherworking school in the realm: Weatherwatch. But as Zayira struggles to find her place, Glorya steps into the daunting shoes of her late mentor, who left behind not only a legacy but a dangerous mystery that could change everything. With time running out, Glorya must unravel his secrets before they fall into malevolent hands. Can they navigate the perilous tides of magic and betrayal, or will darkness consume them both?

Dive into this thrilling tale where loyalty, courage, and destiny collide!

# INVOLUNTARILY IMMORTAL

**Sable Montgrief wishes her curse would let her die. Unfortunately for her, fate has other plans.**

Living alone in a cabin for decades, Sable has done her best to break the spell cast on her that has extended her life for centuries. She never wanted immortality; in fact, she's spent the majority of her long life trying to end it. Her latest attempt has her so close to breaking free she can taste it...until someone breaks down her door to find her.

Adem Ozturk is looking for someone to help his daughter, Ailith, who is plagued with visions of the future she can neither manage nor interpret. They're on the run from an unknown organization with unlimited reach and are up against a wall–until Adem's wife sends a message to Ailith from beyond the grave, sending them to find Sable and recruit her to their cause. If they can convince her to help they may be able to not only save Ailith, but prevent a global cataclysm. The cost: another lifetime of torturous existence for Sable.

**If they fail, she'll be trapped in eternal torment; if they succeed, she'll still lose everything she loves.**

# ABOUT THE AUTHOR

A software architect by day, Emily enjoys reading, writing, knitting, crocheting, sewing, running, and learning martial arts with her family in her spare time. She is supported by her longtime husband and two wonderful children, who endure her eccentricities with enthusiasm.

**For more information and to join her mailing list, visit https://emilybarlowwritesthings.com or scan the QR code below!**